The Forgotten Creatures

An Alumière Sisters' Adventure

Morgan Delaney

Published by Morgan Delaney
Contact: morgan@morgandelaney.info
www.morgandelaney.info

Edited by Julian Barr
Cover images from Depositphotos. Cover fonts by Set Sail Studios.
Cover design by Morgan Delaney

The Forgotten Creatures / Morgan Delaney. —1st edition 2024
Ebook ISBN 978-3-98566-017-9
Audiobook ISBN 978-3-98566-019-3
Print ISBN 978-3-98566-018-6

*For Nadine,
who makes life heaven.*

Welcome to Hawkinge-By-Hythe!

*To make the most of your stay, please note that the spelling is
UK English, the measurements are imperial and the temperatures
are in degrees Celsius.*

*To minimise delays while travelling in England, North American
visitors are kindly requested not to yell "it's my ass on the line"
while using the trains. English railway operators will always stop
if they believe a small horse has wandered onto the tracks.*

Chapter 1

Smack On The Lips

"IT'S RAINING FISH," said Mrs Champion to herself, but she did not believe it. Not even when a sardine slapped her on the shoulder.

Just a moment before, the narrow, hedge-bordered Cairn Way had been empty, as she limped into town to give an afternoon speech at the Cosey Kettle tearooms. Now, sardines poured down around her. Their wet, silver scales glinted in the sunlight as they fell, then flopped helplessly on the ground.

She locked eyes with one. It seemed as surprised as she was. Standing on the neat road, surrounded by tumbling fish, Mrs Champion felt she had been transported to some magical underwater kingdom. One didn't see the sky full of fish every day, and Mrs Champion enjoyed the moment, though the poor sardines' plight spoiled it somewhat.

Anywhere else in England, it would doubtless later be described by the local newspapers as a "mysterious", "peculiar", or even "freakish" event, depending on how low the editor would stoop to cajole the pennies out of his reader's hand. But Mrs Champion lived in Hawkinge-

By-Hythe, where people took this kind of thing in their stride.

Most towns grow around crossroads or bridges, good fishing waters or some other natural advantage. But not Hawkinge-By-Hythe. The founding members of Hawkinge—the town's original name—were more ambitious. They set up camp near the top of a hill in the county of Kent, said to be directly under that bit of heaven where God's throne was located.

Such, at least, is the explanation in the town's official history book, and it would explain the place's particular charm. Not only did it enjoy mostly perfect weather, but there was always something interesting happening to keep people entertained.

So much so, in fact, that religious scholars made a circle around the place throughout the Middle Ages. During a period of history when hordes of academic scholars roamed the globe, searching for that elusive *nescio quid* their book needed to hit the demonology bestseller charts, they all avoided Hawkinge-By-Hythe like the plague.[1]

Anywhere boasting that much funny business, they felt, must be taking the piss.

So Mrs Champion's problem wasn't that fish were falling out of a clear blue sky in the middle of a beautiful summer day. It was that they were falling on *her*.

She was on her way to give a speech in front of the exclusive Official Women's Club of Hawkinge-By-Hythe (OWCHH). Mindful of the honour, she wore a new buttercup-yellow day dress patterned with green circles

---

[1] Editor's note: Latin for "I do not know what". They were mad for Latin in those days. Today, we would use the French expression "*je ne sais quoi*" instead.

and a tiered skirt. Her outfit also included matching green crocheted gloves and a yellow felt hat.

But it did not include an umbrella, and to be caught in a rain of fish without an umbrella would be terribly unlucky.

And Mrs Champion was *lucky*.

It was even the topic of her speech.

She looked up to determine where the fish were coming from. She saw nothing. A cold, salty smack on the lips from a plunging sardine persuaded her not to look again.

Despite what they were doing to her new dress and hat, her heart bled for the fish. Hawkinge-By-Hythe lay half a dozen miles from the coast, yet the sardines were alive. For now.

They left her without a choice. Suffering the same pangs of heroic sacrifice Abraham would have gone through when God asked him to kill his first-born son, Mrs Champion lifted the hem of her lovely yellow dress to catch the poor fish.

She limped into town with her ruined dress and her slip showing. It would spell the end of her reputation as Hawkinge-By-Hythe's luckiest citizen, but she couldn't leave them on the road.

Her dress filled to the brim, she limped faster to the Cosey Kettle.

During the Great War—finished not quite a decade yet—if things fell out of the sky, they were bombs from a German Zeppelin. These days they were fish. Well, she thought, that was progress for you. She struggled on. The wonder of the unusual rain had worn off. She no longer felt like a mermaid sauntering around the bottom of a clear, azure sea. Sardines are small, but they are wet. And there were so many of them. As she lumbered along, she felt less like she were swimming underwater, and more like she had been caught in a shower of soft, fish-scented hailstones.

As she reached town, fish drummed soggily on the rooftops around her. The beat dictated the rhythm of people's bustle, as they emerged from their homes with buckets, basins, and old metal bathtubs to gather up the sky's bounty.

Hawkinge-By-Hythe rewarded those who thought on their feet.

Late for her meeting, the club members were gossiping around the table amongst themselves when Mrs Champion peered through the tea shop window. With her yellow hat squished out of shape on her head, and her dress damp and bulging with sardines, she had never felt less lucky. She pushed open the door of the tearoom.

"Mrs Champion!" She did not recognise the voice so filled with horror, but it did not matter. She busied herself decanting her sardines into the collection of flower vases and saucepans Miss Cosey rushed forward to provide. The other women gasped and clutched at their necks in vicarious terror at the thought this could have happened to them.

Then Mrs Pengle spoke with an edge to her words that arrested Mrs Champion's attention. "Caught in the shower, were you?"

About to reply, a sudden thought struck Mrs Champion. Usually when she met sardines, they were in a tin and covered in oil. And a rain of tinned sardines would be very dangerous. She might not have made it to the Cosey Kettle at all if tins had been whistling past her head. So that was lucky.

And tinned sardines *without* tins, might almost have been worse. They would have been oily, ruining her dress forever. So she was lucky the sardines had been fresh. Yes, at the moment she radiated a smell that endeared her to every cat within a one-mile radius, but that would wash out.

And, looking at them now, she realised a problem which had vexed her for several hours had also been solved. She smiled at Mrs Pengle. "Most invigorating," she said. "I had been wondering what to make for tea!"

The ladies gasped at this further evidence of Mrs Champion's unrelenting good fortune and called for fresh tea and more buns, eager to get things moving.

For Mrs Champion used to be a mere mortal like everyone else, sometimes helped, sometimes hindered by fortune. Her fame had started with the big toe on her right foot, which had been causing her twinges for a long time.

Not the second toe, longer than the first toe, and which could therefore be considered bigger if by bigger, one meant longer. *That* toe had caused her a lot of teasing in her youth. No, it was the toe that was bigger by virtue of its more generous circumference. The wider one. Her actual big toe.

Or, as she called it when it became the subject of discussion, her Big Toe.

Not so long ago, she had burnt it with boiling water—accidentally—and thereafter suffered twinges of such debilitating intensity that she worried she might need to get it removed. Instead, she heeded the advice of Colette

Alumière, who ran the local apothecary shop with her sisters, and put it in the hands of the local doctor. He diagnosed a fungus and prescribed a strict regimen of foot stretches and minty creams.

Soon her Big Toe was pain free and out of danger.

Barely a month after that, she won five pounds in the *Illustrated Sports Intelligencer's* "Guess the Outcome" competition.[2] She had been doing them for years, and never even come close before. The people of Hawkinge-By-Hythe recognised what must have happened.

What the smug city folk of London might regard as a coincidence, they regarded as a sign.

Mrs Champion's toe. Saved from the surgeon's knife, the toe had—so to speak—spread its wings. Now it was flying high, taking Mrs Champion with it.

In case any smug city folk from London have picked this book up by mistake, perhaps misled by the title, *The Forgotten Creatures*, into thinking it a gritty tale of ennui among "the jazz generation", the author wishes to make it clear that the people of Hawkinge-By-Hythe were not gullible. Far from it. Even the smuggest Londoner should understand that when a woman who has never won five

---

[2] This is a fine example of the ingenuity of newspaper editors. The editor of Folkestone's *Illustrated Sports Intelligencer* wished to include even the results of Scottish sporting events, but was unable to find a reporter brave enough to stay in Scotland overnight for the late matches. He established the "Guess the Outcome" competition to get around this. The event was listed, but the newspaper encouraged readers to submit their guesses about who had won, by how many points, etc. The results were published in the subsequent edition, after the editor had studied the *Lancaster Leader*. Located further North, the *Leader's* reporters could take the last train back to England and safety. With time, the *Intelligencer's* competition grew so popular—and the reader's guesses so ingenious—that the editor started choosing the most entertaining submission as the "correct" one and cancelled his subscription to the *Leader*.

pounds in her life suddenly wins five pounds after having cream rubbed on her toe, that means something.

The villagers were conscientious in their attempts to recreate the exact sequence of events which had created this luck. Their efforts caused a run, not just on toe creams, but on anything even slightly minty.

Mrs Champion's doctor—who requested anonymity to discuss her case—was flooded by so many requests to examine big toes, he developed a twitch and took early retirement.

But nothing worked. No matter what anyone tried, they failed to improve their luck the way Mrs Champion had. Whatever lay behind it, it worked only for Mrs Champion.

How lucky was that?

Amongst other things, Mrs Champion became a much sought-after speaker at the Official Women's Club of Hawkinge-By-Hythe. She often discussed the weighty responsibility that came with being so lucky, but would talk on any subject as a prelude to the principal attraction.

For it was all well and good for Mrs Champion to talk about being lucky. What the ladies of OWCHH really wanted was to get up close and personal with the source of the luck itself. High on sticky buns and strong tea, the meetings ended with them gathered around to touch Mrs Champion's Big Toe, hoping its luck might rub off on them.

Occasionally, things grew rowdy, which is where Mrs Champion's limp came from. Now, a particularly frisky squeeze, administered by Mrs Pengle, caused her to bite back a gasp of pain.

It was a small price to pay for being so lucky!

Before Mrs Champion's rise to ascendancy, Mrs Pengle had been the toast of the club, for she was none other than Dierdre Pengle, the daughter of Alfred Pengle. The man who nearly invented putting salt and vinegar on chips.[3]

Growing up with the great man, the story of how he had almost pioneered this dish had been her favourite, and her father told it to her often. She fell asleep to it most nights, and knew it off by heart, despite it being a long story, and exquisitely detailed.

How he had bought a cartload of wine for a good price after the barrels fell off another cart.

The shocking dishonesty of the man who sold him the wine, for it was bad, not "dry".

His long weeks lost in thought, as he wondered what to do with 730 barrels of incredibly sour red wine.

The day he first started dipping bits of thinly sliced potato into the bottle to chew as an aid to inspiration.

More long weeks, as he wondered whether he might somehow induce other people to dip potatoes into "dry" wine.

His weeks sitting on the bench on Main Street, dipping and chewing for all he was worth, in the hope it might catch on.

How, after more long hours burning the midnight oil, he decided to cook the potatoes, rather than dipping them raw into the bottle.

[3] Editor's note: "Chips" here refers to *hot* fried pieces of potato ("French fries" in America). *Cold* pieces of fried potato—"chips" in America—are called "crisps" in England. In Germany, "chips" ("French fries") are called "*pommes frites*". *Pommes* is French for "apples", however, not potatoes. The fact that Germans don't notice they are eating potatoes after ordering apples tells you all you need to know about Germany's cuisine.

The dramatic improvement in the potato experience.

The ensuing disappointment with how often the cooked potato broke apart and fell into the bottle, plugging up the neck.

His brainwave to leave the potatoes on the plate and add the wine to them, instead of the other way around.

His foolish attempt to "fix" the wine's sourness by adding sugar.

Accidentally adding salt instead, because his wife didn't need the tins labelled, and how many times have I told you not to mess around in my cupboards, Alfred?

The incredible discovery that, in this case, two wrongs did make a right: the combined ingredients made the potatoes delicious!

Their early success selling "salty sour spuds".

The subsequent bankruptcy when Alfred hired England's best lawyers to sue the government for refusing his patent, on the ridiculous grounds that other people had been eating potatoes that way for years.

Before Mrs Champion came along, Deirdre Pengle, like her father before her, had been dining out on the story for years. Mrs Pengle's only regret in life was her inability to talk the local reporter into interviewing her for the paper, despite countless letters requesting one.

She had to request the interview by letter, for he was a young man, and too fast for her to discuss the matter in person.

Yet she had seen him frequently talking to Mrs Champion.

Some people had all the luck.

Mrs Pengle couldn't remember the last time the OWCHH wanted to hear her story.

But she remembered the last time she told it. Because someone—she would love to find out who—had yawned and told her to put a stocking in it, right in the middle of the exciting saga!

She gave the lucky Big Toe another squeeze and bared her teeth at Mrs Champion.

Let her have her lucky toe.

Deirdre Pengle would make her own luck.

Chapter 2

Squirting Toads

THE OFFICIAL WOMEN'S Club of Hawkinge-By-Hythe prided itself on the exclusivity of its member list, despite missing the three most important women in town: Gertrude, Victoria, and Colette Alumière.

The Alumières didn't enjoy clubs, particularly exclusive ones. Even the prospect of coming to grips with Mrs Champion's Big Toe wouldn't have enticed them to the Cosey Kettle tearooms, had they known about it.

Which they didn't. Because none of the Official Women ever invited them.

Instead, while Mrs Champion waded through sardines, and Mrs Pengle stared at OWCHH members, hoping to recognise a yawn, the Alumières were observing the fish phenomenon from the back garden of Swiftwater House, where they lived since moving to Hawkinge-By-Hythe.

The identical Alumière triplets had been drawn to the town for its reputation for having supposedly "supernatural" things happening all over the place. On finishing some business elsewhere, they had been looking for a new challenge. When they spotted a newspaper listing for the comfortable and spacious Swiftwater, they had pounced.

The Alumières did not believe in magic or the supernatural. Their life's work was to prove that a perfectly serviceable scientific explanation existed for everything, if only one took the trouble to search for it.

They found the promise of Hawkinge-By-Hythe irresistible, and it had not let them down. But after spoiling them with a demonic possession, a plague of rats, a well-lit werewolf—and the locals' tendency to think of witches whenever they saw the Alumières—a rain of fish left them cold.

The Alumières loved nothing more than grappling with the inexplicable. They thirsted after knowledge and didn't shrink from pushing the boundaries of scientific knowledge as far as they would go. When something "uncanny" happened, the Alumières needed to understand how the trick was done.

They were scientific to the core. That the locals thought they were witches was the unfortunate flip side of their interest in the odd.

The locals' behaviour resembled that of the old labourer who refused to eat anything though he wasted away. Author George Eliot tells how, offered any delicacy he could imagine if he would just eat, he refused it all.

Too ill to eat his usual plain meal, a lifetime of eating nothing else had robbed him of the ability to imagine anything else.

In just such a manner, so the villagers refused the Alumières' fancy new scientific explanations in favour of those they knew and always got good mileage out of.

Witchcraft.

It is hard not to understand their reasoning.

The three Alumière sisters were identical triplets, emphasis on the word identical.

Most "identical" siblings are nothing of the sort, as they discover when pulling one of those "why-don't-I-pretend-to-be-you-and-you-pretend-to-be-me-for-the-evening" stunts.

But the Alumières were truly identical in appearance. They even moved the same.

And they wore the same outfit: black wide-brimmed pork pie hats, black ruffled blouses buttoned all the way up, comfortable culottes (black) with plenty of discreet pockets. And sturdy steel-capped leather boots.

Black ones that laced up to well past the ankles, for a genuine lady never knew when fancy footwork may be required.

They were aware of the effect of their appearance on others, but they couldn't help the way they looked, and the clothes were practical, comfortable, and stylish.

Their actions, rather than their appearance, would teach their new hometown that witches weren't real.

So far, the lesson had not taken.

What the villagers *had* learned was that the Alumières preferred to be called scientists rather than witches.

Superstitious villagers are quick to learn not to do anything that might annoy a witc… scientist.

Gertrude Alumière, in particular, could be very vocal on the subject.

After what had happened to Mr Harrow and Mrs Goyle (on two separate, very loud, and very public occasions), they were careful only to think about witches in the privacy of their own skulls and when they were sure the Alumières weren't around.[4]

Although most of the world no longer believed in witches a quarter of the way through the twentieth century, Hawkinge-By-Hythe's peculiar history made not believing in witches very difficult. Especially as no sooner did the Alumières arrive but *even more strange things than usual* started happening. In the villagers' opinion, that really gave it away.

Despite this, they were a wonderful addition to the town. They had saved it a number of times already, from what they insisted were either coincidences or as-yet inadequately researched phenomena. Even better, their apothecary shop teemed with creams and ointments, powders, and tablets, which made life a lot more pleasant.

A person only needed to remember one thing before they entered the shop: which Alumière they were talking to.

The only outward difference between the Alumières was the differently coloured feathers in the hat band of their black pork pie hats. Gertrude Alumière wore a carmine red one, Victoria sported safflower yellow, while Colette's looked black, but shimmered silvery grey when the sun shone.

All three of them were equally talented at selecting the specific salve a sore spot needed to soothe it, but only Victoria possessed a bedside manner. Gertrude made the

---

[4] When the Alumières *were* around, the locals resorted to singing loudly in their heads to stop themselves thinking the word "witch". This is the reason why the Alumières had such musical conversations, when they made a sudden appearance. Usually along the lines of, "Good morning, good morning! Good-good morning, Miss 'Lumièèèrrre!"

patient understand it was their own damn silly fault for getting sick. Worst of all, Colette had a sense of humour.

Laughter may be the best medicine, but the two things a patient wishes to avoid while poorly are:

1.   A large thermometer and;

2.   Uncertainty where a grinning young lady intends to stick it.

For the most part, the villagers accepted the Alumières as they were. They might be "scientists" (wink, wink), but they were also handy to have around.

By now, only a small group waited for them to rip off their masks of respectability. Witches or not, one does not joke about certain things. Yet they were officially on the record as stating that all women should get the vote if all men had it.

And even this did not describe the full extent of their moral depravity: they rode bicycles! Their comments in favour of the suffragette movement might have been passed off as girlish high spirits. But their insistence on zipping about the countryside on devilishly fast mechanical contraptions which *showed where their legs were underneath their clothes!* proved conclusively that they must be in cahoots with the Devil.

Or were French, which would be almost as bad.[5]

For a lady did not use foul language. Nor did she perspire. And it went without saying she should refuse to admit to the possession of legs while moving from Point A to Point B, in order to avoid giving offence or inflaming passions.

Luckily, only a small minority of the villagers felt this way. The majority were honest folk who liked to live and

---

[5] According to the exotic postcards Herming Durum once sneaked back from a seaside holiday, *all* the women in France had legs!

let live as a general rule. After all, life in Hawkinge-By-Hythe—a place that attracted the inexplicable like white washing attracts bird mess—presented enough challenges to be getting on with already.

Religion played a major role in Hawkinge-By-Hythe. And what united all the various faith systems was their common belief that, whatever else God might be, He was big enough and powerful enough to take care of things himself, if He didn't like someone.[6]

It seemed presumptuous to assume mere mortals could smite better than He.

Except perhaps the Alumières. They were formidable separately and unstoppable together.

There was no doubt they might even give the Lord a run for His money when it came to smiting people who displeased them.

On this Wednesday, as on every Wednesday, they shut up their apothecary early for half-day closing, because eight-year-old Chloe Dunsloe was coming around to play with their calf, Curly.

They had all been playing Blind Man's Buff together until the sardines stopped the game. Now they collected the fish into pots, pans, jugs, glasses, and anything else suitable.

---

[6] People in Hawkinge-By-Hythe believed in all sorts of religions, and up to a dozen at a time. The main one was the undemanding Church of England, which was nice for getting out and meeting people on a Sunday. A significant Muslim community dated back to the Crusades, when Hawkinge-By-Hythe's plucky crusaders had offered the other side an "away" game, so to speak. After a rocky start, people were also on good terms with the Jewish community. The problem had been the word "*syna*gogue", which caused rumours to circulate. After rebranding it to "agogue", all was forgiven. There were also all the other ones that people didn't wish to talk about. And, of course, the Church of Atheism,* which no one took seriously.

* Because everyone else had a church.

Curly, who had been "it", appreciated the interruption. It is difficult to win a game that requires wearing blindfolds when one has two heads, both of which want to go in different directions.[7]

He was a black-and-white, two-headed, Friesian calf. One head was black with a white curled forelock. The other was white with a black curled forelock. Otherwise, there was nothing unusual about him.

Yes, most bovines possessed but a single head, but anyone who has studied Mr Mendel's pea-based theories understands how physical characteristics are determined by the hidden hand of genetics.

And anyone who has ever played the game of whispers, where a message is passed from person to person, understands how a message gets more and more jumbled in transit.

That summed up genetics in a nutshell for you and explained Curly's two heads completely.

As for his ability to talk. Well, what of it? Speech is a common side-effect of demonic possession. Once the Alumières had removed the demon, only the ability for speech remained. It is only because demons usually possess humans that more exorcists don't realise this.

Curly had been born on the Dunsloe's farm, and adopted by the Alumières, as two-headed, talking calves are the sort of thing that make superstitious people nervous. It was for his own good, rather than that of the locals, that the Alumières adopted Curly. He talked a *lot*.

"And there's a time and a place for everything," Gertrude Alumière liked to caution him, "but Hawkinge-By-Hythe is not the place for a talking calf right now."

---

[7] Try it if you don't believe me.

His best friend was Chloe Dunsloe, eight years old, and small for her age. Short, straw-coloured hair frizzed around her head. Her attempts to get it to lie flat were futile, even when she tried flattening it with her fingers after eating jammy bread.

She was the only girl in the Dunsloe family, which had been blessed by an abundance of male offspring. This is relevant as it explains both why Chloe usually wore boys' hand-me-downs, and her strong aversion to being called either a "tomboy" or a "princess". For now, she was simply Chloe Dunsloe. She would make up her own mind about what else she might be when she felt like it.

Other than the Alumières, she was the only person in town who knew Curly could talk. In the privacy of Swiftwater, he could do so as much as he liked.

Even with his blindfolds removed, Curly did not take an active role in the sardine rescue. Having two mouths to talk with suited him more for a managerial executive role. While the others picked up fish, he searched for stragglers.

Although it seemed unlikely someone would be hanging around and listening through the hedges of Swiftwater's secluded back garden, he agreed to call out a more bovine-sounding "Oo-*ooh!*" when he found a fish.

Should anyone be there, this would sound enough like "Moo-oo!" to allay suspicion, while also making Chloe laugh when he did it in a high-pitched, squeaky voice.

As they gathered up the last of the fish, Gertrude looked into the sky, while her sisters discussed what might be behind it.

"Monro mentions rains of fish throughout the area in his *Description of the Western Isles of Scotland* from 1549," said Victoria. "He draws no conclusions, but they seem to occur with greater frequency west and north-west of the Gulf of Corryvreckan."

"Where the whirlpool is situated?" Gertrude watched Colette slide another sardine into her green enamel basin of water. Once it hit the water, the fish shot out of her fingers to confer with its fellows. None of them knew any more than it did. "Sudden changes in the usual conditions might turn a whirlpool into something more akin to a geyser."

"Precisely," said Colette. "During gale force conditions, standing waves of up to fifteen feet in height have been recorded for certain. Any fish caught in them would likely become airborne. And there's no knowing how strong the winds get. The worse the storm, the fewer people are standing around measuring things."

"Aunt Victoria!" called Chloe, and Victoria left them to see what she wanted.

Gertrude wondered how one became an aunt. She didn't recall anyone discussing the matter with her, yet here was Chloe, using the term for Victoria.

"The Honduran town of Yoro has an annual rain of fish, and have done ever since the 1860s," said Colette.

"A town with all modern conveniences. How lovely! Because?" Gertrude turned the garden hose off. They had been filling their old aquarium with water and salt to accommodate the sardines. The aquarium originally held the world's largest monkeyfish. Upon liberating her from a travelling sideshow, it had been in storage ever since.

"Because the inhabitants were hungry, so their priest, Father Subirana, prayed for extra food. They got fish."

"Oo-*ooh!*" called Curly from near the far hedge. Chloe snorted a laugh and ran to see what he had found. Victoria returned to her sisters.

"And really because?" asked Gertrude.

"By a bizarre coincidence, the fish invariably arrive at a time of meteorological disturbances. Stormy weather."

"That sounds more like it," said Victoria.

"Poor fish!" said Chloe when she and Curly joined them. "But we got them all, Aunt Colette."

Aunt Colette! thought Gertrude.

Chloe beamed once the final fish slipped into the enormous aquarium.

"Snatched up by wind and carried along until the wind loses force. At which point the fish plummet to the ground," said Gertrude, to make sure Chloe noticed the presence of "Aunt Gertrude", should she be required. "Of course, this usually culminates in a cessation of life, missing from the current situation."

Chloe's smile faded away.

"It's just nature, angel," said Colette to Chloe. "Often, it's just birds, and they have to eat too. Sometimes, they get airsick and vomit up what they've eaten, including bits of fish."

"Ew!" said Chloe.

"Oi/Stop it!" said Curly. "There are gentlemen present!"

"In which case they are *definitely* dead," supplied "Aunt Gertrude" helpfully.

"Or what also happens," said Colette, giving Curly a grin that stood the hairs on his necks straight up, and made his ears twitch. "Is that people see fish on the ground where no fish should be and assume they must have rained down."

"Or toads. Sometimes people see toads," said Victoria, joining in the game.

"The fish—or toads—might be from a nearby river. Perhaps a heavy rain has fallen. The river has burst its banks, flooded the streets. Left the fish behind. But no one saw it, because they were inside out of the rain, or it happened at night while they slept. When they go out, they see fish on the ground and assume they fell from the sky."

"What is the value of this speculation?" asked Gertrude, wondering how she and her sisters could be so alike, and yet they could be so *silly*.

"Because where else would they have come from?" wondered Victoria.

"Where?" said Chloe.

"Where?" said Curly. "Don't tell me!"

"From *below!*" Colette knelt down to put one arm around Chloe and another around Curly's black head and stage-whispered the answer.

"From below?/From below?" whispered Chloe and both of Curly's heads in unison.

Colette nodded grimly.

"Really!" said Gertrude.

"Underground rivers, subterranean cave systems. They fill up during strong rain, and then they overflow. Just like a river," said Victoria.

"But there's nowhere for the water to go, so the water—and the animals—are squirted out of the ground.

"Squirted?/Squirted?" said Curly.

Chloe squealed, then laughed as Colette tickled her.

"Is this true?" Curly asked Victoria.

She nodded. "No need to worry."

"No need to worry?/Frogs squirting into the air, and no need to worry!" Curly gave himself an exasperated look.

"Toads, not frogs."

"Fine. But nothing larger than that?"

"Of course not."

"Right. So, no *calves* raining down?" his black head clarified. His white head watched Colette, in case she knew more.

"No," said Victoria.

"Certainly no calves who go to bed nice and early, anyway," said Gertrude. She would have liked to take part in the fun, but it seemed no one wanted her to.

She knew they regarded her as the bossy one. Usually, she relished the role. It helped her get things done efficiently. But watching them play made her wish she didn't always have to be the tough one. But Victoria was so soft-hearted people took advantage of her. And Colette never took anything seriously. Which is why it fell to her, Gertrude, to be tough. The sun was setting. Tomorrow was Thursday, and Chloe needed to get a good night's sleep for school.

"Night, Chloe!/Nighty-night, everyone!" said Curly.

"Can't we play a little longer?" Chloe asked Victoria, in case there might yet be a reprieve.

"It *is* bedtime," said Victoria.

"But the fish! There might be more in town. Can't we go see? They're suffering!"

"Unlikely. Any fish left in town are almost certainly undergoing a process rendering them into useful energy," said Gertrude.

Chloe stared.

"Being eaten," explained Colette with a sympathetic glance.

"Oh!"

"But maybe not *all* of them." Victoria gave Gertrude an exasperated look as Chloe's face fell. "Saddle up, Curly. Animal patrol!"

Gertrude ground her teeth. The only thing she hated more than being contradicted was letting people see them argue amongst themselves. She watched Victoria and Colette help Chloe onto Curly's back, armed with basins, jugs of water and a packet of salt in case they encountered saltwater fish.

"You're too *nice*," said Gertrude, when they were gone.

She fumed. Not only had Victoria contradicted her, but before she left, Chloe gave Colette and Victoria grins and a hug before riding off.

To Gertrude, Chloe had said, "Thank you for having me stay, Miss Alumière." She understood it wasn't personal, but it rankled. If she wanted, she could be the nice one getting hugs. If Victoria ever displayed a bit more steel.

As if rubbing it in, Victoria now glared at her, as if it were her fault! *Typical,* thought Gertrude. *As nice as kittens with everyone else, but if* I *say anything, she's only too ready to show her claws!*

"Oo-*ooh!*" came Curly's distant call.

"You know there has *never* been a rain of animals in Hawkinge-By-Hythe?" said Colette in the silence as her sisters glared at each other.

"No?" asked Victoria, staring at Gertrude. Gertrude should have been proud. Normally Victoria would have backed down, or said something to defuse the situation. Obviously *she* wasn't going to apologise. Victoria had contradicted her in front of their guest.

"No," confirmed Colette.

"Noted," said Gertrude, waiting for Victoria to break the staring match they were now locked in. She would stand there all night if necessary. Victoria was *forcing* her to be a bully!

"I'd also like to note something," said Victoria, without blinking. "A certain entity which has been making its presence known on several recent occasions."

"Carfax!" said Gertrude.

As she spoke, the clouds, which had been massing over them, were split by a flash of lightning and a peal of rumbling thunder, like a filthy, deep-throated laugh.

Chapter 3

Dead Twenty Years

WHEN ANOTHER SHOWER of sardines fell the next day, all eyes in The Groat and Ball pub turned from the window to Professor de Glube. The generous locals were eager to give credit where it was due, and he had arrived, calling for refreshment, only seconds before the downpour.

The professor was a cheerful, dapper gentleman of advanced years with a shock of wild white hair, though his clothing delivered the real shock. He favoured colours of such intense brightness, that even the more bohemian students at the University of Fontissen in Luxembourg, where he worked, found them loud.

"Nothing to do with me, thank you," he said, after draining almost half his pint of malty beer. He had been wandering the countryside all morning, and it was thirsty work. Not only that, but the fish rain had upset him. He was dressed in a suit of discreet emerald green tweed with crimson lining. The thought of how close he had come to having this gorgeous garment sardined on left him atwitter. "Should we go and see if there's anything we can do to help the poor fishies?" he asked once the fish stopped falling.

This raised the other drinkers' suspicions again.

Professor de Glube was the town's very first tourist, and the prevailing sentiment was that they had picked a winner.

Originally from Luxembourg, he had studied theology in his wild youth at the same seminary as their local vicar, the Reverend Gresstart. While the reverend had stayed the course, the professor had given it up for epigraphy, the science of hunting down headstones to note what was written on them.

De Glube came to Hawkinge-By-Hythe to catch up with his old friend while tackling a couple of pet research projects, for he was none other than Professor Lucius de Glube. One of Luxembourg's most well-respected epigraphers.

He had always been popular in town, and the villagers were eager to believe the best about anyone. The word "fishies" struck them as sinister, however.

No honest man referred to fish as "fishies" without an excellent reason.

As it happens, de Glube had one: he was in love. He might have come to town for the Gresstarts, but he stayed—for the moment—for the Sniffacres.

A lifelong bachelor, he had fallen head over heels with Hawkinge-By-Hythe's longest-serving widow, the enchanting Jennet Sniffacre.

After a single glance, he had realised she was the woman for him. And he had believed she felt the same about him. In his mind, they were a modern-day, maturer version of Romeo and Juliet. They walked together, they ate their meals together. They even used to go to the cinema together, before the place collapsed. De Glube burned for Jennet Sniffacre, but though he burned for her, he never forgot his upbringing.

He was a gentleman.

And as a tourist, he represented Luxembourg with every word and act. Accordingly, he held himself to the strictest standards of Luxembourg's fastidious rules for lovers. His behaviour remained exemplary, therefore.

When it came, the realisation Jennet could never be his had crushed him.

For despite everything, it seemed she still pined after her dearly departed husband: the late Mr Sniffacre.

De Glube had hoped that being alive might offer him some natural advantage over his deceased rival. But it was not to be. Whenever he broached the subject, she switched the conversation to what hot stuff her now cold husband used to be.

Despite being dead some twenty years, Mr Sniffacre's hold on his former wife appeared as strong as ever, and de Glube did not stand a chance.

Just the other day, she had said something about Mr Sniffacre shortly hurrying home for his tea.

Dead twenty years, and she still hoped to see him come through the door! But de Glube could not help his feelings. He loved Mrs Sniffacre, and this had led him into the terrible habit of lovers around the world. He found everything cute.

Fish were "fishies". When he fancied a stroll, he went for "walkies", and, only the other week, in Grunnion's butcher shop, he had requested "a pork choppie".

His beer finished, de Glube headed outside to see what might be done for the fishies. The other drinkers followed him, and soon a human rescue chain was in operation. At one end, the landlord passed fresh glasses out to the volunteers, who added a sardine, then sent it back.

Fish would be on the Groat and Ball's menu for a while.

The professor was glad of the opportunity to help. The physical effort allowed him to forget his woes for a while.

And when the rescue mission led to a heated discussion, with the pub's patrons remonstrating with its owner on the sardine-beer exchange rate, that suited the professor too.

He stole away without any of them noticing. He needed to see a man about a bird.

As well as a broken heart, de Glube also had a secret...

Chapter 4

Nodding Dean

THERE WERE TWO reasons de Glube found Hawkinge-By-Hythe and the surrounding countryside so interesting from an epigraphic viewpoint.

Like so many before him, he had been lured into epigraphy by the tales of legendary English astronomer, alchemist, and mathematician, John Dee.

Grown to man's estate, de Glube no longer believed the wondrous claims that Dee made. Such as being able to converse with angels in a language he called Angelic, now known as Enochian.

Dee had transcribed 48 verses of this Enochian language, together with 19 "Calls" to translate them. De Glube believed in an alternative translation, along with some ideas about where he might discover some fresh inscriptions written by Dee himself. If he were right, then he would settle the matter of the Enochian Calls one way or the other.

And he had been right. While most scholars avoided Hawkinge-By-Hythe to prevent getting their toes embarrassingly wet in the sea of superstition that surrounded the place like a moat, de Glube dived in head first and grabbed the jackpot.

There was no mistaking his findings. At times, it even seemed like Dee—or someone—guided him, an unsettling but rewarding feeling. Just the other day, while wandering around an old graveyard, enjoying the headstones, and making notes inspired by a standard, "Here lies ol' Whassisname", ol' Whassisname hinted that de Glube might like to check the next headstone along.[8]

And ever since the business with the werewolf and statues, de Glube held proof that his new translation worked.

He needed to be careful before he tried again.

For he would try again, despite the stern talking to dished out by a furious Gertrude Alumière.

His eyes were set on a much bigger prize than they could grasp and nothing should stand in his way.

With a little care, they would never find out about it.

Not before it was too late, anyway.

When de Glube first made Mrs Sniffacre's acquaintance, he took her with him while he rambled around the countryside for his researches.

No longer. Luxembourg's rules on courtship forbade it, even if it had not been too painful for him.

Left alone to ramble as he pleased, de Glube left at the crack of dawn, before even the farmers yawned and cursed their alarm clocks.

This is exactly what he had done the day after the rain of sardines outside the Groat and Ball, after making sure

---

[8] Ol' Whassisname's *inscription* seemed to hint that. It had been drilled into Ol' Whassisname throughout his long life that when he died, he was expected to lie quietly until the Lord came along and said otherwise. The six feet of dirt on his coffin were to make sure he took the hint.

to dress in his second least favourite suit (bishop purple with truffle brown/white pinstripes), and pack a large umbrella in case the weather should again turn fishy.

He needed the early start, because de Glube's plans required privacy, and he knew of no other way to get it.

When a man dresses like a peacock on hallucinogenic drugs, is the very first tourist a town has ever seen, *and* is well known for dispensing sixpences with a lavish hand, that man can find privacy hard to come by.

De Glube needed to find a spot far away enough from prying eyes to suit his purposes.

A keen walker, de Glube had by now explored almost every corner of the Kent countryside around Hawkinge-By-Hythe. But a quirk of geography encouraged people to wander south and west. It is a fact that very few of the local roads led east or north, despite the usual argument of pedants, that a proper road must always have two ends.

Or, they hasten to add, two starting points.

This is why de Glube had never before come across Nodding Dean.

Even by the standards of small English towns, Nodding Dean was titchy. De Glube might well have missed it this time, too, except that a sudden noise behind him made him leap off the road. He pushed his way through a lacklustre hedge and over the fields to get away from it. It might be someone he knew, which would foil his plan to get away from everyone. Determined to be left alone to stew in his misery, he continued over the fields until he found another road.

He stepped out through another hedge and turned south. Then he realised that actually he wished to try north for a while and started walking.

After a while, he realised he was still headed south. He turned around and continued walking. Then he stopped, because—he double-checked the position of the sun—he was still walking south. Again he turned north, yet when he continued walking, he found himself going south once more.

He stopped and summoned up all his determination and started walking, sweat breaking out on his brow.

Finally, he was heading north, and the road fought him every step of the way.

His perseverance was rewarded, for in just a very few minutes, he came across the Church of Nodding Dean.

As he would later discover when updating his meticulous notes, the church in Nodding Dean was administered by the parish of Nodding Dean.

The parish of Nodding Dean consisted, in its entirety, of the town of Nodding Dean.

And the town of Nodding Dean comprised the church, the church grounds (including graveyard), and the rectory, where the church's pastor would have lived, if there had been one.

But what Nodding Dean lacked in size, it made up for in ambition when it came to ecclesiastical architecture.

The church had been constructed in the Byzantine style, wide and broad, rather than narrow and tall, like most English churches. Square, of cream-coloured sandstone blocks of various sizes, the smaller stones expertly "snecked" into the spaces among the larger ones to add solidity and style to the design.

De Glube moved closer, his heart pounding. Not only were the stones snecked, but they were bull-nosed, too. He wished he carried a camera on his person. He had always been a fool for snecking, and when the stones were bull-nosed into the bargain, his knees practically turned to jelly!

If Mrs Sniffacre were with him, he would have spent the rest of the day pointing out each block. How the mason carefully rounded them for that distinctive shape—like a bull's nose, which is where the term came from—thereby lending the majesty and grace of said animal to the finished building. She would have liked to know that.

He walked around the building once, noting the lack of windows in its walls, until he returned to the entrance, a bright red arched doorway. When he pushed at the door, he found the interior was not dark, as he had assumed it must be. The church was topped with a large central drum tower with large stained-glass windows running the entire way around it.

It represented the usual scene of Jesus or someone doing something nice for peasants, as far as he could tell. He found the window's story less interesting than the spectacular light which flooded the church through it. He felt like the lightbulb inside a Tiffany lamp. The nostalgic scent of ancient incense and wood polish from the half-dozen pews lined up before the altar soothed him further.

The building could never have held more than two or three dozen people, despite how imposing it seemed from outside.

De Glube nodded to himself in satisfaction.

Really good snecking did that for a building.

He strolled through the church with his hands out, watching the greens and blues and reds of the stained-glass window dapple his skin. The sense of peace the place gave him was stunning.

When he started feeling light-headed from the quiet and kaleidoscopic patterns, he left again to examine the church grounds. He headed first towards the graveyard, looking in at the tiny little rectory house set back in the greenery, which is where the vicar would doss down.

One could always find something to sit on in a graveyard. After that, he would take a wander around. In his mind, plans formed themselves. He had been looking for somewhere private to do what he planned to do, and this might very well be the spot.

Besides, he had yet to come across a church which did not have some concealed secret.

It might be the trace of witch marks half-hidden by plasterwork to ward off evil. Or a choir boy's honest opinion of his choirmaster, after an unsatisfactory exchange of views.

Something.

As expected from such a small place, the graveyard was not large. It consisted of half a dozen headstones, all with railings marking out their territory and he quickly found the something he had been seeking. Despite the graveyard having enough space to accommodate it, a seventh headstone lay outside the graveyard, at the edge of the church's property. Almost hidden between thick bunches of wild angelica bushes on either side.

What captured de Glube's interest was that, while the headstone itself appeared newer than all the others, the inscription was illegible.

Either the inscription had somehow been particularly affected by weathering, or it had been poorly inscribed.

Or, some letter-like shapes had been scratched into the stone with a chisel to fool careless visitors.

Its location only added to the mystery. Separate from the other graves, it suggested a person of great infamy.

But when he knelt to examine it, de Glube found the presence of weathered wood peeking through a tiny hole at the back of the headstone most interesting of all.

Checking to ensure he remained unobserved, de Glube unfolded his pocketknife to pick away at the hole in order to reveal more of the wood.

As anyone who has ever enjoyed scratching an itch can testify, the trick is knowing when to stop. De Glube's curiosity itched at him, and he quite forgot to stop scratching.

Within an hour, he had removed the entire back of the headstone. Under it, he revealed a convex wooden shape only slightly narrower and shorter than the "headstone", which turned out to be an artful mix of gravel and cement. This mix covered the wooden object, which appeared to be shaped like a very large soup bowl turned to stand on its edge.

Lost in his work, he poked next at the ground. First with his pocketknife, then with a branch.

As far as he could tell from the resistance he encountered, the "bowl" continued into the ground.

He brushed his hands, dusted off his trousers and completed another circuit of the church while he thought.

When he finally made his way home, he felt more cheerful than he had done in days.

His conviction that where there was a church, there was a hidden secret, had been vindicated.

And this secret looked like being a large one.

Chapter 5

Germanic Wise Man

WHILE DE GLUBE made exciting discoveries in Nodding Dean, Victoria Alumière attempted to do the same in the Records Office at Hawkinge-By-Hythe's Town Hall. Colette and Gertrude were managing their chemist shop, the Alumière Apothecary.[9]

Victoria loved delving into a place's history, and her claim to be writing an updated history of the town gained her access to the town's official secrets. It helped that they were friendly with the alderman, who was delighted to help. The other council members had been less enthusiastic, but the knowledge they had burnt the good stuff years ago provided them some measure of comfort.

Currently, the alderman's friendship proved as much a curse as a blessing, however, because he kept popping into the dusty room to see if Victoria needed anything. He found it difficult to accept her assurance that she did not, for he himself found the room oppressive. So many files chafed his guilty conscience.

---

[9] Trial and error had enabled them to ascertain that two Alumières represented the maximum recommended daily dosage for Hawkinge-By-Hythe's adults.

To be alderman, a man—or woman—must possess two qualifications.

An ability to cope well with boredom.

And looking like someone who reads all the paperwork laid in front of them.

The Records Office troubled Fawsick the way a doorstep full of empty bottles would trouble someone unable to give up stealing their neighbour's milk.

Essentially, an alderman does the same job as a mayor. The difference is that the population of the town elect a mayor, while the town's board of councillors elect an alderman.

He is, in effect, their mascot.

One that can take the blame whenever the natives get restless.

Having been elected by the citizens of Hawkinge-By-Hythe, Alderman Fawsick was the mayor, but he liked the sound of alderman.

A dictionary he had once read informed him it came from the Germanic word for "wise man", which he liked the sound of.

When his 53rd birthday rolled around and no one knew what else to get him, the councillors clubbed together for a pewter mug with "ALDERMAN" on it.

The title had stuck after that.

Having already pretended to have read all the paperwork on his desk for the day, popping in to make sure Victoria was comfortable helped him pass the time. He never stayed long, though, because every time he opened the door, he experienced the unpleasant sensation that the assembled records raised their metaphorical eyebrows as if to say "You? Here? Really?"

Despite the interruptions, Victoria was making good progress through the town's written archives, searching for something *relevant*.[10]

Although she couldn't have said exactly what she was looking for, she would recognise it when she found it. A lot of strange things had happened in Hawkinge-By-Hythe over the years. Victoria wanted to determine whether this was natural, or whether she could discover a certain, unmistakable *nescio quid* which would indicate Carfax was somehow involved.

She made one interesting discovery right before the alderman buzzed in the last time. She didn't yet understand how it fitted into the grand scheme of things, but it positively leaped out at her.

A massive bill for goldbeater's skin paid for from the town's coffers.

For those unfamiliar with it, goldbeater's skin is simply a tissue-thin material made from animal intestines. The intriguing name comes from its use during the process of beating gold into gold leaf for gilding. And Hawkinge-By-Hythe had no history of metal working, jewellery, or

---

[10] When the town council said that the Records Office contained the town's "written archive", they weren't joking. Aware that destroying *all* the town's records would arouse suspicion, they had come up with a scheme similar to that of Minister D-, the antagonist of a short story by Edgar Allan Poe. In that story, Minister D- conceals a purloined letter by leaving it lying about with the rest of his correspondence, on the assumption that anyone sent to retrieve it will be searching for a hidden letter. Likewise, the council had collected so much paper that finding something useful should be well-nigh impossible. As well as official meeting minutes and notes, the Records Office contained all the local newspapers, receipts, fourteen copies of every advertisement ever posted within the town's jurisdiction, several books of poetry, the complete set of journals outlining the process behind every bye-law ever passed, a mountain of doodled scrap paper, and every note ever intercepted by a teacher during school hours.

printing. It was as she made a second interesting discovery that the alderman buzzed back in again. This time in the company of Mrs Pengle.

The alderman seemed to be dancing with Mrs Pengle, for he bobbed around her like a rubber duck in turbulent bathwater, but most likely he merely wished to keep her away from the room's ornate, disused fireplace. The alderman's particular contribution to the Records Office was to allow the town's reporter to use it to store his correspondence from Mrs Pengle.

Letter after letter concerned with her father's supposed claim to fame, coupled with an enquiry as to when an interview might be convenient for the reporter. But Mrs Pengle was only at the Town Hall because she had followed the town constable there while he answered a question she had asked him.

The Constable was one of the area's hardest-working law enforcement agents. He combined his duties as a constable, with those of the alderman's chauffeur, as well as being his personal bodyguard.[11]

Mrs Pengle had encountered him outside, and, remembering her vow about Mrs Champion, she was picking his brains on the subject of toes and public indecency. He had been holding her less than spellbound ever since.

As they entered the town hall, Mrs Pengle saw an Alumière in the Records Office. She realised she might have found something even better than the law to squash Mrs Champion. When she saw the yellow feather and

––––––––––––––––

[11] One doesn't get to be alderman without kissing a lot of babies. Although none had so far threatened revenge for this heinous act, Fawsick wanted to be prepared for when the day of reckoning finally came.

realised she was looking at Victoria, Mrs Pengle wondered if she might not be a little lucky herself.

She would have been prepared to tackle Colette, or even Gertrude, in her quest. But Victoria was the nice one.

Well, nice for a *witch*.

The OWCHH didn't invite the Alumières to their meetings because they didn't seem like "joiners". Nor was it possible to imagine Gertrude idly sitting by while other people talked, and as for Colette…

Naturally the members of the Official Women's Club of Hawkinge-By-Hythe were all for both progress and a good time. A *woman* with a sense of humour, however, seemed like a bridge too far.

But, Mrs Pengle asked herself, what about Victoria? Such a shame she couldn't attend the meetings, just because her sisters weren't Club material.

Who would blame Mrs Pengle for taking pity on the poor lonely girl and inviting her to come along one day out of sympathy? *There she sat, reading old newspapers by herself*, Mrs Pengle imagined herself saying. *Including the one with the photograph of my father with his wine bottle full of potato. I remember it well. Taken on the day he almost invented putting salt and vinegar on chips. It was like this…*

And if Victoria *did* bring her sisters… well.

Mrs Pengle would bet Mrs Champion wouldn't dare flash her Big Toe with Gertrude at the table. The mind boggled at what Gertrude would say to that kind of provocation.

And if nothing occurred to Gertrude, Colette would have something up her sleeve to remove the toe's shine!

"I'll leave you here, Constable," said Mrs Pengle. It meant interrupting the saga of the 1842 Poultice Reform

Bill, just as the constable reached the climax of his blow-by-blow recounting of the most interesting bit, but she had work to do.[12]

"Lovely to see you, Miss Alumière," she called as she navigated her way around the jittery alderman. He planted himself in front of the fireplace. Just in case.

"Good morning, Mrs Pengle," said Victoria.

"I thought of you just the other day. I told the ladies it's a shame we don't see more of you." Mrs Pengle waited for Victoria to ask who the ladies were.

"That's very kind of you, I'm sure," said Victoria instead. "If only there *were* more of us! But it's only the three, and when we're not in the shop, then we're busy on our other projects."

"Victoria is writing a book!" said the alderman.

"Fancy!" said Mrs Pengle. "I'm sure… *ahem*… The Ladies… would love to hear about it." She nodded, head-butting the ball back into Victoria's court. Now, Victoria would be forced to ask who the ladies were. Then Mrs Pengle could spontaneously explain the OWCHH and invite her to take part.

And then watch the sparks fly next time Mrs Champion unsocked the secret of her success!

"They can read the book!" said the alderman.

"Exactly. There's not much to tell at the moment, as I'm still gathering the information."

"I see," said Mrs Pengle, and she meant it. "There are buns, as well." She held out little hope that this would

___

[12] This concerned the lawyers' protracted discussions whether they should shove in another simple "wheretofore" so that the strength of their legal argument would not be overwhelmed by the elegance of its language, or wow the crowd with a well-deserved "whereof the hereaforementioned" in the fourth sentence of the third last paragraph of the fifteenth clause of the ninth Act.

make a difference, but she had shot her best powder and it was all she had left.

"Ooh!" said the alderman. Then he caught Mrs Pengle's eye.

"Thanks, but—" said Victoria.

"Wonderful! It's very exclusive," continued Mrs Pengle, aware that if she let Victoria say anything, the battle would be lost.

"Really, I—"

"That's settled, then! It's at the Cosey Kettle, but I'll pick you up at home, shall I? So we all arrive together?" In her mind's eye, she heard the ladies gasp as she entered with three Alumières.

"Sorry, I'm afraid I can't," said Victoria. "Too busy with all this—"

"I'll pick you up at home," said Mrs Pengle.

"I—"

"I'll pick you up at home," repeated Mrs Pengle. She had once seen a hypnotist, and that was all he did, repeat the same thing over and over again until people did it.

"No!" said Victoria. Then she turned away and continued reading. The word stopped Mrs Pengle in her tracks like a head-on collision with an omnibus full of nudists.

The alderman had watched the tense scene unfold before his eyes. Now he made himself useful for the first time that day. He hurried himself and Mrs Pengle towards the door before either of them caught cold from the room's sudden drop in temperature.

"Well," said Mrs Pengle to the alderman. "I just wanted to be *nice*..."

"Shh!" said the alderman, in case it set Victoria off again. He turned to check it was Victoria. Yes, a yellow feather adorned her black pork pie hat, for all that she sounded just like Gertrude.

"It says in the Bible, doesn't it? That people should be nice. Of course, I wouldn't expect one of *them* to know what's in the Bible!"[13]

"He that is without sin among you, let him cast the first stone," said Victoria, who knew exactly what was in the Bible.

The door slammed.

As it turned out, Victoria's injunction to Mrs Pengle had the opposite effect to that intended. As usual.

"Without sin," mused Mrs Pengle. "Stones. There's an idea."

"Scones?" enquired the alderman, whose mind still wrestled with the buns she had mentioned.

"*Stones*," said Mrs Pengle.

Alone in the Records Office, Victoria packed up her belongings. Gertrude might have applauded her firmness, but Victoria felt seedy from being mean to Mrs Pengle. She needed to walk it off.

And time was running out.

The Alumières were due to meet their arch enemy that evening.

---

[13] Editor's note: The Bible does not say this. In fact, the word "nice" does not appear at all in the King James Version of the Bible. Possibly Mrs Pengle preferred the Douay-Rheims Bible, in which case it is worth noting that the DRB uses the word "nice" in its original sense of "ignorant".

Chapter 6

Beast That He Was

IT'S NICE TO be righteous. But it's not always enough.

For some people, even knowing that one day they will receive their eternal heavenly reward for leading a good life seems like a poor bargain. Especially when a quick glance around shows how much fun other people are having *now*.

In Hawkinge-By-Hythe, these people coalesced around the local vicar, Reverend Gresstart, who seemed like the gloomy type who might sympathise. Since the Alumières had arrived in town, they coalesced even more, sensing his antagonism towards them. They reasoned that when witches arrive, the clever villager searches out a strong champion to protect them. And who better than that imposing man of God, the reverend? They need not fear the devil's thermometer, with the reverend at their backs, as it were.

And *of course* the Alumières said they weren't witches. Witches always said that.

Gresstart remained unaware they had nominated him the People's Champion. He did not like the Alumières, but he did not like anyone. Except, of course, for his wife,

Tabitha. He *loved* all his flock. His job required it. But with so much on his mind, it left him little time to go around liking people.

For their part, the Alumières were sceptical of the reverend. In their experience, a man with that much on his mind must be up to something.

The Reverend Gresstart and the Alumières only had one thing in common. Professor de Glube, who was determined to get them talking to each other.

So they were gathered around the table in the dining room of de Glube's cottage at 7 p.m. that evening, in response to his invitation. Conversation did not flow, as each side expected the other to say something that would ruin the evening.

Even de Glube, their host, regretted it now. His original idea had been that, what with the Alumières' interest in the unusual, and Gresstart's belief in God, they must have tonnes in common over which to bond. It just needed someone to make the first move.

De Glube prided himself on his cooking skills (people often complimented him on his dishes being "unforgettable"), and he had looked forward to the evening being a smashing success. In turn, seeing him lead the feast would turn Jennet Sniffacre into putty in his hands.

This, she would think, *is what married life is all about. Good food, brilliant company, and a cook who wears spats in the kitchen!*

Afterwards, he would pop the question. She would gasp her answer, and they would settle the thing without further delay.

Of course, he had planned the evening back before he realised she did not love him. Things looked different now.

To save something from the wreckage, he decided the dinner should be his farewell party instead. It was a depressing thought, though not as depressing as the anguish of catching Jennet Sniffacre's eye. In his mind there lay no doubt that he detected her impatience to get away from him and return home.

He would not be joining the strength of Hawkinge-By-Hythe's population, after all.

He remained passionately in love with Mrs Sniffacre. Her smile unleashed butterflies in his stomach, and she meant more to him than even his favourite lucky pen had done while he was a young student writing his first dissertation.

Foolishly, he had attempted to woo the woman, unaware of her feelings for her dear dead ex-husband. She had rebuffed his every attempt, and he would soon return to his lonely university chair. Perhaps from that distance they could be friends, if she liked.

He might yet have stayed were it not too dangerous. Proximity had turned him into a volcano of burning passion, and it was only a matter of time before he lost control completely.

On several occasions, he had kissed her in public. Nor could he plead extenuating circumstances. He had kissed her, simply because he wanted to. His cheeks burned. He had acted monstrously. No doubt her neighbours talked about nothing else.

Beast that he was, he must leave for her sake. And so he would, after one last task.

As soon as his eagle arrived. Or on the last day of the month.

Whichever of the two came second.

Even the novelty of fish falling from the sky did nothing to help the conversation along.

The guests ate in silence. The full guest list, starting under the still life painting of a dull apple and leering banana and moving clockwise towards an even worse painting of a green waterfall, comprised Victoria Alumière, de Glube, Colette Alumière, and a Mr Oaten, who could always be relied upon to make up the numbers, on that side of the table.

Continuing clockwise on the other side of the table sat Gertrude Alumière, Jennet Sniffacre, the reverend Aubrey Gresstart, and his wife, Tabitha Gresstart. It was not correct to seat the Gresstarts together, but when one invites three Alumières to a dinner party for eight people, one's options are limited. Even at his most optimistic, de Glube would not have risked seating the reverend beside one of the scientific triplets.

Even leaving aside the supernatural—or scientific, depending on whom one asked—aspect of the rain of fish, there had been something beautiful in the silver flashes of sardines raining between the clear azure sky and the juicy lime green of the countryside. And yet, except for Mr Oaten, nobody mentioned it. And even Mr Oaten had little to offer on the subject of raining fish. Other than that, like Mrs Champion, he did not believe it.

He wanted the assembled diners to understand that when fish fell from the sky, they fell, too, outside the bounds of his credulity. That was all. He felt that they should know this and repeated it often. After which, he relapsed into an uncomfortable silence, wishing de Glube had invited a few real men to the party so they could talk about football.

The Alumières did not want to mention the fish, in case the Reverend said something religious on the subject.

And the reverend did not want to touch the subject in case the Alumières said something scientific about it.

De Glube realised it must be his responsibility to ensure everyone enjoyed themselves. His love for Mrs Sniffacre distracted him too much to allow him to make conversation, however.

For her part, Mrs Sniffacre said nothing because she was depressed. The man she loved most in the world— Prof de Glube, *not* Mr Sniffacre—had led her on, until she assumed they were soul mates. Then he dropped her as he prepared to return to Luxembourg.

Mr Hyssop acted as de Glube's butler for the evening. When he cleared away the potato and leek soup, which they had eaten in near-total silence, Victoria opened proceedings by mentioning her discovery from that morning.

The item was interesting and uncontroversial. Besides which, Colette was looking at the cruet-stand in a way that signalled she would shortly make her own attempt to liven things up by loosening the top of the saltshaker.

Gertrude sat there and waited for someone to say *anything*, so she could tell them they were wrong.

Well, just let her try!

After brow-beating Mrs Pengle, Victoria felt about ready to tackle a menace who deserved it! "I came across an interesting article today in an old newspaper," she said.

"Oh yes?" said Mrs Gresstart, after a moment, when no one else said anything. Mr Oaten was still shaking his head that fish lacked the common sense needed not to fall from the sky. Her husband stared at the table in front of him. No doubt lost once more in gloomy rumination of what to do about the church roof.

It is one of life's ironies that church roofs are particularly susceptible to leaks and loose slates. And that the men and women who work there belong to one of the few professions which requires looking earnestly skyward at regular intervals, making it impossible for them to ignore it.[14]

"A newspaper from the 1750s, contained a report about Lord Collopy Muir setting up a committee to rename the constellations of the night sky. It seemed to be all the rage for a while," said Victoria.

The Muirs were the local big wigs. Normally, they lived at Muir Hall outside town. The current Lord Muir had whisked himself and his family off to see the world before the Alumières arrived.

Before leaving, he had mentioned something about wishing to broaden his family's horizons. By now the Muirs had been gone for years. Significant money changed hands in the town's drinking establishments whether they would return with Britain's broadest horizons, or whether they possessed the kind of horizons which couldn't be broadened, regardless how much effort one put into it.

Gertrude eloquently grunted her opinion of the Muirs, but otherwise said nothing.

"I'd love to name a constellation," said de Glube sadly. He would have called it *Jenneta*. That way, he could see her wherever he went.

______

[14] The Reverend often mused on how similar his lot was to that of King Jehoash, who waited 23 years—in vain—for someone to fix his leaky Temple (2 Kings 12:6 in the King James Bible, hereafter KJV).

"And then everyone lost interest in it. The entire business just died." Victoria looked in the reverend's direction, ready to pass him the conversational baton, should he wish to take it.

"Ah!" said de Glube. "Death!" Yes, if he could have neither Mrs Sniffacre, nor even a little constellation named in her honour, then perhaps death was best. The Alumières knew what they were talking about.

"What did they want to call the constellations?" asked Colette, though it seemed unlikely the story would have a good punchline, as they were in polite mixed company.

"Well, it seems to have started with an article praising the efforts of Nicolas-Louis de Lacaille, a Frenchman who named fourteen different constellations in the eighteenth century. From reading between the lines, I received the impression it was a dig at Lord Muir's astronomical efforts. At any rate, he seems to have taken it personally. There's a letter to the editor complaining that between Ptolemy and de Lacaille, the French and Greeks had it sewn up between them. His argument was that the stars would look nicer with proper English names and set up a committee to do something about it. The Mayor, a certain Catchpleen, loved the idea. Said he knew someone at the Astronomers' Royal Society of England who could help."

"Like the Smith Constellation? Or Brown Minor? Major Muir?" asked Colette. "He can't have considered fortune tellers. Just imagine: 'Oh, do be careful, I see great danger for you ahead when Major Muir enters—'"

"Colette!" said Gertrude.

"'Aquarius'," finished Colette. "Yes, Gertrude?"

"Well, more along the lines of British wildlife. The Red Deer, and the Great Crested Newt, and so on. British names for British constellations," continued Victoria.

"They have Great Crested Newts in France. And across most of the continent," said Gertrude, glad to have spotted an obvious mistake.

"Yes, but they're only *called* Great Crested Newts in *English*," said Victoria. She tried out a glare.

"I'm guessing they didn't get very far with it," said Gertrude, unwilling to start a fight in public. She shifted her own glare to the reverend. Victoria understood her reasoning. His manner as he ate his soup had been suspicious, and it behoved them to be prepared in case he suddenly lunged at someone with his spoon.

"Fish, though! A rain of fish. I'll tell you this: I couldn't believe it!" said Mr Oaten.

"What a lovely idea," said Tabitha Gresstart. "Although I'm no good at spotting those constellation things."

"The Reverend Hennessy might have been involved in that," said the Rev, rubbing his ankle, where his wife had kicked him under the table. "There were some notes and sketches. Something about a squirrel constellation?"

"How adorable!" said Victoria, drowning out Colette's comment about nuts. "As I say, the papers were full of it for a couple of months, then nothing."

"Oh, you know how it is," said the reverend, talking to de Glube. Triplets made him nervous. "People get interested in something, then something else happens and they forget. I must say I don't like the idea. They've been named. Leave them be," said the Reverend, inflating his chest. "He allowed us to name His animals. We mustn't seek to name His stars, too!"

"Are you interested in astronomy, Reverend?" asked Victoria.

"A bit," he said. Hyssop came in with the salad, and Gresstart dived at it to escape the conversation.

The Alumières slowly relaxed. His sudden movement had made them tense for action.

"A bit? He loves it," said Tabitha. "It's all I can do some nights to get him away from his telescope."

"It's where He lives." Gresstart addressed the table.

Gertrude coughed. This was too much for her.

"Fish, though? Unbelievable," said Mr Oaten. "Mind you, rain's nothing but water, and fish like water. But still."

Conversation flagged after that, but it wasn't an inauspicious start. Even when the professor served *quetscheflued*, a plum tart, and speciality of Luxembourg, the evening might yet have been regarded as a success.

Until the time came to leave and they saw what was waiting for them outside.

Chapter 7

A Clown With Mange

AS MRS PENGLE stormed out of the Town Hall after her interview with Victoria Alumière, she had second thoughts. And then third thoughts.

Her first thought, it will be remembered, was "stones". The second was "throwing". The third was the worst: "serve them all right!"

But as she stomped along Main Street, she calmed down. Enough to have a fourth thought: if she didn't confess these terrible sinful ideas, she might not get into heaven. So she hurried off to find the reverend.

Mrs Pengle had been looking forward to heaven for a very long time. The longer she lived, the more nervous she grew about passing away with some tiny sin on her conscience, preventing her from getting in.

In her imagination, the pearly gates to heaven were at the front of a very white and fluffy cloud. Holy golden balls topped off the railings around it to keep out the riff-raff. St Peter stood in front of the gates, wearing biblical robes, but also a posh black hat and gloves like the doorman at an expensive London club. If she arrived with a stain on her soul, he would know it, and cut her dead. And then, of course, Mrs Champion would turn up and waltz right in! There Mrs Pengle would be, excuse me-ing and can-I-speak-to-the-manager-there-must-be-some-mistake-ing, getting all flustered. Meanwhile, through the railings, Mrs Champion would be flashing her Big Toe at the angels, and Queen Victoria and so on. Grinning while Mrs Pengle landed in purgatory.

Not that there was anything wrong with purgatory. But, by all accounts, it wasn't great, either. Perhaps something like a busy dentist's waiting room, with green flocked wallpaper, windows painted shut, and too few magazines to pass the time. It was not how Mrs Pengle intended to spend her afterlife.

So, as soon as she had all these thoughts she headed for the reverend like a hound after a fox. Not finding him at home, she stalked the town until she found him. It was easy to find him thanks to the small, devoted clique who followed him everywhere in case he suddenly smote someone.

Mrs Pengle could count herself lucky that smiting wasn't the Reverend's style. He would have been more likely to smite Mrs Pengle than anyone else. Purely out of self-defence.

Her constant need to confess everything had done more to wither his open and exuberant nature, than even worrying about the state of his holey roof. Bright and vibrant in his youth, he now resembled the last lemon in the greengrocer's window. A bit sour, but mostly jaded.

It was both the quantity and the quality of the material. She led such a blameless life that, it seemed to him, the thrill of confessing to impure thoughts was the most exciting thing she would ever experience. Which was good, and exactly what he wanted, of course. Better than her getting her soul in trouble. But it irritated him. As an Anglican, he didn't like talking about sin and that type of thing.

But he couldn't break her of the habit and yearned to hear something shocking. Just for the variety.

Looking on the bright side, it meant he could rely on her to always do the right thing. If she didn't, she would tell him all about it afterwards.

Compared to this, the Alumières didn't bother him at all.

He disliked them, but in a general way. They were new in town (he didn't like that), and they possessed that elusive quality of being modern (he didn't like that).

The reverend didn't like anything modern, particularly the Church of England's current inclination to ape what the Catholic Church did, rather than going its own way. Like this matter of confessions, for example. When he had been a boy, the vicar gave the congregation a single minute's silence to reflect and ask for forgiveness. "The Lord knows what you've all done. So you'd best say sorry and mean it!" Yet his current bishop told him he should encourage Mrs Pengle to seek him out and whisper sorry nothings in his ear, "if it makes her happy!"

That was what he disliked about the modern age. People wanted to be happy all the time. Only one thing irritated him more than people being happy all the time, and that was people treating him as an equal.

He did not regard anyone—man or woman—as an equal who could not recite Bible passages on command, or perform half a dozen baptisms in a single morning without breaking a sweat. After years of practice, the reverend's technique allowed him to dunk babies through the fountain, like he worked on the production line at one of Mr Ford's new factories. He was proud of his skill.

And perhaps it didn't help that the reverend and the Alumières both wore black. Gresstart was a tall man, with a long face, long unruly hair, and a hint of the Byronic about him. He looked good in black and resented the Alumières infringing his copyright.

His devoted following had picked up on it. They conflated his apparent disapproval with their own suspicions that the Alumières might be witches—French ones!—and waited for the fierce battle for the souls of Hawkinge-By-Hythe that must shortly be enjoined by these rival forces.

This would have shocked the reverend. He was prepared to stretch a point and believe in witches, if God insisted, but, in his opinion, modern people were the real scourge.

Who in hell could stand being happy all the time?

"Will he be long?" Mrs Pengle asked the reverend's inner circle as she joined them in the road outside de Glube's cottage where the reverend dined with the Alumières.

Secrets are hard to keep in a small town, and the news of the reverend meeting with the area's most scandalous sisters had quickly made the rounds. And as it travelled it had morphed and grown into a tale of how the reverend intended to forcibly demonstrate the errors of their ways to the three ladies. Possibly even signing them up for a nunnery. His fans outside waited with bated breath for the cries of repentance and gnashed teeth they expected to ensue. So far, things remained quiet. Mr Nooney shrugged, then returned his gaze to the walls of the mysterious cottage.

Unperturbed, they continued to wait, no matter how long the mighty battle within the walls of the cottage might yet rage.[15]

"What's that?" asked Mrs Pengle to change the subject. As one of the reverend's best customers, she knew this crowd well. They did not enjoy speculation.

The world was a bad place.

The reverend was a good man.

Beyond that, they were not prepared to go.

"Rowan," mumbled Mr Ball, showing her the little cross he held.

"Keeps *them* away," explained Mr Nooney. From the way he said it, it left little doubt who he meant. And Mrs Pengle knew the rowan tree's reputation as a powerful protection against witchcraft.

"Very nice," she said, making a mental note to add this lie to her confession.

The cross was not nice. It was two bits of twig bound with a bit of greasy string into the crude shape of a cross. The upright twig still had a wilting head of red rowan berries, giving it the appearance of a stick figure representing a clown with mange.

Her compliment went down well, however, and the entire group of a dozen squeezed closer to her. Each held out their own rowan cross to get her discerning opinion of them.

---

[15] In their belief that a mighty battle raged, they weren't far wrong. At that moment, the diners were dealing with de Glube's *quetscheflued*. What with the viscosity of the baked plums, and the pastry's tendency to bond immovably to the chewer's teeth, it was a dessert which never went down without a fight.

She did her best and wracked her brain for the perfect compliment for each hideous specimen pressed upon her attention. Could she get away with saying the stains on this one's dirty twine were "unique"? Then de Glube's door opened.

The crowd backed away from Mrs Pengle as the Reverend Gresstart came out.

Mrs Pengle realised she still held the rowan cross, as the Alumières appeared behind him.

She threw it onto the ground, not sure if she was more worried at the implied insult to the Alumières (she still harboured a hope that she might get Victoria to come to an OWCHH meeting), or the fact that the reverend would think she indulged in heathen beliefs.

The cross flew into the flowerbed of de Glube's front garden, but not far enough to be easily overseen. In fact, with two shrivelled red berries, like bloodshot eyes, this one seemed to be crying out for someone to look at it.

The crowd murmured as they saw the reverend and the Alumières together, smiling awkwardly.[16]

"Mrs Pengle!" said Reverend Gresstart, and all eyes slapped against her like *quetscheflued* attaching itself to enamel.

For all that she had come to see him, Mrs Pengle was terrified. Had he spotted her holding the rowan cross before throwing it away? Was he even now about to tell her she had committed idolatry and littering?

The reverend strode through the rowd to take her arm.

"What are you doing with these people?" he asked. His eyes darted around the assembled faithful.

---

[16] A really good *quetscheflued* can keep people smiling awkwardly for days, before it completely dissolves and the mouth can move freely again.

"I wanted to talk to you," she said, swearing it was true. She hadn't meant to pick up the cross, nor intended to throw it on the ground.

"Good," said the reverend. "Good. I can rely on you, can't I? Can you… keep an eye on them?"

Mrs Pengle nodded. She would have said something, except she was too busy having an epiphany. For the first time she understood what the phrase "God helps those who help themselves" meant.

She had come to atone. For guidance. Yet it seemed she had known what to do. Instinctively, she had thrown the symbol of heathen faith aside, to be rewarded with the reverend's confidence.

If she had held onto it, or apologised, and asked to confess, he would no doubt already be sighing and demanding whether it couldn't wait until the morning. Like he usually did. Instead, he squeezed her arm in gratitude, and entrusted her with this position of power as he collected his wife and said goodbye to the others.

Another epiphany hit her. "God is everywhere" including, thought Mrs Pengle, *in Mrs Pengle*. He helps those who help themselves, because He is everywhere. Even in sinners, such as herself. Even in these wretches who stood around bothering the reverend, while hedging their bets with heathen beliefs.

She almost fainted when a third epiphany hit her, bigger than the previous two. So big that it almost certainly came directly from God himself. These wretches might be very useful to her. In turn, she might save them from themselves. They should have confessed to the reverend that they kept crosses made of rowan wood, instead of hiding them in their pockets. That was a sin.

But if they assisted her, then she would show them how to repent and be saved. Confessing had not yet caught on with anyone else in Hawkinge-By-Hythe, but why else would God give her control of these poor souls' destiny?

As the reverend left, his faithful attempted to close in around them, but Mrs Pengle, strengthened by the reverend's faith, stood in front of them.

She would start helping God help those who helped themselves right now.

She hadn't dropped the rowan cross, she realised now. The Lord had thrown it from her grasp to help her get the respect she deserved. She no longer needed the OWCHH.

The Lord and Reverend Gresstart had ordained that she lead her very own group.

And with them, she would do her very best to make sure everyone was sorry.

How else would they get into heaven?

"Look," she said. "They can't get past it." She raised her arm to point at the Alumières.

In fact, the Alumières were still saying goodbye to de Glube, but they had already spotted the cross, and were annoyed.

"Come!" said Mrs Pengle, leading her righteous flock away from the scene of their first triumphant battle.

They were long gone before the Alumières strolled down the path.

Colette picked up the rowan cross. "Rude," she said.

"The berries make a lovely jam, though," said Victoria.

Gertrude said nothing. Instead she subjected the departing group to a non-witchy, but very evil eye.

Chapter 8

The First Shall Be Last

OVER THE NEXT few days, fish continued to pour down. Fewer sardines now, and more mackerel or perch. Hawkinge-By-Hythe was ready. People left buckets and basins out overnight, so when Chloe Dunsloe and Curly rode into town on Animal Patrol the following Wednesday, there wasn't much for them to do.

Meanwhile, Mrs Pengle did what the reverend wanted and kept an eye on the more active members of his flock.

She also talked to them, measured them up, and sewed them white woolly tunics like the crusading knights used to wear while marching to the Holy Land. What the reverend didn't know wouldn't hurt him.

For the same reason—to avoid hurting the reverend—she refrained from telling him she referred to them as "The Reverend's Right Handers", a name they willingly embraced.

And to avoid hurting *their* feelings, she avoided clearing up an innocent misunderstanding that he knew all about it.

She would straighten things out with everyone, eventually.

To help him get used to the idea of these Right Handers—without spoiling the surprise—she didn't wear the tunic herself when she met the reverend for confession. When Mr Nooney, Mr Ball, and the others paraded past St Dunstan's Church as arranged, she was left without any doubt. He had been impressed. So much so that he even stopped talking, despite her enquiry about his choir, a subject on which he felt strongly.[17]

It had been difficult to get him talking again afterwards. He kept asking her if she was really keeping an eye on "certain people".

She confirmed it. And the only reason she didn't wear the white tunic herself, she explained to her Right Handers afterwards, was because she didn't quite feel she had earned it yet. There were still one or two things she needed to get off her chest first.

But she was the leader of the group, all the same. Right?

Right!

She reminded them of what the Bible said about the last being first, and all that. So she'd don the tunic last, in order to be first through the gates when heaven opened for business. If that was fine with everyone?

Fine!

In the meantime, they had work to do to prevent the town from turning into a modern-day version of those sinful towns with the Irish-sounding names, Sodom and Gomorrah.

Only through confession could they hope to avoid hell. Everyone had done something wrong at some point. It was only human.

---

[17] So strongly that he was forbidden from mentioning it at home anymore.

For example. To pick an example at random. Something she didn't care about in the slightest. Not that she cared at all. Off the top of her head. Once, as she embarked on the tale of how her father had almost invented putting salt and vinegar on chips, someone had muttered "put a stocking in it" and yawned! It was possible that she might have told the story once or twice before, but not enough to warrant such rudeness! Someone needed to get that off their chest if they wanted to get to heaven.

Mrs Pengle would forgive whoever it was. Of course she would. But she needed to know who it was first.

So, once the Reverend sat safely ensconced in the Church, interviewing the builder about his last bill for roof repairs, she brought her Right Handers to Main Street.

Let the confessing commence!

Although Mrs Pengle knew for a fact that most of the town's inhabitants were human, and therefore sinful, business was slow. It seemed no one wanted to confess to anything. After a couple of hours standing in the sun outside Town Hall, even her, that is to say, *the reverend's* followers were losing interest. They had thought their new roles would mean seeing more of the reverend, but they hadn't seen him for hours. What was he doing without them? And wasn't the builder due today? Who wouldn't want to see a builder get smote? Just then, the Lord swooped in and saved Mrs Pengle's bacon once more. Two people strolled in their direction, right when she needed them most.

Humanity's need for religion is deep-seated. All around the world, people believe many things. Different gods, different hells, different prayers. But they all agree on one thing.

Young people are up to no good.[18]

Therefore, the sight of a young man and woman walking and talking together without looking married made Mrs Pengle's day.

"Confess!" she cried out as they approached.

"Ar!" said the Right Handers, righteous in their shiny new woolly tunics. Their moment had come. It was one thing to hang around waiting for the reverend to start smiting, it was another to do it themselves. The knowledge that they were taking action went straight to their heads, jamming their vocal chords on the way. So they could only manage an "Ar!" What they meant was, "Excuse me, sir and madam, but we are worried about the state of the world today, and wondered if you would like to unburden yourselves of anything sinful? You'll feel ever so much better afterwards, plus the Lord will be sending fire and brimstone if things don't improve, so do think about it, won't you? Thanks!"

"Morning Mrs Pengle," said the young lady, Miss Tinfeld, and continued walking with the young man, who turned out to be Huffam Pyle. Miss Tinfeld would have stopped to confess if it meant getting rid of Huffam. Her parents were very strict, however, and didn't allow her to have any sins. She looked forward to the day when she moved out, got a place of her own, and could give them all a try.

As for Huffam Pyle, the delivery boy for Cappledrum's Grocery, he naturally assumed they weren't

---

[18] Whether young people are naturally more sinful, the Devil works harder to tempt them, or they are just lucky enough to have the *energy* for sin remains a mystery.

talking to him. He only walked with Miss Tinfeld because he required information. She had made the mistake of telling him a joke as he brought her order. He still hadn't understood it.

"Morning, Mrs Pengle. But *why* did it want to get to the other side?" he demanded again as they left the group behind.

It came as a sore disappointment to the Right Handers. They wanted to be taken seriously. They were wearing white woollen smocks in summer, so people would take them seriously, and nothing had happened. "Ar," they said, but Mrs Pengle read volumes of dissatisfaction in those two letters.

"Stop!" cried Mrs Pengle, spying another young mixed couple approaching from the other direction four minutes later. The young man carried a box. It seemed to Mrs Pengle that he did so in a lascivious manner. Well, she would stop the moral rot from going any further.

"Oh, is there a problem with tomorrow, Mrs Pengle?" asked Miss Cosey, the female half of the duo, when she heard Mrs Pengle. Mrs Pengle helped her clean the tearooms every second day.

Mrs Pengle cleared her throat when she saw Huffam Pyle. Returning from the other direction, like one of those Hellfire Club rakes who can't bear to be alone, he carried the box of Miss Cosey's provisions.

Like Miss Tinfeld, Miss Cosey would have been delighted to stop and chat, even if meant a problem. Huffam kept telling her there was a chicken over the road, then grinning. She worried he might soon turn dangerous.

"No," said Mrs Pengle. "No problem."

Miss Cosey and Master Pyle passed on, and the grumbling around her grew louder. It gave Mrs Pengle a taste of why they made the reverend so nervous. They had been grumbling for years, and had it down to a fine art. They were very eloquent.

Despite not being able to make out any individual words, they left her in no doubt that they were not happy, and disappointed in her.

It stung.

Well, they weren't so great themselves, in Mrs Pengle's honest opinion. If they were worth the woollen tunics she had made, they would have done something to be a bit more intimidating. Instead, they left it up to her, despite her being in just her normal clothes.

Or perhaps the town was already so far gone that even the righteous white of the saved could not shine its saving light through the murky sins of the townsfolk?

That might be it.

Truth be told, she felt ever so slightly self-conscious. What they needed was some practice. Find somewhere a bit more private, and work their way up to accosting people.

Somewhere where neither the reverend nor the Alumières would catch them, ideally.

Out in the countryside, for example. No doubt all kinds of sinning went on out there, and there wouldn't be as many nosey parkers checking up on any righteous who were fed up with it, either.

Out in the countryside.

Where Mrs Champion lived.

Sinful Mrs Champion who let people worship her Big Toe. Like it was a pagan god.

Let him who is without sin cast the first stone.

Or her, of course.

"Follow me," said Mrs Pengle.

"Why?" asked Mr Nooney, whom she had marked down as one of the keener onions in the fire. So keen he might be trouble. When the Lord came back, Mrs Pengle would make sure he was first to be taken. That way he would actually be last, and with a bit of luck the Lord might forget to take him at all.

The rest of the Right Handers were mumbling again, and even looking sheepishly at their white smocks, as if wondering what they were doing.

"We're going to cast the first stone," said Mrs Pengle.

This time, the chorus of "Ar!"s around her sounded just right.

Chapter 9

Adventurous Crouch

DE GLUBE'S MYSTERIOUS find in the graveyard kept him busy in Nodding Dean while Hawkinge-By-Hythe found religion.

He couldn't keep away, despite the late hour, for he was starting to make progress.

By rights, he should have already penetrated the mystery, but kept getting lost whenever he tried to follow the road to Nodding Dean. Even a compass had not helped. He had wasted a lot of time wandering the country roads, certain the one he wanted lay close by, but quite unable to find it.

Finally, he gave up on the road and resorted to using the "shortcut" through the hedge, to get there. It meant concentrating hard to make sure the road didn't fob him off with the wrong direction when he came out again, but was otherwise the easiest option.

He assumed it must be something to do with magnets, but tried not to think about it. Because magnets reminded him of things being attracted to each other. Which turned his thoughts inevitably to his hopeless love for Jennet Sniffacre.

On the road to Nodding Dean now, a full moon hung over him, and the crisp smell of leaves slow-baked in the summer heat scented the air. Alone, de Glube made it to Nodding Dean, challenged only by owls. He ignored them and hopped over the church wall.

The gate hung open, but he considered it unsporting to walk into the graveyard he was plundering.

He carried a torch for emergencies, but kept it switched off. Should anyone come by, he would rather not be noticed. His current project was nowhere near as naughty as what he planned to do once his helpful young friend, Lorry Tassel, delivered his eagle, but still.

Something about digging up graveyards in the middle of the night demanded solitude and a lack of nosy gawkers. No doubt most resurrectionists were only captured because they operated in groups.

If, say, famous body snatchers such as Crouch and Harnett had snatched their bodies alone, they might, in all likelihood, have done so indefinitely. It was their penchant for company that undid them. De Glube found it too easy to imagine what must have happened. As one dug, the other kept watch. While the digger operated his shovel, the watcher would have grown bored and wanted to chat. No sooner would they have started chatting than Harnett—or Crouch—would have insisted to the other that the corpse *he* had dug up the previous night was much bigger than the current one. Crouch—or Harnett—would have been stung by the insult, and insisted that although the current one might be a tiddler, Harnett—or Crouch—should have seen the corpse that he, Crouch—or Harnett—almost landed when he, Harnett—or Crouch—went off for a cigarette.

That one had been massive.

At that point, it was almost irrelevant whether they came to blows or kept arguing. Either way, tempers would have frayed, voices would have been raised, and they would have been spotted, apprehended and locked away.

Along with his torch, de Glube had brought a shovel with a retractable shaft and a flat cushion. Soon, he knelt on the latter, digging around the back of the headstone with the former to reveal the graveyard's secret.

Although, as an epigrapher, his forte was inscriptions, epigraphy falls under the broader umbrella of "adventuring". Like treasure hunting, exploring remote valleys with dinosaurs in them, and teasing Egyptian mummies to test the strength of their curse. And any adventurer worth his salt would back de Glube up that anything hidden in a cemetery is fair game.

It wasn't a simple task. Whenever he remembered he was in a grave, he thought of Mr Sniffacre. Which reminded him of Jennet Sniffacre, which reminded him of his heartache. But he persevered. It would be worth it.

He worked carefully to avoid damaging his trophy, but finally the entire front of the "headstone" lay exposed before him. Under the cunningly fashioned gravel, cement, and plaster, he uncovered a simple length of wood.

Sturdy ash, if he were any judge. Round and concave from the front. Or round and convex from the back, if one preferred to approach the matter from that direction. Either way it tapered into a long, thick beam.

His preliminary scientific poking told him that the object went deep into the ground. Freed from its cover, he saw it entered the ground at an angle from back to front.

This precluded the existence of a body underneath the headstone. That was good news, at least. De Glube didn't like to think of himself as the sort of adventurer who went around desecrating graves when he didn't have to.

Satisfied that further investigation would not disturb anyone's final rest, he returned his attention to the round head of wood on top. It was about three times as large as his own head (not including the ears). Combined with the long narrow shaft of wood below, it looked to de Glube a bit like a spoon.

A giant wooden spoon. Stuck in the ground and covered with plaster like leftover porridge to hide it. This gave de Glube pause.

Though a foreigner, he understood English customs well enough to understand that the English did not bury giant spoons in graveyards without a good reason. He should at least consider what that reason might be before continuing his work.

For he would continue to dig. Possibly he would find an epigraph engraved along the length of the spoon's shaft. That would mean he was well within his rights as an epigrapher to dig it up.

But possibly it lacked an inscription. In which case he might face every adventurer's worst nightmare. The question why he hadn't taken the easier, more sensible, and obvious option of *just leaving everything alone.*

Either way, the mystery demanded to be solved before he left Hawkinge-By-Hythe.

For all it looked like a giant spoon, de Glube suspected it must be something else. But he would make sure before he committed himself. Speculation was a fool's game, and a dangerous one, too. A keen student of history, de Glube again thought of Crouch and Harnett and how speculation might have led them to their terrible fate of digging up graves.

He saw them as young men, sauntering arm in arm through a cemetery on their way to watch the ballet.

Then Crouch, spotting the recent date on a headstone, would have turned to Harnett. "Bet you a pound that the eyes have already gone on this one," he might have said. No doubt he intended only to remind his friend that they should enjoy the ballet, even if it turned out disappointing. For their time on Earth would be brief.

And Harnett, who hated ballet, and whom de Glube imagined to be the more imaginative of the pair, would have replied, "Nonsense! I'll bet you ten pounds Grandad has skipped town with the barmaid, and there's nothing in that grave at all other than... oh, let's say, a giant wooden spoon."

In need of cash—ballet tickets aren't cheap—Crouch would have insisted on digging up the body to prove his point, and the rest is history. Having dug up their first body, digging up the rest would have come ever easier to them. Especially if Harnett insisted on doubling down on his spoon theory after every lost wager.

And de Glube did not doubt that, were he here now, he would have lost again. For buried in the cemetery of Nodding Dean, was something potentially a lot more dangerous than a giant wooden spoon.

Chapter 10

Nipping Buds Or Butting In

A WEEK LATER, Victoria once again occupied the Records Office, continuing her research into Lord Collopy Muir's efforts to rename the constellations. Colette preferred to use her half-day off to spy on Mrs Pengle, intrigued by a mob clad head-to-toe in white woollen tunics in the middle of summer.

And at Swiftwater, Gertrude prepared the makings of a rather fine tea party for a guest.

She had hurried home after shutting up the apothecary, determined to make a better impression on Chloe when she came to visit Curly. And if she could decant all the incriminating fruit punch, eclairs, sticky buns, etc. into the intended recipients before her sisters turned up and noticed, so much the better.

"Thank you, Miss Alumière," said Chloe, when Gertrude let her in, and brought her to a seat at the wrought iron garden table on the terrace in the back garden. Curly was already there, though he remained standing. He found it easier to reach the food that way.

"Like a picnic," explained Gertrude. She seldom lacked for confidence, but something about small people—

children—made her nervous. And Curly's sceptical glances weren't helping. Gertrude and Chloe sat.

"Well," said Gertrude. "Help yourselves!"

"Thank you, Miss Alumière," said Chloe.

"You can call me Gertrude, if you like." She tried doing that thing Victoria did so well. Smiling.

Chloe and Curly stopped chewing for a moment to give Gertrude's smile the attention it deserved. "Yes, Miss Alumière," said Chloe.

And that seemed fair enough to Gertrude. Smiling had never been her strong suit, and the thing felt weird even to her.

"Have an eclair, Curly?" She meant it as an offer, but it came out as a reprimand, because he kept muttering to himself, which put her off. Likewise the heat. She hadn't realised before, but the day was a scorcher, and she was perspiring with the effort of trying to get the conversation going.

Politics? Religion? The modernists' rejection of traditional literary conventions? What on earth *did* children talk about?

She would start small. "How do you like school?" she tried.

"School's fine," said Chloe, swinging her legs. Gertrude noticed and deduced this indicated comfort with the topic. If she ignored how Curly was staring at her, she might make progress.

"And your teacher?" She poured them both another glass of punch and added a sticky bun to Chloe's plate.

"She's fine," said Chloe. "Am I in trouble?"

"No! Not at all. I just wanted to chat until the others come back. I'm usually so busy." Gertrude blushed. Did that sound like a boast?

Curly's mouths dropped open, and Gertrude realised the flaw in her plan. She should have bought more eclairs to keep him busy. He had sucked up all half-dozen from the plate, and now had nothing better to do than goggle at her with his mouths open. Like she had two heads or something.

She admitted defeat—for now—and gave up. She would need to pay more attention to how Victoria did it before she tried again.

Hopefully, her sisters would return soon.

She cleared her throat to frighten away the silence that had swooped down on their picnic table.

"So," she said. "What do you think of Churchill's decision to re-introduce the gold standard for the British pound?"

There was no sign of Chloe, Curly, or Gertrude when Victoria and Colette returned to Swiftwater.

Once the treats were gone, Chloe had taken pity on Gertrude and suggested a game of hide and seek. She had seen the eldest Alumière sweating and wondered if the sun might have boiled her brains. In which case, the best thing would be to keep her somewhere cool until the others returned. After a quick conference with Curly, Chloe announced she would seek first. Curly led Gertrude to "one of the best hiding places" behind his shed in the back field, which had plenty of shade. He hid himself nearby, behind the pile of lumber Colette was seasoning for future projects, from where he could check on her.

Chloe had hidden to avoid agitating the patient should she return demanding to know why she hadn't been found. Or resume the conversation about Chancellor Churchill.

So when Victoria and Colette arrived in the back garden, a large potted *cotoneaster horizontalis* beside the terrace in the back garden told them what had happened. "I'm sorry," it whispered. "But I think Miss Alumière has had a touch of the sun."

Then Chloe popped her head out from behind the pot, now it was safe to do so.

"Oh dear," said Victoria.

"She's been saying some very peculiar things."

Colette finished her survey of the table with its empty plates and came to a conclusion. "Was she being *nice?*" she asked.

Chloe nodded.

"Oh dear. I hope you weren't frightened?"

"No, but it was strange."

"Ah, there you are!" called Gertrude, coming into view from the bottom of the garden, emerging from the hedge, which she had used to sneak around Curly undetected. "Did I win?"

"Yes, Miss Alumière," said Chloe. "I was just going to tell you." The sound of pounding hooves announced Curly.

"Fish/Fish! I saw fish!/Let's go!"

Conversation was constrained while the Alumières helped Chloe onto Curly, loaded him up with basins and petrol cans filled with water to rescue any fish they found. He and Chloe waddled into town on their mission of mercy.

Colette collected up the plates and made tea. Gertrude and Victoria waited in silence. Gertrude felt embarrassed.

Not only did she know exactly what Victoria must think of her efforts to impress the small person, but she would realise they had been unsuccessful.

A dreadful thought suddenly crossed her mind, requiring her full reserves of control not to squirm. Had Chloe *let* her win the game?

Birds chattered in the trees to cover up the uncomfortable silence.

"I'll tell you what I found out, shall I?" said Colette when she returned.

"Please," said Gertrude. She couldn't believe Colette hadn't been laughing her head off in the kitchen, but without proof she remained civil.

"They call themselves the 'Reverend's Right Handers'. Mrs Pengle keeps them all worked up, and they have a slogan: 'Lambs on the outside, lions on the inside'.[19] They stood around in a field praying, then shouting. Once they were excited enough, she brought them around to harangue Mr Kelby."

"We can't have that," said Gertrude. After her frustrating afternoon, the chance to shout at people sounded wonderful. She sat up straighter in her chair and threw her shoulders back.

---

[19] While she was sewing up the tunics, Mrs Pengle came up with the idea of using that bit from the Bible about lions lying down with lambs. It sounded good, and she had always felt that people treated her like a lamb when she would have preferred to be treated with some respect. Like a lion. So it was a shame that bit wasn't actually in the Bible.

Although the prophet Isaiah forgets the punchline, he relates a story about a bunch of animals living together in the Bible. There's no lion in it, but there is a *wolf* and a lamb. Briefly, the wolf is staying at the lamb's house, because the leopard's house was full. The leopard's house was full because he shared it with a young goat, a calf, a lion, and a second calf. This second calf is fat, Isaiah tells us. Also living there, for some reason, is a small child who acts as head of the household (Isaiah 11:6).

Anyone who's ever lived in shared accommodation will know exactly how the poor leopard must have felt, and why the wolf decided to give it a miss.

One must assume this is the bit Mrs Pengle was thinking of, and simply got the *dramatis personae* muddled up.

"What were they shouting about?" Typical, Victoria always wanted to hear both sides, to try to make excuses for people.

"They accused Mr Kelby of being sinful for liking dark beer, despite not having sheep. I'll admit I don't see the connection."

"Hmm," said Victoria. "There is a bit in the Bible that says 'But he that entereth in by the door is the shepherd of the sheep. To him the porter openeth….' It's in John, somewhere."[20]

"Which? The quote, or the porter?" asked Colette.

"Oh God!" said Gertrude. No wonder people didn't take them seriously.

"Well, never mind," said Colette. "Should I continue to monitor their behaviour, then? It sounds like they might hurt someone, even if only themselves."

"Monitor their behaviour?" scoffed Gertrude. With her blood up, she couldn't face the prospect of letting a bunch of *people* get away with things.

"Yes," said Victoria.

"And then—"

"What on Earth is the use of that? We understand enough about mobs to guess what happens next. They need to be nipped in the bud, before they come around here talking about you-know-what," said Gertrude.[21]

"But if we want to get at the root cause, rather than address the symptoms—"

"Poppycock!"

"How come you're allowed to say that, and I'm not?" asked Colette.

Gertrude hadn't intended to, it had slipped out.

[20] Editor's note: John 10:2-3.
[21] Editor's note: witchcraft, presumably.

She had just been through a trying experience, all because she didn't have time to practice being nice. Because someone needed to look after them all.

Victoria and Colette couldn't do it. It all fell on her shoulders. Her sisters were "Aunt Victoria" and "Aunt Colette", because Gertrude kept everyone in line.

She would have loved to be Aunt Gertie… well, no. Not that.

But maybe Aunt Gertrude, if only her sisters would do their fair share and give her a chance!

"Do continue," said Victoria to Gertrude, and Colette rubbed her hands in anticipation.

"Well, why are you both so nice all the time? It doesn't actually help, does it? Eventually you end up having to put your foot down and—"

"I'm not nice. I'm witty," said Colette. Gertrude ignored her.

"I'm sorry your afternoon with Chloe didn't go as planned," said Victoria.

"That!" Gertrude sniffed. "I thought you'd never get back, and I'd be stuck with her for the rest of the day."

"It's alright to be upset," said Victoria.

"Yikes! Another cup of tea?" asked Colette. "Or perhaps something stronger?"

"I'm always in favour of something stronger," said Gertrude. "We need to nip buds!"

"No," said Victoria. "We keep them under observation until we have a reason to go *butting in!*" They had both stood up when Colette rose to get a hot drop from the kitchen.

"Butting in? You're scared people won't like you if you ever dared to stand up for yourself," said Gertrude.

"Not at all. But I promised the alderman we would refrain from inciting any more riots for at least a little while," said Victoria.

"See? You care too much about his opinion."

"Why go looking for trouble? They haven't done anything yet."

"*Yet!* You'd rather wait until they make trouble for me, when I have to save everyone!" Gertrude ground her teeth.

"You don't want to save anyone, just boss them around!" Victoria was surprised to find herself almost shouting.

"And you refuse to make the hard decisions that need to be made!"

"You don't understand that people have feelings!"

"They still need to be led!" said Gertrude, tossing her head back.

"And you're unwilling to lead by working *with* them, because it's harder to do. Shout and move on, that's your style!"

"Why waste the time?"

"Because it's much more rewarding!" said Victoria. As Colette returned at that moment, it meant she managed to have the argument's last word for a change.

"I have to say, I'm with Victoria on this one," said Colette, setting out a set of fine teacups and a teapot which used to belong to an ex-nun from Limerick who now lived near Piccadilly Circus.

Gertrude was so furious that she let them have their way. That would teach them a lesson.

Let them get pushed around, if they liked. She would enjoy watching it.

But they needn't expect her to mop up the mess afterwards!

Chapter 11

An Eternity In Hell, Or Half An Hour At Home

IT WASN'T THE Reverend Gresstart's fault, for he didn't know Mrs Pengle was leading people astray under the name of "the Reverend's Right Handers".

Mrs Pengle could hardly be blamed, as she just wanted to get to heaven.

And what would be the point of blaming Leviticus? It forbade *everything*.

An impartial observer might therefore come to the conclusion that it must have been Kelby's own fault.

While drinking a glass of porter in the Groat and Ball one evening that week, he carelessly mentioned to Mr Nooney and Mr Ball (no relation to the pub) in the course of a dry conversational spell, that he had clover in the fields. Though he would have turnips in again, once the clover came out.

The next day, while casting about for something to say to Mrs Pengle, they had mentioned this to her. She had decided it was exactly the kind of depraved sinfulness which couldn't be allowed to stand. As a sign of her favour, she allowed Mr Nooney and Mr Ball the honour of explaining to Mr Kelby why he would burn in hell. She stayed back a bit so as not to get in the way. So far back, in fact, that Kelby couldn't see her.

It took quite a bit of coaching before they were ready. Then they descended on Kelby's farm to urge the farmer to drop crop rotation for the good of his immortal soul.

Leviticus 19:19, explained Mr Nooney and Mr Ball, made it clear that God didn't like crop rotation. He subscribed to a one-field, one-seed policy for farmers. A chorus of people saying "Ar!", with the occasional "Arlelujah!" behind them, prevented the two preachers from feeling silly as they did so.

Despite it all, Kelby remained unimpressed, enquiring merely whether God had up-to-date figures on the cost of running a farm in post-war England.

For this they labelled him a "turnip-lover".

Kelby admitted to enjoying turnips, and Mr Nooney enquired whether he liked them enough to spend eternity in hell for them.

Mr Kelby informed him they cooked in half an hour at home. Less if he cut them up first.

From there, the conversation moved onto his taste in alcoholic refreshment. The Right Handers insisted that if he didn't burn for the turnips, he surely would for the stout.

It took all the reverend's skill to calm Mr Kelby down when he complained afterwards.

Naturally, Mr Kelby assumed that the reverend must be behind a group calling themselves the Reverend's Right Handers.

In turn, the reverend called on Mrs Pengle to demand answers. He had specifically requested her to keep an eye on this group of people and look at the upshot.

Mrs Pengle claimed they must have slipped off without her noticing. She thanked the reverend for letting her know where they had gone. It would be useful for next time.

The reverend was mollified enough that he even offered to hear her confession. Apart from the little white lie she had just told for his own good, Mrs Pengle had nothing to confess for a change. But, so as not to disappoint him, she made up a couple of things for him to be getting on with.

Later that night, as he stood in front of his wardrobe to pick out pyjamas, it occurred to the reverend to wonder what she meant by "next time".

The next morning, the Reverend decided he might need more help than just Mrs Pengle. It wouldn't be the first time his more devout parishioners had gone a bit over the top. So he dusted off a favourite old sermon about tolerance for Sunday and practised hard for the rest of the week.

Mr Sporkmann visited the reverend at the rectory first that Monday, desirous of an explanation of why the reverend wanted people to smash his windows.

Mr Sporkmann managed the estate for the absent Lord Muir, which involved a lot of work, including occasionally selling a slice of land. It appeared, Mr Sporkmann explained to Reverend Gresstart, that the woolly ones were against this, claiming it flew in the face of Leviticus 25:23, as it all belonged to God.[22]

The reverend did his best to reassure Mr Sporkmann that despite what the Bible said, there wasn't actually a

---

[22] Editor's note: "The land shall not be sold for ever: for the land is mine." Leviticus 25:23.

problem. The whole thing came down to *interpretation*, you see?

Mentally, he re-ran his sermon to spot where he had accidentally quoted this bit in his sermon.

Still, although it may not have been the lesson he wished his congregants to learn, he was nonetheless pleased they were reading the Bible.

Yet, a little learning can be a dangerous thing, so he resolved to fish out another old favourite for Sunday. The one about taking the word of the Bible too literally. Yes, the book contained the complete and absolute word of God, but that didn't mean one took it literally. What would be the point of the clergy, if anyone could just pick it up and understand it?

But first he needed to pay a visit to Mrs Pengle.

When he arrived, he was surprised to see the very people Sporkmann had complained about in her kitchen. Especially when Mrs Pengle invited him into her house, but only as far as the hall.

"How are you, Mrs Pengle?" he asked.

"Fine, thank you, Reverend."

She looked fine, too. Although a bit skittish, as if she had a secret. Which was a joke, of course. How could Mrs Pengle, who confessed everything, possibly be hiding anything?

"That matter I asked you to keep an eye on..." He nodded at the woolly mob in the kitchen. Some of them nodded back when they caught his glance.

"Oh!" said Mrs Pengle. "Yes!" She exhaled a long breath, as if relieved. "Exactly! *That's* why they're here! So I can keep an eye on them."

"Sporkmann tells me they tried to smash his windows."

"They didn't," said Mrs Pengle.

"I assure you, Mrs Pengle!"

"Well, let him try to prove it!"

"And last week, Mr Kelby told me they demanded changes in his farming technique."

"His word against theirs! But I've spoken to them, and that's all in the past. A misunderstanding."

"You've spoken to them?" Somehow the conversation refused to go the way he expected. Mrs Pengle's answers were *odd*.

"I have," said Mrs Pengle. "Just as you wished, Reverend." She said the last part louder, almost as if she wanted everyone in the kitchen to hear it.

"And they listen?" asked the Reverend.

"Indeed they do."

"Good. Great. Wonderful. Then if I could ask you to keep just a tad *more* eye on them in future? I really don't wish to hear about any more little misunderstandings. Mr Sporkmann and Mr Kelby are God-fearing men who shouldn't be troubled." What he meant was that Mr Sporkmann and Mr Kelby were always good for a few quid whenever the church roof got too thin on top.

"Right you are, Reverend. I understand." She winked at him.

The reverend departed.

"Well," said Mrs Pengle back in the kitchen. "People are talking."

"Spreading the Word?" asked Mr Nooney. "Perhaps you should start wearing your wools now, as well?" The kitchen was hot.

"Not spreading the Word, telling tales. And I'll wear my whites when I've earned them. Like you have, Gavin."

And once I'm sure the reverend is used to them, thought Mrs Pengle. "You were wonderful with Mr Kelby. You heard what the reverend wants from us now?"

The Right Handers grunted. The grunts could have been yesses or nos, depending on what was required.

"Good. He wants us to continue our good work. And as a reward for what we have done so far, he has a special position in mind for myself and two others." She picked out Mr Nooney and Mr Ball.

The reverend had not told them to stop what they were doing. He had said he didn't want to hear about it. So she would make sure that either she, Mr Nooney, or Mr Ball would always be around to stop people telling him.

Chapter 12

This Involved Grapes

A TERRIBLE WEEK for sinners followed the reverend's visit to Mrs Pengle.

The Right Handers chased Little Betty home for petting a dog. Dogs, Leviticus tells us, are unclean.[23] Luckily, as it was her bath night, she was spared having to wash twice that week. But her prayers were more petulant than usual that night as she knelt by her bed. She *liked* dogs.

Bills fell overdue, and several people celebrated lonely birthdays when they chased the postman out of town for going "from house to house" despite Luke warning him not to.[24]

They gave Mr Oaten a stern talking to regarding his comments to the local post mistress, Mrs Boff. Nonetheless, he regretted nothing, for she had tried him sorely. It had taken him ages to summon up the courage to request a special manual for married couples. But Mrs Boff, whose hearing was not good, instead ordered him a government pamphlet. The pamphlet dealt with how

---

[23] Editor's note: "And whatsoever goeth upon his paws... those are unclean unto you." Leviticus 11:27.

[24] Editor's note: "Go not from house to house." Luke 10:7.

recent income tax increases were improving England, and given the optimistic title, "The Joy of Tax". Mr Oaten's disappointment had been great, leading him to run afoul of Leviticus 19:14.[25]

But the hardest blow came when Grunnion, the butcher, dashed everyone's breakfast rashers from their lips, until he could guarantee that his pigs were grass-fed.[26]

As if to signal God's approval of their work, irregular showers of fish continued to fall, with a particularly large shower on the day Grunnion made his announcement.

People discovered there was little use in attempting to talk to the reverend about matters. He appeared to have gone to ground, and whenever someone attempted to see him, Mrs Pengle, Mr Nooney, or Mr Ball turned them away.

And yet, every cloud has a silver lining. Professor de Glube unexpectedly benefited from the unusual lifestyle set out by Leviticus. Although the book forbade pretty much everything else, it was solidly pro-foreigner and encouraged everyone to keep them happy.[27]

Cross-referencing Leviticus 19:33 with Leviticus 19:10, it seemed the best way to do this involved grapes.[28]

De Glube's popularity suffered a brief dip when he mentioned to Mrs Goyle that a French friend of his had once cooked him some snails (Leviticus 11:28–29 did not approve), but God was merciful. He would naturally give foreigners the benefit of the doubt. When the time came

[25] Editor's note: "Thou shalt not curse the deaf."

[26] Editor's note: Deuteronomy 14:8.

[27] Editor's note: "And if a stranger sojourn with thee in your land, ye shall not vex him." Leviticus 19:33.

[28] Editor's note: "...neither shalt thou gather every grape of thy vineyard; thou shalt leave them for the poor and stranger..." Leviticus 19:10.

to weigh their lives and decide between admitting them through the pearly gates, or casting them down into eternal, agonising hellfire while being whipped by demons and insulted by the horned one himself, He would remember they might not have understood the Bible properly, as they didn't speak very good English.

Sometimes it seemed they didn't understand the Bible at all. Witness, for example, de Glube's insistence that he didn't want any more grapes now, thank you very much. He even claimed not to like them that much when Leviticus 19:10 insisted that, as a stranger, he must be mad for them.

Assuming people were making an extra effort because he was heartbroken, de Glube appreciated their kindness at first. It quickly became a nuisance. The constant supply of grapes caused him to break out in spots along his chin. He also hated to put everyone to the effort and expense of supplying them. All he wanted was to be left in peace to dig up his mysterious object and attend to some other urgent matters.

For example, bringing Mr Sniffacre back from the dead.

Surprisingly, even if he had told the Right Handers this, he would not have got in trouble with them. The Bible does not waste time on such frivolous matters as raising the dead, when more important matters need to be attended to. Preventing people from eating shellfish, for example.

After reading the Bible, one comes away with the feeling that reanimation is such a bagatelle that even Leviticus didn't think it worth his while to forbid it.

Legally, it was much the same. Hawkinge-By-Hythe's constable would have been hard-pressed to find a single judicial ruling which explicitly forbade it. No doubt he would come up with something if he had to, but de Glube was prepared to take the risk.

As long as he managed to stay out of trouble with the Alumières, he was happy with his chosen course of action. Given the choice, he would take an eternity burning in a lake of fire while devils pointed at his bits and laughed, over five minutes with an angry Gertrude Alumière.

He had always hated the cold, anyway.

Chapter 13

Friendly Or Foe-ly

DE GLUBE DIDN'T catch up with Lorry Tassel at his home near Muir Hall until the following Wednesday. He needed Lorry's assistance to put his plan into action, and Lorry had been avoiding him.

Lorry Tassel was what Irish-French economist Richard Cantillon had in mind when he talked about entrepreneurs being risk-takers. It was Lorry Tassel's fault the Damme Billett pub had burned down. Lorry Tassel had founded Hawkinge-By-Hythe's first detective agency. And who else but Lorry Tassel had personally broken into the Victoria & Albert Museum to research what the art world considered "in" for the educational pamphlet, "This Is Modern Art, And This Is Why You Must Like It"?[29]

He lived in a small cottage near Muir Hall, while he attempted to convince Ruth Leeds to marry him. Ruth spoke her mind, and his willingness to marry her regardless showed just how intrepid he was. In Lorry's opinion she was the jammiest bit of all the jam he had ever met. His life would be a barren piece of toast indeed if she wouldn't be a good egg and marry him.

[29] Available now from Tassel's Correspondence Courses for only one shilling!

To put it briefly: if you were in Hawkinge-By-Hythe and needed something special (without wishing to go into explanations), then you needed Lorry Tassel. His disreputable past was now behind him for the most part and he intended to pay for a ticket the next time he visited the museum. So when de Glube asked him to provide an eagle without delay, he only did so for old times' sake.

However, according to his contact in Folkestone, the world was in the middle of an eagle shortage. Without coming right out and saying it, he left Lorry with the impression that this was a delayed after-effect of the Great War. On the bright side, it meant that when eagles did flow once more, any bird he got would likely be a war hero.

When they were both seated around the kitchen table of his home, Lorry passed on this exciting development to de Glube, but it did nothing to assuage that man's impatience. He was not political and just wanted an eagle for his own purposes.

Still, it reassured him to learn the young man was working in his interest, and de Glube headed from Lorry's cosy cottage in the woods to Nodding Dean. Going through the woods turned out to be a good idea. Gangs of woolly Right Handers occupied all the town's major thoroughfares, armed with grapes. With them safely behind him, he could enjoy a pleasant day digging in the graveyard.

He whistled as he made his way back home that afternoon.

His excavation had progressed enough to confirm his suspicions. For whatever reason, somebody had buried a catapult under the fake headstone. He enjoyed being proved right, but really it was the whimsy which cheered him up.

He would tell Jennet all about his discovery the next day. It was momentous news and he had no one else with whom to share it. Tact would prevent him from giving her all the details right away, for it was always better to exhume… *dig* first and apologise afterwards.

Although perhaps he should mention the thing to his friend Aubrey Gresstart first, to make sure he followed the proper procedure.

De Glube had given up his seminary studies after a single year and forgotten most of it. He retained only a vague idea that a bishop might wish to say a few words before it came out of the ground. He would hate to get anyone in trouble by neglecting this.

Finding the catapult had quite raised his spirits, so it was a shame that a bream spoiled the mood by slapping him on the head on his way home.

He had quite forgotten about the fish.

A pike followed the bream, landing on the ground in front of him, and he stumbled to avoid stepping on the flapping fellow. Another bream followed it. And so the thing carried on.

One of the poor chaps smacked the blade of de Glube's shovel with a hollow ringing sound and lay still. The rest seemed lively enough, though not, obviously, for long.

With fish above him, fish before him, and fish to either side, de Glube used his shovel to cover his head and carry on. The last time the shower—no, he corrected himself, remembering his English lessons, the *school*—of fish had consisted of little chaps. These were larger. He risked a pike in the eye to look up, but saw nothing out of the ordinary. He wasn't sure what he expected to see. The chances of him observing a rogue fisher trawling the skies and dumping his catch overboard as some sort of industrial protest action were slim.

But then, he reflected, until a few days ago, he wouldn't have expected to find a catapult buried in a graveyard either. He sighed.

He would miss England when he left. The whole place was loopy.

He looked up again. All he saw was a blue sky decorated with cottony wisps of gentle cloud.

And fish, of course.

There were too many for him to save them all. He scooped up as many as possible, filling his pockets and carrying a wriggling armful with his shovel, then hurried home to slip them into his bath.

With that done, he returned twice more with suitcases. By the time he closed the door of the cottage for the night, he was gasping like the fish. It had occurred to him to ask his neighbours for assistance, but recognised it would be easier to do it himself. There were occasions when being a foreigner did not help. This was one of them.

He knew exactly how the interview would have gone. He would knock on his neighbour's door and wait for it to open.

"There are fish on the road," he would say, when the householder showed himself. Or herself.

"Oh yes?" his neighbour would reply with a tolerant smile. "Fish, are there?"

"That's right. Can you help me pick them up?"

"Oh yes? Pick them up, shall I?"

"Yes, please. Before they expire."

"Before they expire, is it?" By now his neighbour's eye would be twinkling at how amusing people from other countries were when they tried to talk simple English. "Is it milk you want? DO YOU WANT TO BORROW SOME MILK?"

"No thank you, just your help in rescuing these fish."

"He says he wants to rescue some fish. Do you think he might want sugar?" By now, the householder would have given up on de Glube and be addressing the house's other occupants, who wished to know why they were letting a draught in. "It's the accent. I can't understand a word he's saying. Can you see if we have any grapes for him?"

It wasn't worth it.

The next morning de Glube rose late and in the mood for fish for breakfast. He settled instead on the rest of the *quetscheflued* which had continued to mature since the dinner party a couple of weeks ago, instead.

He didn't have time to prepare anything else as it was an odd Thursday, which meant Mrs Sniffacre expected him for breakfast. (On even Thursdays, they dined *chez* de Glube.)

When he arrived, she showed him into the parlour for breakfast. Once tea had been poured, de Glube opened proceedings by telling her about being caught in a rain of fish.

"Oh, yes?" said Jennet Sniffacre. "My husband got caught in a shower once when we were married. If I hadn't stripped him off and cuddled him warm, he might have caught pneumonia. As it turned out, one thing led to another, and he only strained his back." Her heart wasn't in it, however, and the conversation dried up after that.

Mrs Sniffacre had only ever regretted having kept her married name since she met de Glube, in case it put him off. She couldn't just think of herself, however. Not only did she owe it to the postman to keep things simple, but she needed to consider the bank, too. It kept all her money, and the name on the account was "Sniffacre".

Banks are not built to deal with their customers changing their names. Bank staff lack the training required to surf the tsunami of paperwork involved.[30]

Still, being called Mrs Sniffacre had not seemed to daunt de Glube in the beginning. She and the professor had hit it off immediately. As if destined for each other, like Harry Houdini and his handcuffs.

She had fallen for him hard and he had done the same, she thought. They had connected in a way that she hadn't with her original husband. They had loved each other, and were happy, but it had been more, as you might say, physical. What with them both being younger at the time.

De Glube was more her soul mate, though she believed a certain fire smouldered within him too, if she could but stoke it. Yet he always seemed to pull back, and, liking a bit of heat, she had done her best to encourage the flame of his passion.

He continued to pull back when she would have liked him to push on. She grew to believe she had been

---

[30] To this day, noted adventurer, Richard Francis Burton, holds the record for having changed the name attached to his bank account in under a year. He changed it to *Francis Richard* Burton over the period June 1859–March 1860. But as well as being brave, he was also irascible, with a nasty habit of challenging people to duels. And even he failed in his subsequent effort to change his name back again.

mistaken all this time for the more she pushed, the harder he pulled away.

In the beginning they chatted and went for walks and kissed. She had hoped for more of the same, but it seemed de Glube wished only to be friends.

Or not even, for she had learned while visiting the town's combined library and post office, that he intended to return to Luxembourg.

No doubt he thought her too coarse for his refined sensibilities, and her subtle hints that she wasn't made of china had shocked him.

Lost in gloom, they ate the rest of their breakfast in silence.

Once it was over, de Glube asked if she wanted some fish. They made their way in silence to his cottage, where he asked her to take her pick of the fish in his bathtub, then blushed madly.[31]

After that, Mrs Sniffacre summoned her group of concerned citizens/lawless vigilantes, the Wait Watchers. She had formed the group in response to a crime wave, against which the Constable had been powerless. As chickens disappeared, practically from under everyone's noses, Mrs Sniffacre had realised that something would need to be done. She had been sitting at home watching out the window for the rumoured werewolf when the inspiration hit. If she and all her neighbours banded together and watched out for each other, they would soon find out what was really going on.

And so, the Wait Watchers had been born. Any criminal would think twice knowing that the concerned

---

[31] Editor's note: there's a very famous—and very rude—joke in Luxembourg, of which this is the exact punchline. Luckily, it's untranslatable.

citizens of Hawkinge-By-Hythe were waiting and watching out for them.

Today's agenda concerned itself with the newly formed Reverend's Right Handers, and whether they should be regarded as a friendly organisation, or a foe-ly one.

Chapter 14

Exotic Lemon-Scented Spider

DE GLUBE MADE his way to the rectory after leaving Mrs Sniffacre, hoping the reverend would be available to chat. The reverend might know something about the reason for a catapult being buried on church grounds.

It was just as well that de Glube made his way straight there. If he had first asked in town about his chances of seeing the reverend, he would have been told that it was a pointless quest. Nobody got past Mrs Pengle, Mr Nooney, and Mr Ball, who dogged the reverend's steps. Neither Grunnion, the butcher, nor Mr Oaten, nor Little Betty's parents had succeeded.

But different rules applied to de Glube, as the town's only real proper stranger for people to be nice to.[32] When he therefore turned up looking for Aubrey Gresstart, he was allowed to waltz straight in.

Barely had he rung the rectory bell before Mrs Pengle opened the door. Behind her were two sweaty men. He recognised Mr Nooney and Mr Ball, but did not know which was which. Not because they looked alike—like the

---

[32] Technically, the Alumières were also strangers, but it would take a brave man indeed to offer Gertrude Alumière a bunch of grapes she hadn't asked for.

Alumières—more that they possessed the type of face which his brain registered as not being worth remembering, poor chaps.

For a moment they all looked fierce, then their faces fell, enabling de Glube to deduce that he had caught them grapeless.

Mrs Pengle hurried off to tell the reverend about his visitor, while Mr Nooney and Mr Ball entertained him in the parlour until his host arrived.

"Very, er… very…. Very…" said one.

"*Warm*," said the other.

"That's it," said the first one. They nodded at each other. Job done.

It certainly must be warm in all that wool, thought de Glube, but these were not the men to explain it to him.

Eventually, Mrs Pengle returned. "Thank you," said de Glube, when she told him that the reverend would see him now. "No, thank you," he said, when she offered him a grape, which she must have picked up somewhere on her travels.

He believed the grape was along the lines of a parting gift, but this turned out not to be the case. When he hurried into the back garden to talk to Aubrey, they hurried with him.

Seeing the reverend therefore presented no problems. Seeing him for a confidential chat would be trickier. Mrs Pengle, Mr Nooney, and Mr Ball stuck closer than the grape seeds between de Glube's teeth.

After years of wishing people would pay him a bit more attention, even the reverend found it a bit much. He walked faster, ignoring how Mr Nooney and Mr Ball grew redder and more liquid in the day's heat. The reverend's mien grew ever more Old-Testament-Prophety as they panted behind him, but the more it did, the more his followers did exactly that: followed him.

Finally, near the second last row of the graveyard, he and the reverend achieved sufficient speed to escape, leaving the entourage panting behind them, and de Glube free to bring up the catapult.

He mentioned having read something interesting about church catapults and wondered if his friend could tell him any more about it.

"It seems like such a quaint practice," said de Glube, for nothing charms the English like being told they are "quaint".[33]

"There was something," said the reverend. He spoke disapprovingly.

There was always something.

He had become a minister to spread love and hope. Instead he spent most of his time listening to confessions, playing diplomat for his choir, or, worst of all, worrying about the church roof.

"You'd expect a church roof to be particularly sturdy," he said, following his own train of thought. "We haven't needed to do anything to the rectory since we moved in, except freshen up the downstairs walls with some paint. Mrs Gresstart likes reds, and I like green, so we painted the parlour blue, you see? Red is a very, er, *strong* colour for a vicar, in my opinion. But I have to go begging for funds every year to patch up another hole in the church, if I don't want my organ to get wet."

[33] Except in London, where everyone wants to be taken seriously. It unites everyone from cockney costermongers to blue-blooded bankers. Even judges, who should have received enough further education to know better, are offended if someone smiles when they wear their silly wigs.

"Perhaps vicars used catapults to throw new tiles up at the men who fixed the roof?" asked de Glube.

"Oh no, the parents would complain," said the reverend, his mind now on the latest disappointment in his efforts to make Hawkinge-By-Hythe's choir something special. "It's a thought, though. They might be willing to pay to throw things at the *other* children? There's *intense* competition to get them into the choir. But as soon as they're in, they lose interest. But if they were hurt...it's only their caterwauling that covers up the infernal squeaking of the door's hinges when people leave."

"Catapults, Aubrey," said de Glube. "I'm more than happy to listen to whatever it is that's bothering you, but I asked first. Do you know anything about church catapults?"

"Catapults?" said the reverend, finally paying attention. "Trebuchets, Lucius."

"Oh, *trés*, Aubrey. *Trés*, indeed." Gentle encouragement was the only way to make progress with Gresstart.

"No, I mean, they are called trebuchets. A kind of catapult, but more powerful. All the churches used to have one."

"So you are aware of them?"

"Not really. One of my predecessors had one, for whatever reason." His mind was already wandering again, as it sifted its way through all the problems confronting him.

"It's not part of the normal service, then?" asked de Glube. "The Anglican Church doesn't, say, shoot the deceased into the sky to see if they can get to heaven before they are buried, or anything?"[34]

---

[34] It had been a *looong* time since de Glube had studied at the seminary.

"Noo-o…" He would only have to do it to a couple of the ringleaders the next time they made trouble, thought the reverend. Or was he too strict? Perhaps God, in his infinite wisdom, loved even the remains of boiled sweets sucked to within an inch of their lives and stuck under the pews, where they gathered lint and hair until he discovered them.

The number of times he had been on the verge of a heart attack, sure the thing his unwitting hand rested on must be some form of exotic lemon-scented spider…

No, decided Aubrey Gresstart. Even the Lord, with infinite love, would draw the line at hairy, sticky lumps of sugar and saliva.

But he would probably frown at the retaliatory use of a catapult, too.

"Just some old fad from a hundred years ago or so," he said in answer to de Glube's question. The sooner de Glube left, the sooner he could go back to checking whether the hole over the pulpit really was getting bigger. "A fad. Like the, eh, ahem, *ladies* mentioned about the constellations when we were having dinner. You know small towns. Someone does something, and either everyone laughs at them, or copies them. If they copy them, they try to do it bigger and better, until someone gets hurt. Then it stops. I do know we had a trebuchet here. The Reverend Hennessy's idea."

"How interesting!" said de Glube. "You've never wanted to build one yourself? Whenever I feel out of sorts, I like to undertake some physical activity to take me out of myself." The reverend always seemed so glum.

"I don't have the time," said the reverend. "Hennessy was lucky enough to be around when Mayor Catchpleen closed the village. Thank God it didn't catch on again. The roof is in bad enough condition without people playing with ballistic devices. Dear Lord! The money and time I've spent on that roof..." He raised his eyes up imploringly towards his ultimate employer.

"Perhaps the roof gets damaged from the eyes of the Lord as he gazes down lovingly at you," suggested de Glube.

"Well perhaps we shouldn't have a roof at all!" The Rev stopped for a moment.

His ears buzzed, the way they did when he had a great idea. Why *did* they have to pray indoors? Why *shouldn't* they be out in the fields, praying within sight of their creator? Then he remembered he lived in England, a country bounteously provided with the most precious of all the Lord's gifts: water, without which life could not sustain itself. He shot a look at the sky. "Thank you very much indeed, Lord!" he said, and the two men continued on.

They didn't get far, however, when the sound of piping voices alerted the reverend to the fact that his presence was needed again. The choir had arrived and resumed their debate on whether girls should join the choir. Both sides of the argument were represented by passionate orators who would discuss the matter until they came to blows.

The reverend himself didn't mind one way or the other, and the Bible provided no assistance: it was neither for nor against women singing in the choir. The problem was that half the boys were far too shy, and the other half were far too keen....

He hurried off.

When he had left, de Glube checked no one was observing him, then darted into the graveyard to steal a handful of consecrated earth.

Chapter 15

Deeply Sinful Culottes

THE REVEREND KNEW exactly what he was talking about when he mentioned how an idea could take over a small village under the right conditions.

Barely had de Glube discovered his catapult (or trebuchet) than Colette Alumière decided she would like one of her own.

It was only a small model, which she constructed in what they called the War Room at Swiftwater. The War Room was where they gathered all the material together for whatever case they were working on at that moment. As they didn't currently have a case, Colette decided to use it for her trebuchet instead. Once she had worked out the loads and tensions to her satisfaction, she intended to knock together a full-sized machine in the back garden.

Neither the reverend nor de Glube had mentioned trebuchets to her, so this coincidence might have seemed uncanny to many people. The fact of the matter was, however, that Colette simply liked making things, and she had never yet built a trebuchet, so why not do it now?

Or perhaps it was a reaction to the growing animosity of the Reverend's Right Handers in town, which set her thinking about offensive weapons.

Or it may have been the triplets' unerring, intuitive ability to be one step ahead of the game that might have explained it.

She could already think of a use for the model catapult too, and would test it out the next time Chloe came around to visit. If it turned out to be as accurate as she hoped, then it would be a very popular addition to the Alumière Apothecary. It could turn the distasteful and occasionally frightening task of taking one's tablets into a carnival pleasure.

Once she had the catapult ready, the only other thing she would need to do would be to mark off the floor of their apothecary. Then children of different heights would know where to stand when opening their mouths, if they wished to play with the world's very first Tablet Tosser.

The Alumières did not have a family motto, but if they did, it would have been "There's Nothing Like Keeping Busy".

For although the Alumières were never bored, they nonetheless felt a sense that they were experiencing a lull in the "supernatural" activities which had drawn them to town. Honestly, a fish rain barely rated on Colette's Odd-O-Meter, built during a stopover at the Palazzo Dario in Venice.

While Colette's intuition drew her to catapults, Victoria's drew her to further investigation of the short-lived craze for renaming the constellations. She found it significant.

Especially the lack of information about what had happened beyond those first few newspaper clippings.

Hawkinge-By-Hythe had hung onto an anonymous pupil's note dated 1631 which revealed that "Mastyr Hugh The Mathes Teecher Smells Of Cabbidge", and every receipt from every sale of the town's most famous invention.[35] Yet it professed to be unaware of the results of Lord Muir's and Mayor Catchpleen's attempts to make astronomical history.

Victoria knew it for an indisputable fact that no matter how ridiculous or unpopular an idea is, there will always be someone to keep believing it. People still believed you could tell if someone was a criminal by looking at them, after all.

That an idea should die out so completely was very unusual, suggesting there may have been more to it than met the eye. The archives revealed nothing. For two entire months, the newspapers were full of Lord Muir's plans and activities. It even included an offer of £100 to anyone who proved that none of the constellations looked anything like de Lacaille said they did.

And then no further mention. Nothing in the council minutes. No more updates on Lord Muir's efforts.

Not a single letter to the editor blaming juvenile delinquency on the lack of proper British names for the constellations.

---

[35] The town's most famous invention were Salty Trousers. This ingenious device was a pair of otherwise normal trousers with a discreet compartment at the back, which could be filled with salt. Fabric was stitched in such a way as to create two channels, one down each leg, allowing for a steady flow of salt to empty itself behind the wearer. It was therefore possible to go about one's daily business without having to manually throw salt over one's shoulder to prevent bad luck. "Good Luck Can Be Yours, With Salt In Your Drawers!" trumpeted the slogan.

A full-page notice advised that Mayor Catchpleen, who had eagerly taken up Lord Muir's cause and made it his own, was closing the town. Due, he said, to continued concerns about people falling upwards after the moon came too close to town.

It would have been enlightening to know more about this, but at the relevant meeting the reporter had instead allowed himself get distracted by an exchange between the Mayor and Lord Muir. Lord Muir had enquired of Catchpleen on whose authority he would close the town, then taken exception to Catchpleen's answer.

Catchpleen insisted he had merely been clearing his throat, suggested they all go for drinks, especially "our esteemed and hard-working journalists", and they closed the meeting.

When Hawkinge-By-Hythe reopened two weeks later, no one mentioned the stars anymore.

With Colette building toys and Victoria reading newspapers, Gertrude felt they left it to her to take care of the important stuff. This suited her natural inclinations, as she enjoyed being around people. Ideally, people she could order about, but in a pinch any people would do.

Having been told that her scheme to nip people in their buds was a non-starter, she had decided on an alternative plan.

With Victoria's scolding in her ear, Gertrude wanted to prove that she found nothing easier than working with people.

So, she had taken over observation of Mrs Pengle and her woolly friends, with a plan to get to grips with them later on, once she had closed the shop.

Emboldened by their white tunics, the Reverend's Right Handers were taking a firm line against identical and scientific triplets—or "witches", as they called them. To this end, a permanent delegation was installed across the road from the Alumière Apothecary. They had been there all day, with every customer who entered the shop getting an unfriendly stare. They had tried to intimidate Gertrude with stares as well, before giving up.

Their stares were designed to make the recipient feel like he—or she—had been caught wandering into the church wearing the wrong clothes, smelling of pig and burping during the quiet bits.

But that didn't work with Gertrude. Occasionally she stared back, and her stares made the recipient feel they had wandered into the wrong church wearing only a tutu and squeaking a humorously shaped balloon whenever the priest paused for breath.

They were undeniably bad for business, however, and the day passed slowly. As much as she enjoyed terrorising potential customers (and the people now giving her dirty looks would soon come crawling again), she had little else to do other than think.

Like her sisters, her intuition was working overtime. For whatever reason, a rain of fish made people think about rooting out sin and begging for redemption. It seemed to Gertrude that a God who threw around free food—assuming one liked fish—did not sound like an angry God. Something else must be motivating them, and Mrs Pengle had something to do with it.

Why was she heading up a group of religious zealots? Mrs Pengle had always been the equivalent of a supporting actor in village life up to now, and no danger to anyone. As long as one avoided saying anything that would prompt yet another re-telling of her "famous" father's almost-invention, of course.

Perhaps Mrs Pengle really was worried about the fate of the town's souls, but Gertrude doubted it. Then she heard a commotion outside, which clinched the thing and pointed the way forward.

A smashed window. If required to guess, Gertrude would have said it belonged to Spottleton's barber shop one street over.

The Right Handers outside the apothecary seemed to have been expecting it, for they cheered and grinned amongst themselves.

Then they wobbled as they forgot themselves, looked at Gertrude Alumière through the window, and caught her stare. Gertrude activated Plan B.

For all that the Right Handers claimed to be about purity and righteousness, they were a bit rough in their methods.

But they weren't the only game in town. Mrs Sniffacre's Wait Watchers had been formed to help people *now*, not after their death, and Gertrude would join them, and get involved with whatever was going on. Then she could rub Victoria's nose in it when she proved she was as good at working with people as anyone else.

Of course, it would be crucial that she join as only one of the group. That way, if things spiralled out of control, well, it wouldn't be her fault…

She locked up the shop, then swung her leg over the saddle of her bicycle instead of stepping through the frame as she would normally do.

It was a direct challenge to the people watching her, and the group gasped. Gertrude wore culottes. Black, comfortably baggy, with plenty of pockets for all occasions. Not trousers, but dangerously close to trousers, which were men's clothes. Anyone who has read the Bible knows the Lord doesn't approve of men wearing women's clothes and vice versa. Presumably because even an omniscient being finds His subjects tend to look a little same-y from watching all of them all the time. Doubtless He appreciated anything that made it easier to work out who was which.

Gertrude realised they regarded her culottes as deeply sinful, but didn't share their opinion. Why shouldn't a woman wear trousers if she wanted? Unless, of course, the Lord was embarrassed by women's legs. Which would be strange if He had made them in the first place.

The group mumbled behind as Gertrude sped off, but they didn't dare do anything.

Which was a pity for the town. Attacking Gertrude would have been the fastest guaranteed way to end their reign of woolly terror.

Although unsuccessful getting the reverend to tell him why it was buried underground, de Glube was thrilled to have found a catapult, *trebuchet*, at Nodding Dean. And if there was one, there might be more. The thought reinvigorated him as he made his way home from the rectory. His high spirits were so noticeable that even the Right Handers hesitated before making their offering of grapes. They regarded it as a self-evident truth that the truly righteous refrained from smiling when not absolutely necessary.

Do not the upturned corners of a smiling mouth resemble the horns of the Infernal One? And God-fearing folk don't invite the cloven-footed one to perch on their lips.

If they could have seen de Glube alone in his cottage, which backed onto Mrs Sniffacre's back garden, their doubts would have increased.

Approaching his abode, his manner turned furtive. He glanced over his shoulder. And by the time the front door closed behind him, he had undergone another change, and despair claimed him for its own. For entering his cottage reminded him without fail of Jennet.

She too lived in a cottage, and no doubt also entered it when she wished to go inside. He sighed. They had so much in common!

Before arriving in Hawkinge-By-Hythe, de Glube had been a confirmed bachelor, and when he fell for Mrs Sniffacre, he fell as hard as only a confirmed bachelor could fall.

De Glube loved everything about her, from the way she smiled to the way she said "So!" when she sat down opposite him for a chat. He loved the shape and the size and the smell of her. He loved her voice and the house she lived in.

He even loved the livestock she kept in her back garden despite the smells her goat produced, which always found their way towards him, regardless of how the wind blew.

In summary, he loved everything.

Even now, in his daydreams, de Glube imagined returning to Luxembourg with Mrs Sniffacre, or, if she didn't want to go, retiring to Hawkinge-By-Hythe to be with her. But not while she was in love with her husband. That, he couldn't do.

Instead, he planned to make one final grand romantic gesture.

The kind of thing Romeo would have done if Juliet had loved Count Paris instead.

Cost what it might, Mrs Sniffacre would be happy.

Chapter 16

A Bucket Of Cold Mr Sniffacre

IN MRS SNIFFACRE'S kitchen, crowded with Wait Watchers, and redolent of ginger biscuits, Gertrude Alumière's arrival caused quite a stir. Everyone paused their discussion of what to do about Mrs Pengle and her troublemakers, while they waited for Gertrude to tell them what they were doing wrong.

But Gertrude had been practising her smiles and convinced Mrs Sniffacre she only wanted to help. If they wanted her.

She sat, smiling encouragingly whenever anyone else spoke, and hardly saying a thing herself.

A minor incident marred the tea break. Gertrude had jumped up to hand out the biscuits, despite this being Mr Hammond's role. Mr Hammond hadn't dared say anything, and it had been up to Mrs Champion to fill Gertrude in. Gertrude apologised, but the eye she turned in Mr Hammond's direction made her true feelings clear.

Then, after the tea break she gave Mr Hammond her biscuit plate, even though gathering the plates was Mr Comer's job! People looked away, thinking harsh thoughts about the country of France, if this was how people behaved over there.[36]

After these shocks, the discussion regarding the Right Handers picked up only slowly, everyone on edge waiting for the next bloomer. It remained a back and forth between those who felt that perhaps the ends justified the means, and those who disagreed, until Gertrude attempted once again to contribute.

"They are breaking windows, aren't they?" Gertrude attempted another smile, and this time the thing came out perfectly. "That's not nice."

The crowd remained non-committal.

"I wouldn't like it, if someone broke my windows, would you?" She looked around and people shook their heads. Still, perhaps windows were a small price to pay to get rid of sin?

"Would you like it, Mr Hammond?" She gave him a smile. Mr Hammond shook his head, unable to look away. "Raise your hands anyone who would like to have their windows smashed? Even if it's for a good cause?"

No one raised their hands.

"The problem..." She stopped and looked around. "Oh, forgive me, I don't want to interrupt!"

"No, no, go on!" said Mrs Sniffacre.

"Thank you so much." Gertrude coughed and switched from a smile to a thoughtful frown. Her cheek muscles were starting to ache. "I just thought, even if someone does want their windows smashed. For the good of their soul and to make up for being naughty, for example..."

"Yes?" Mr Hammond edged forward in his chair.

---

[36] The Alumières had never claimed to be French, this had just been assumed. Of course, what with the name, the culottes, and their manners, where else could they have been from?

"Well, what about the *glass?* The Reverend's Right Handers leave it on the ground. The shards of glass are just as sharp whether the owner is good or bad. Young humans—I mean, *lovely little sweet dinky kiddywinks*—might hurt themselves on it."

"Yes," said Mrs Sniffacre. That was it. As Wait Watchers they didn't need to concern themselves with ethics and theology and all that tough stuff. They were against criminal behaviour and people doing things that might be dangerous for kiddies.

Let Mrs Pengle and her lot worry about getting people into heaven. The Wait Watchers would make sure they didn't make a dangerous nuisance of themselves in the process.

Mrs Sniffacre nodded, and the group nodded back. Now they knew where they stood and it was a relief.

But if her mind was now lighter, her heart remained heavy.

Gone were the days when the love of her life, Professor Lucius de Glube, would pop around for a cup of tea and a chat in the evenings. Her kitchen emptied as the day grew dark and her troops started their patrols. She stood at the kitchen window from where she could see into de Glube's kitchen. Even as recently as a few weeks ago, if one of them spotted the other light click on, it meant popping around for a shared pot of tea. No longer.

He wanted to avoid her. She felt sure of it, for although his kitchen light remained off, she noticed movement in his darkened kitchen.

The breakup was so much worse for how promisingly it had all started. With a gentle, though definite bang, the very first time she had seen him, despite the pain in her eyeballs. The professor favoured suits so bright they would make even the sun cry out for its tinted glasses. The first time they met, he had worn blue trousers with red stripes below an orange and yellow waistcoat.

As he had rather overdone the sunscreen, a pure white face topped of the ensemble. But she found him kind, suave, handsome, and clever, and he crashed into her world like a rainbow meteorite, and she had fallen head over heels in love.

When he spoke, he became animated, his wild white hair blowing and tossing towards her. As if it wanted to whisper sweet nothings to her.

His flashing eyes too, had been full of an unmistakable message in Morse code. She did her best to assure him there was no Mr Sniffacre in her life any more, but it made no difference.

She had hinted that he, de Glube, was the wall on which the shelf of her happiness hung, but, again, nothing.

She had even resorted to attempts to rouse his jealousy by mentioning her late husband, to let de Glube know she would not to mind should he desire to get a bit more physical. But his momentary interest in her had passed, leaving her lonelier than ever.

In her desperation, she might have been too frank. That must be why he avoided her. No doubt he valued her as a friend, but recoiled from how shamelessly she threw herself at him whenever they were together.

They used to walk together in the countryside, but now he walked alone, staying as long as possible, so he wouldn't bump into her when he returned to his cottage.

Now when she looked out her window, she saw only her own goat, with disdain for her neediness in its yellow eyes.

She wished it were not so, but she couldn't help looking out and torturing herself this way. If the light was on, then he had returned safely, yet preferred to sit in the dark, rather than risk her coming over to say hello.

And if he were out, she worried he might be lost, or have come a cropper in the dark where no one would see until it was too late.

Clearly he cared not a whit for her feelings, and she would remain Mrs Sniffacre for the rest of her life, despite her desire to become Mrs de Glube.

She had even reconciled herself to the fact that he would upstage her at the wedding. It seemed impossible to imagine that a man with his exuberant style would turn up wearing a simple black suit for the big day.

By now, any reader who has been carefully following the story, rather than merely moving their eyes from left to right across the page for exercise, might be wondering what is going on.

De Glube, they will realise, had taken one look at Mrs Sniffacre and decided that she was the specific reason he had remained a bachelor all his life.

Mrs Sniffacre believed that, without de Glube, life was not worth living, though the alternative meant going to heaven to listen to Mrs Pengle tell a story everyone already knew off by heart.

So how did things come to this unsatisfactory pass? The answer, of course, is culture.

Luxembourg has some of the strictest rules around courtship anywhere in Europe. It's the principal reason the country remains so small. De Glube, shy and unsure of himself in a foreign country, had made the mistake of sending home for a copy of his homeland's book of relationship etiquette.

Mrs Sniffacre, being neither too skinny, nor too plump, but exactly right. With hair the way he liked it, and a laugh like warm sweetened cream, was the woman for him.

They talked, they strolled, they drank tea together.

In those early days, de Glube even felt bad for Mr Sniffacre. He would be heartbroken to lose the world's most perfect woman, when de Glube married Jennet. His only consolation the knowledge that he had never been quite good enough for her.

So when he learned there *was* no Mr Sniffacre, de Glube rejoiced. Nothing, it seemed, could stand in their way.

Except, it turned out, for Mr Sniffacre.

In Luxembourg, romance is a slow process. The Luxembourger is not hot-headed like his French or Italian counterpart. In Italy, romance happens fast. Relationships exist solely to pass on *Nonna's* secret pasta sauce recipe. As soon as a couple agree on which recipe they prefer, *bambinos* sprout from the woodwork.

In France, things go even faster. If someone takes a French person's fancy, they blink at them through cigarette smoke. If that someone blinks back, then it's all over save for throwing the rice.

Even the placid German, who only bestows his heart after doing his homework to check the object of desire is tax deductible, is considered a quick worker in Luxembourg, where patience is the hottest thing going.

De Glube's own parents hadn't kissed until their sugar wedding anniversary, and even then the scandal had been immense. Unaware that de Glube therefore believed he was already moving faster than Captain Pol Scholl-Kroll (Luxembourg's famous human cannonball), Mrs Sniffacre tried to hurry things along by mentioning how eagerly the late Mr Sniffacre used to snap into things.

They were neither of them getting any younger.

But de Glube had not realised that English lovers move just as quickly as their mainland counterparts. Somehow he had remained ignorant of the long list of legendary English lovers throughout the ages. He must have missed school that day through illness. Thus he proceeded with his courtship as slowly as the fire of love in his belly would allow him to save Mrs Sniffacre's blushes.

And every time he thought he made progress, Mrs Sniffacre would dull the blaze of his passion by pouring a bucket of cold what-Mr-Sniffacre-used-to-do over it.

Eventually he concluded that she wanted them to be friends. Someone with whom she might gossip about all the things she and her husband got up to.

Their romance, after starting with a bang, was ending with a fizzle, like the depressed efforts of a damp firework after everyone has left the party.

Chapter 17

The Scientific Cesspit

MRS SNIFFACRE AND her Wait Watchers were not the only ones finding the Right Handers trying. Reverend Gresstart, in whose unwitting honour they were named, didn't like them at all. And as he did not realise that they worked for him, he did not know he could have told them to get lost and mind their own business. For all sad words of tongue or pen, the saddest are these, "if only he had known he could have told them to bugger off."

The Reverend, as he had admitted at dinner at de Glube's cottage, followed astronomy keenly, though the new belligerence of the people wearing white tunics forced him to be discreet.

Used to being the one who spoke sharply, it astonished the reverend when the diminutive Mr Nooney wagged his finger in the reverend's face on learning that yes, he possessed a telescope with which he looked at the stars.

Well, Mr Nooney had wagged his finger somewhere between the reverend's eight and ninth ribs, what with the difference in their heights, but still.

And he couldn't give it up.

As with epigraphy, so too is it with astronomy. No one chooses to spend their nights staring into a tube for the thrill of being the first to spot a distant speck of light. It is a vocation. A compulsion. Possibly it is hereditary.

Aubrey Gresstart was an astronomer first, and a reverend second. The shimmering flecks of light in the night sky had always fascinated him. On mastering his scripture, his interest in the stars only intensified. Out there, somewhere in the depths of space, God waited.

Unless one needs to steer a ship at night, no hobby is of less practical value than astronomy, but the reverend could not have given it up if he tried. He knew this because he had tried.

He had reduced the number of hours he spent in his back garden looking at mostly nothing—literally—after marrying Tabitha. She insisted, and she was right to do so, of course. And now, Mr Nooney informed him, his telescope would be the vessel through which the devil would enter him.

"Witchcraft." Mr Nooney looked around to make sure there were no Alumières listening in. "Is forbidden, as per Revelations 12:8, and Galatians 5:19–21, not to mention Deuteronomy 18:10–13, and all the rest, amen."

"Ar," said Mr Ball, to drive the point home.

The reverend did his best to explain the difference between astronomy, the science of celestial objects, and astrology, divination based on what those objects are up to.

Mr Nooney remained sceptical. Mr Ball said "Ar." The claim of "science" had already been tainted by the Alumières saying the same thing, despite obviously being witches.

And now here stood the reverend, their direct line to God, being sucked down into the same scientific cesspit. Mr Nooney grew so upset that Gresstart promised to tone it down in future.

But not stop.

He needed it. Yes, he knew God was everywhere. But with the universe so vast, he couldn't help but search for a sign there was something else out there. That humanity was not as alone as it had always seemed to him.

Deep in his soul, he hoped to one day spot God out there, looking back.

For the sake of a quiet life, he moved his telescope and equipment to the belfry of the church's bell tower. This presented no problem as the tower lacked a bell in it. The bell tower was wide enough to accommodate his beloved Dolland refracting telescope. And finally the bell tower would get a bit of use.

It gave him a better view of the stars too, while nobody would see him there as the tower sat back a way from the road.

As a bonus, only a ladder led to the top, so it also provided the reverend with some daily exercise. Just the other day, Tabitha asked if he had developed a muscle.

Everyone was happy. Tabitha liked to think he was living healthily. His congregation liked to think they had saved him from himself, and he was happiest of all. Safe in his bell tower, he could use his telescope to his heart's content, knowing that even Mrs Pengle wouldn't come to get him at the top of a ladder. It was marvellous to get away from it all. No one, other than an author of romance novels, could have *that* many lewd thoughts in a single day, surely.

It reminded him of his boyhood. As a child, he had watched the heavens through the window of a small tree house built by his father. Now his telescope pointed through the belfry's arched, un-louvered openings. It soothed his soul, despite the enormity of the black void pressing in around him.

And for the first time ever, the reverend saw something in the sky.

Not a star, for it moved. Not a shooting star, for it was black.

A speck of black against the velvet dark of night. It lasted a second, then disappeared, before he thought to track its movement.

A sign!

It filled his soul with awe that God had signalled He saw him watching, while his astronomer's soul sang at having seen something. All those years staring at nothing had paid off.

And what could it portend other than God approved of his decision to become a vicar? It was a tiny token of appreciation for the good work he put in minding the sheep of Hawkinge-By-Hythe. He noted the coordinates in his book, his handwriting shaky as butterflies tumbled and turned in his stomach.

He would tell Tabitha! His parishioners! God was truly out there, watching us!

Then he reconsidered. It had only been a speck. He would wait to see if it turned up again. Just in case.

He wouldn't put it past the Alumières to be flinging things into the sky to catch him out and make him look foolish.

Chapter 18

A Most Unholy Place

GERTRUDE BECAME A regular Wait Watcher to show Victoria she had been talking through her pork pie hat with the yellow feather. Working with people was easy.

Mrs Pengle might not have agreed. Her Right Handers remained tricky despite all she had done for them.

She had given them a glorious name. Sewn them lovely woollen tunics so that they looked the part and even assured them—bending the truth here for the greater good—that the reverend liked what they were doing. Yet the glamour had gone out of the thing. Even she had to admit that it got boring standing around on Main Street telling people to confess, when no one wanted to. The occasional broken window when no one was looking hardly made up for it, and they were getting cold feet.

"No, thank you, not today," was the usual response when they accosted passers-by to inquire whether there might be some little thing they wanted to get off their chest? Otherwise they might burn in hellfire for eternity? No?

And although they were getting cold feet, the rest of them were roasting hot, for Mrs Pengle had been generous with the wool while sewing the tunics. The Right Handers felt they were already vouchsafed a pretty good idea of what the heat of hellfire would be like and were staying home.

The crowning humiliation came when she, together with Mr Nooney and Mr Ball, met Mrs Sniffacre. Asked if Mrs Sniffacre wouldn't like to confess anything, the sinful woman had brushed her off.

"No impure thoughts?" teased Mrs Pengle. She wondered how the woman dared to show her face with all the smooching going on between her and de Glube. And Mrs Sniffacre had laughed.

Laughed!

"I might head home, now," said Mr Nooney, and Mr Ball nodded. They had been standing on Main Street all morning. And nothing to show for it, but their shoes full of the sweat rolling down their legs under the wool.

Mrs Pengle regretted her thoughts later when she went home. She usually did, and prayed, even though she had to do it on her own. Her husband only prayed on Sunday. "The rest of the week's my own," he always said. God, he said, had given him free will. If he prayed when he didn't want to, that would be throwing God's gift back in his face. She didn't want him to do that.

She retired early to bed, in order to catch the reverend first thing in the morning to confess her uncharitable thoughts. It would mean she could get there before her Right Handers arrived. Although they were the Reverend's Right Handers, really. She just needed to find a way to pass the information on before he found out for himself.

And she'd be sure to confess that bit too once she was sure they were all saved.

Except for Mrs Sniffacre. She could save herself. If de Glube didn't do it for her.

The Reverend turned his groan into a cough when he saw Mrs Pengle waiting for him again the next morning outside his church. He had hoped giving her something to do might help her find a useful focus for her time. It seemed not, however, and he wondered if he had somehow made a mistake.

She seemed more confident. Or at least louder, and when not hanging around the church waiting to confess, she hung around the rectory following him about the place.

All he wanted her to do was act as a restraining influence on the other members of the congregation, but he supposed he couldn't complain. She did, after all, drag them off for a few hours each day, which allowed him to mull over the latest thing weighing on his mind.

He almost wished he had given up astronomy. He had seen the speck again the previous night, flashing past overhead. Did he only imagine it had flashed ever so much slower than before?

He hoped so.

It would be just his luck that the thing, whatever it was, would land on his roof, taking it beyond all hope of repair.

These were the thoughts going through his mind as she sat in her accustomed pew and told him what was on her mind.

What if it landed on his roof right in the middle of a sermon, destroying his rook *and* squashing his flock?

Mrs Pengle droned on.

And what about the fish? Did that perhaps prove it must be the ark? The thing had been moving at an incredible speed. The fish could be falling overboard as Jesus whipped around the curves a bit too fast.

Mrs Pengle ground to a halt. He advised her to think more kindly of others in future and she promised she would.

Same as every time.

"How are you getting on with the others?" he asked.

"They are worried about the town," she said.

"Of course," said the reverend. "Why?"

"All the sinning," said Mrs Pengle. "I realise it's not the done thing, but I've always said that if people were able to get the bad stuff off their chests, like I do…"

"Good God!" Luckily, the reverend was sitting when Mrs Pengle spoke. Otherwise he might have collapsed at the idea of everyone in town coming for advice every time they did something they shouldn't. One needed to be reasonable when partaking of the Bible's wisdom.

Just the other day, the reverend himself had torn his trousers in a most unholy place. He and Tabitha were moving the rhododendron away from direct sun, now that the plant had outgrown the shade of the rectory's porch. Yet he hadn't worried, despite the obvious threat of drawing God's displeasure on the entire parish.[37] And Mrs Gresstart had borrowed his gloves to add some soil to the pot afterwards, despite both of them knowing that too was forbidden.[38]

If Mrs Pengle had her way, half the population would be around every morning to ask whether there wasn't *anything* they could do to get on Mr Leviticus' good side.

---

[37] Editor's note: "… Uncover not your heads, neither rend your clothes…." Leviticus 10:6.

[38] Editor's note: "The woman shall not wear that which pertaineth unto a man…." Deuteronomy 22:5.

The Reverend resorted to another cough to buy himself time to think. "The good Lord, I mean to say, would surely be delighted, but we are not Catholics!"

"No," said Mrs Pengle.

Probably the only way to get Mrs Pengle to stop seeking his advice every time she sinned would be to avoid going to church altogether. If her fellow parishioners were around, she might not unburden herself quite so often.

At that moment, they heard the unmistakable sound of something hitting the tiles of the church roof, and hurried outside to see what it could be.

It turned out to be voles. Just what I need, thought the Reverend, as he and Mrs Pengle watched them scamper off. Orkney voles, for they were larger than the voles he was used to. Everyone knew Orkney voles were the big ones.

So, although he didn't understand why they were raining on his roof, at least he knew where they ultimately came from.[39]

And then de Glube's words came back to him. About the loving gaze of the Lord looking down on them from on high, the damage a mere unwelcome side-effect.

After all, what about the speck in the night sky? Perhaps the Lord wanted his attention. Was it such a leap of faith to imagine that he wanted their attention so much that he tossed a few fish and voles his way to get it?

It made sense to Gresstart. It explained why the Lord constantly drew his attention to the roof of St Dunstan's Church.

---

[39] Editor's note: Although they are called Orkney voles, they can also be found on one of the Channel Islands, Guernsey, illustrating the danger of jumping to conclusions.

With the speck he was seeing in the sky at night, the message became clear. God wished to talk to His flock in Hawkinge-By-Hythe directly. He did not like the roof of the church, and although there would be challenges involved, the reverend must hold his services outdoors from now on. He didn't dare tempt fate again.

If God did not like the roof, then let Him smash it. There would be no one inside.

And here perhaps even Mrs Pengle might be useful, if he recruited her. It was a risk worth taking.

"Of course, we *could* confess," he suggested.

"Yes?"

"Yes," said the Reverend. "But outside. If we confessed in the purifying light of day, it might be alright."

He hinted at his plans during the next service by quoting Matthew 5:1 at them "seeing the crowds, he went up on the mountain," to get them in the mood. They weren't convinced. There were no mountains in Hawkinge-By-Hythe, just the hill.

It was, insisted the reverend, close enough.

They had, therefore, only one question. "What," they asked, "shall we do when it starts codding?"

Chapter 19

Pure At Heart (Weather Permitting)

IF LISTENING TO Mrs Pengle confess and ask for advice was the worst part of Aubrey Gresstart's duties, then holding the sermon was his favourite. He spent hours each week writing them, searching for ever the right word and the right topic. His aim was to illuminate, inspire and comfort in equal measure.

And that had been while officiating from within the fusty, if sacred, confines of a weirdly shaped building with poor acoustics.

The next Sunday, he brought a makeshift altar close to the top of Bagnell's field, which overlooked the countryside on a fine sunny day. Not at the very top of the field, because that was where the Hanging Tree stood, but a respectable distance away. Far enough that the presence of it behind him didn't give him the creeps. Not one for superstition, but they had hanged witches there in the past, and something about the tree suggested it still held a grudge because of it.

Spread below him in the field, his parishioners hung on his every word, although the white-tunicked members of the congregation, which he overheard Mrs Pengle call

"Right Handers" on their way into the field looked occasionally distracted. No doubt worried what all the grass would do to their lovely white uniforms.

Knowing his forte lay in putting his foot down, he did so now to reclaim their undivided attention.

He wanted to Stop the Grumbling.

There had been a lot of this when he first mooted his outdoor service. Most of his flock received their fair share of fresh air from Monday to Saturday. They enjoyed the sit down that religion offered them on Sunday, but the reverend had marshalled his facts, and presented them now in a manner that brooked no argument. Not quite fire and brimstone stuff, but it sounded good nonetheless. If he looked Byronic, then it was a fed up Lord Byron. Imagine a Byron who had got his finances in order, only to receive a letter from the tax authorities informing him they were bumping him up a category. Meaning that in the future he could kiss an even larger portion of his writing income goodbye. He would have looked just like the Reverend Gresstart did now, as he explained why the pure at heart prayed outside. At least as long as the weather permitted it.

Below him the countryside of Kent stretched before his eyes. Beyond that, the glittering water of the English Channel dividing England and France. He might have reminded his parishioners of Lord Byron, but he felt more like Moses. He didn't mind the feeling at all.

Pride was a sin, so the reverend held no pride in the fact that he spoke well, he accepted it as a fact. He found it all the more impressive because he often worried that he lacked the conviction that a man in his position should have.

Sometimes he woke in the middle of the night, terrified about what would really happen after he died. Sometimes, as he passed their apothecary shop in town, he envied the Alumières their certainty in science. But when he spoke, he felt damn sure of everything he said. His sermons were to convince himself as much as his congregation.

Especially now he had received confirmation from God that He was really there. He owed it to his parishioners to convince them, too.

It would be wise, however, to refrain from immediately mentioning where his certainty came from, so as not to worry them. Possibly they, untutored peasants, would be worried about seeing a black speck, which he now thought of as The Message, hurtling through the heavens.

He longed for The Message to appear in the sky right now, but God would reveal all to the faithful when the time came. Further proof of God's unerring sense of timing came when it started to rain cats: *after* the collection plate went around and come back again. Proof positive He was watching.

One moment the reverend was exhorting his parishioners to love one another, which included, as per Psalm 101:5, not gossiping—he gave Mr Oaten and Mrs Delbing piercing looks, which turned them the red of boiled lobster. The next, out of a clear blue sky, cats were pouring down on top of them, like graceful furry snowballs.

Only a small shower, perhaps twenty cats, but it took them by surprise, and Gresstart called it a day. He would have to meditate on what this latest sign might mean.

Even the Alumières were getting interested.

There seemed no real pattern when the curious rains would occur. Each shower was sudden, short-lived, and very specific. On Wednesday, Mr Harcombe had been disturbed by the sound of his slates being abused. Rushing out, he was in time to receive the last of the sprats on his head. Altogether, there might have been half a dozen fish in the shower. Two Saturdays before that, several kilos of fish had briefly decorated the entire rose garden at Muir Hall, much to the consternation of the head gardeners who transported them to the pond.

Yet despite some small showers, the total mass showed a trend of overall increase. This was an interesting and potentially dangerous development. While a rain of sardines might be unpleasant—though nutritious—a rain of heavy fish risked causing light injury. And while voles were not heavier than fish of the same size, they were more likely to bite.

Colette and Victoria had tended to some villagers who had been fished on. The severity of the injuries suggested the animals were coming from quite a distance. The kind of distance that would make even a duck dangerous to a human if it scored a direct hit.

This seemed to hold true even for the recent voles, though they couldn't be sure, for the voles hadn't stuck around long enough to be weighed, measured and asked questions.[40]

Traditionally, a rain of fish was precisely that (except for when it comprised toads). Now there were voles and cats, too. There seemed no telling where nature intended

---

[40] Why not? One never knew.

to draw the line. And as the animals kept getting bigger, the risk of serious injury, or worse, grew with it.

The only positive thing Colette could point out was that fish fell faster than other animals, as they were shaped to reduce drag. The speed of a falling object is significantly affected by the drag force, which is influenced by the object's projected area. Moving efficiently through one fluid (water), they moved equally efficiently through another (air) while falling, as they were built to reduce friction. Cats, voles, and, for example, ponies were not built to navigate fluids, and hence lacked an optimised projected area. They would cause friction like billy-o while falling, with the air dragging at them and reducing their speed.

Then again, they would only reduce their speed relative to a fish making the same journey, while weighing a lot more.

Put simply, when choosing the winner of a hypothetical race between a falling fish and a falling horse for a bet, choose the horse. (Assuming the race starts at a high enough altitude to make drag a factor.)

But if wondering whether to stand under a falling fish or a falling horse, choose the fish.

The Alumières labelled it fauna-based precipitation in the case notes they now opened. What they needed was more data. And Gertrude would be the one to get it.

As a member of the Wait Watchers, she could stroll about, working with people as she poked her nose into whatever she fancied. Nosiness in the public interest.

The most unusual aspect of the fauna-based precipitation was that the animals, whether marine or mammalian, reached the ground alive.

It is widely accepted that God is all-knowing and all-powerful. Yet, when He added gravity to the planet, He neglected—no doubt for excellent reasons—to add sufficient rubber to His creatures to ensure they possessed sufficient "bounce" for it not to be fatal.

He did give cats the unlikely ability to always land on their feet, so *they're* all right. It is because of this clear evidence they are God's favourites out of all creation that cats possess such supreme confidence.[41] Fish were not so lucky, and they avoided becoming airborne even more strenuously than they avoided going ashore.

Yet all the creatures landed in the best of health. Slightly bruised perhaps. Undoubtedly confused about recent events. But not in dire straits.

Even the reverend had noticed this and pointed it out to his flock. They were still somewhat sceptical about moving their prayers outdoors, and the reverend was glad to reassure them—and himself—that the miraculous rain was a good omen.

In the privacy of his own thoughts, he was not quite as sanguine.

---

[41] According to a small Scottish sect, known as the Tossers, cats' ability to always land on their feet was negotiated with the Lord by the cats themselves. In exchange for being able to always land on their feet, buttered toast must always land butter side down. On the day that toast lands butter side up, the Lord will return, cats will be banished from the Earth, and haggis will get the respect it deserves.

Chapter 20

The Thing With The Hideous Face

OF COURSE, FISH don't last long when they are scattered over hill and vale, which is where Chloe and Curly's Animal Rescue came in.

It soon became a normal sight in Hawkinge-By-Hythe to see mysterious fish flopping around on the ground, before being scooped up by a young girl riding a two-headed calf.[42]

The rescue mission's headquarters were at Swiftwater as the grounds of the house encompassed plenty of land. Enough for Chloe to argue that the rescue missions should continue even if it was now raining voles and things which could move about on their own.

The Alumières agreed and waited for her to go home for the evening before discussing the matter more thoroughly.

Although they were convinced there must be a simple scientific explanation for everything, that didn't mean it would be a nice one.

They were wondering, in fact, whether it might be the nastiest one of all. The one they had hoped wouldn't show its hideous face for a while yet.

------

[42] Well, call it "normal", then.

"It isn't Carfax," said Colette. "Not his style."

Carfax was the thing with the hideous face.

"Agreed," said Victoria. "Fish and voles splatted all over the ground might be Carfax, but alive?"

"How are they still alive?" asked Gertrude.

"Tell me where they are coming from, and I'll tell you how they're still alive," said Colette, fiddling with her catapult.

So it seemed the game was afoot.

When Victoria returned that evening, she had armed herself with both a meticulous list of previous similar events, piping hot green tea, and fingers of cheese on toast with a bowl of sticky chutney to dip them into.

As ever when their keen scientific minds wrestled with esoteric matters, they were assisted by Curly. As a two-headed calf, he liked the old saying that "two heads were better than one." He stood outside, with his heads poking in through the War Room window.

"There have been a few previous instances of fish falling, and possibly mice," said Victoria. "As previously mentioned, however, none in the vicinity of Hawkinge-By-Hythe."

"Which itself is unusual," said Colette. "For *here*, I mean, one would almost expect them on a regular basis."

"But did you know that the moon is particularly strong over Hawkinge-By-Hythe? A little quirk in its rotation means the moon passes unusually close overhead on a regular basis."

"Typical!" said Gertrude.

The other two agreed.

Somehow that sounded exactly like Hawkinge-By-Hythe.

"This might explain the—short-lived—interest in astronomy. Mayor Catchpleen's assertions that people might fall up into the sky on those nights when the moon is particularly low seem a bit far-fetched, however."

"Handy for keeping people off the streets, when you're up to something, though," said Colette.

"And a Mrs Fondwright near Monks Horton claimed to see animals. Mostly Labradors, which she assumed 'appeared from nowhere', but her reports were dismissed."

"Because?" said Gertrude.

"Because she had been claiming for years that men were looking in her cottage windows when she wasn't there to stop them. Also, that the reason her house burned down is that a man knocked over her candle one night while she was alone in bed."

"So they dismissed her as mad." Gertrude's fingers hovered over the plate. She looked at Victoria. "May I?"

"Of course!"

"They were looking in her windows when she *wasn't* there?" asked Colette. "I suppose Mr Fondwright or someone told her about them?"

"No," said Victoria. "She said when she came back home she saw the greasy spots where they pushed their noses against the glass."

"That's creepy!" said Curly's white head. His black head scanned the darkness behind him in case any greasy noses were sneaking up on him.

"I'm sure Mrs Fondwright didn't much like it."

"Even if she wasn't there," said Curly's black head, allowing his white head to take over guard duty.

"Especially if she wasn't there. Who knows what they were looking for?" asked Victoria.

"Curly!" called Colette. She fired the catapult when his white head turned to her and he snapped the sugar lump out of the air.

"You do love your toys," said Gertrude indulgently. "Any thoughts on *why* there are no reports of larger animals raining down?"

"Aside from Mrs Fondwright's reports?"

"Yes," said Gertrude. "We can discount those. She doesn't seem the most reliable source."

"Which doesn't mean she's wrong," countered Victoria. Normally she would just have continued looking into the thing on her own account, without bothering to say anything. Gertrude's insistence she was too soft still rankled and she wouldn't just let this go.

"Fine!" Gertrude rolled her eyes. "*If* we were so unwise as to disregard Mrs Fondwright's valuable testimony, then why doesn't anything with a mass larger than a fish tend to fall more often?"

"Force," said Colette. "And frequency. We seem to be assuming that this is a meteorological occurrence. So an event, a storm, with enough force to pick up small fish, is rare enough hereabouts. One with enough force to pick up, for example, a herd of cattle is exponentially rarer. A waterspout can reach speeds of one hundred miles per hour, which is more than enough force to suck up water, along with any fish, frogs, etc. that might be in it. A tornado travelling over land can reach over three times that speed, so should be able to pick up heavier animals, but there aren't many tornadoes in England. Ergo, only fish are usually observed, as the weather conditions allowing for other animals, say, a calf, don't exist."

"Oi/Oi!" protested Curly.

"Agreed." Victoria nodded. Next time, Gertrude would *not* get the last cheese finger. "But a pond with fish in it might also have toads, so why do we only ever hear of one or the other?"

"The force of the meteorological phenomenon acts like a sieve. It may well pick up water, toads, fish. Seaweed. All from the same area, but as it loses force, it drops things according to weight. Unless the fish and the toads are exactly the same weight, they won't fall at the same time."

"Wonderful, but disappointing. We seem to have solved the matter already," said Gertrude. "Perhaps a last cup of tea, and then off to bed. I'll make it." This last was by way of apology.

Colette patted Victoria's hand when they were alone. "She does her best!"

"Poor thing!" said Victoria sarcastically.

"It's a skill," said Colette. "You're the only one of us who has it."

"It doesn't seem to bring many benefits, does it? I get all the jobs neither of you want to do."

"You get the jobs we *can't* do. Let's not fight."

"Tea!" announced Gertrude from the hall, so they would have plenty of warning in case they were talking about her.

"Allow me," said Colette, after Gertrude poured three steaming cups.

She loaded a sugar cube into the bucket of her trebuchet, then adjusted the spring. When she released the catch, the cube whizzed through the air to plop into the dead centre of Gertrude's cup. She judged the spin so perfectly that it didn't even cause a ripple.

"Cute!" said Gertrude, eliciting an annoyed look from Colette.

Gertrude didn't mean it to be patronising. It was just how her vocal chords worked.

De Glube remained unperturbed by any "fauna-based precipitation" he encountered. It meant he couldn't wear his absolutely finest clothes, but it did give him the chance to buy a fishing cape. He had always wanted to, and this was his chance.

Not realising that fish were no longer falling, De Glube also had a large waxed bag and some canisters of water. Should he come across any fish in need of assistance, he would once again do his bit. He was prepared for anything. For his cape kept him dry and presented the perfect cover for a man needing to bring his own equipment to dig up a trebuchet. There was little else for him to do until Lorry delivered his eagle.

His mood briefly darkened as he thought of Lorry Tassel, who had called around with a pair of budgerigars the previous day. What good were budgies to a man who hoped to re-awaken the force of the Angel's language?

There'd be the Devil to pay if the Alumières found out, however, so he told Mr Tassel that when he said eagle, he meant eagle. Nothing less than a *bona fide* member of the family of *accipitridae* would satisfy him. Furthermore, Mr Tassel should continue not to tell anyone about it, unless he wanted his budgies—

Possibly his agitation at being presented with budgies caused him to lose his train of thought. It caused him to spoil the punchline of another of Luxembourg's famous rude jokes by telling it to Mr Tassel out of context.

Luckily, Lorry Tassel did not understand Luxembourgish, and their budding friendship survived. After all, it was hardly Lorry's fault that he brought budgies where eagles were required. De Glube had not told him what he needed them for. Naturally he did not understand the position de Glube would be in if all he had were budgies when angels turned up to do his unholy bidding.

And Nodding Dean seemed to be the safest place for de Glube to spend his time. He could avoid as many grapes as he wanted if he made sure no one followed him, and summon up anything he wanted, for the place remained abandoned.

It was only a shame that the trebuchet would have to remain here when he decamped for Luxembourg. But as a respectable gentleman grave robber, he would naturally put everything back where he found it when he was finished.

On this day, de Glube dug a couple of other holes outside the grounds of Nodding Dean's church and filled them with water should any fish decide to fall from the sky.

At one point, a rustling close by in the bushes behind him caused him to pause. Indeed, it almost caused him to swallow his tongue as he desperately tried to remember what excuse he had thought up should anyone ask what he was doing. But there was no need for him to worry. It was just a quick shower of small kittens.

Not that de Glube realised this. Deep in his hole, his visibility was poor. And it was a very small shower.

Four kittens.[43]

---

[43] Meaning four random slices of buttered toast would need to be sacrificed by breakfast time of the following day to preserve the natural balance of the universe, according to the Tossers.

Of this, de Glube remained equally unaware.

The kittens sailed gracefully through the sky, only rustling as they disentangled their paws from tree branches on the way down, twisting in mid-air. They gave de Glube a look as if daring him to say something, but he was too busy digging to notice them. Satisfied, they stalked off to find somewhere comfortable to sit. The wild-haired human seemed busy, but they were prepared to wait. He would naturally be eager to spend the rest of his life catering to their every whim as soon as he realised they were there.

Chapter 21

Whistling Pounding Mystery

DE GLUBE CONTINUED not to notice the kittens for a while. Once he finished digging for the evening, he built a lightweight lattice of branches to cover up the hole he had excavated.

It was not until on the road making his way home that he realised he had company. The little cats had elected him their host for the evening. They liked the cut of his gib, deciding that a man who dressed that carefully to dig a hole could be trusted.[44] Where he led, therefore, they would follow. When he finally noticed them and stopped, they came closer to have their chins scratched. After that, they strolled in front of him, so he might appreciate the majesty of their twirling tails. De Glube, fooled by their natural self-confidence—and wishing to put off going home for as long as possible where only the light in Jennet's kitchen would be waiting for him— started to follow *them* as they twined their way along the lanes.

---

[44] On this evening, de Glube's "gib", underneath his cape, consisted of a pale pink suit jacket with tweed orange plus fours, red leather shoes and matching gloves. A beret like a flat navy cherry topped off the confection.

Soon, they were all lost, and de Glube stopped to remove his cape.

The kittens returned to tumble around his feet. When he decided to sit for a spell, they meowed and head-butted his ankles until he rose and continued on, in case he might use this excuse to wriggle out of his duty to provide milk.

He didn't know where they were, and the thought that his furry friends might not be heading home to a farmhouse, but heading out for the night, worried him. At this stage, though, he saw no choice other than to keep following them, while they felt they may as well see it through now. They had allowed him to scratch their chins, so he owed them *something*.

The moon was up, the night scented with fresh hay. It reminded de Glube of Jennet, despite his efforts to think about something else. Many a time and oft had he observed the moon in her presence, and the world seemed empty without her there to observe it with him now. As for the hay-scented breeze? After all the mornings spent feeding and sweeping up after her goat, hay and wind were inextricably linked in his mind with this animal, which made him think of her.

Normally, of course, the smell of hay came first.

Then the rumbling of the old goat's stomach.

Then the wind.

But still.

So clear was the association in de Glube's mind that when he heard a rumbling sound, he thought it must be his imagination.

Then a howl joined the rumbling, and he looked around. First for Mrs Sniffacre's goat, then for a wolf.

If this was where the kittens were going, they would have to go alone, but they too had stopped in their tracks at the noise, puffing their tails into feather dusters of alarm.

Although no wolves had been seen in the area for many hundreds of years, there had been a werewolf knocking about the locale recently. It caused no end of trouble, and de Glube didn't feel in the mood to deal with another one at the moment.

He suffered from a low boredom threshold, and werewolves quickly became repetitive. De Glube was tired, and midnight strolls with a werewolf required a good deal of concentration. It seemed unlikely to prove soothing or enlightening in his current frame of mind.

Nor would the werewolf enjoy it, for de Glube was accompanied by a quaternary of kittens.[45]

He knew all about cats, having had plenty of experience of them as a boy. He understood what would happen if the two parties met. The cats would find the werewolf too doglike for their tastes and would sit motionlessly staring at it until it felt like an idiot.

A better idea would therefore be to avoid a meeting for everybody's sake.

As if the werewolf also realised this, the sound faded.

Then it returned, louder.

It was, de Glube mused, somewhat closer to a whistle rather than the high-pitched squeak of an aged goat's stomach, or the bass howl of a werewolf. And the pounding sounded more like drumming than hay going down with difficulty.

---

[45] Editor's note: A translation of the second half of this sentence into normal English would be, "de Glube was with four cats." One can only assume the family dictionary was dropped on Delaney's head when he was a baby.

Almost like a happy uncle blowing across the top of his empty jug of beer. Although, from the low, almost ultrasonic vibrations that came with it, it sounded more like a whale playing a plaintive note through its blowhole in a subterranean cave. He turned his head and paid attention to the way the sound shook his hair to locate it.

Yes. Over *there*.

"One moment, please." He addressed his small cats, who were ignoring the noise as irrelevant to them. They wound their way around his ankles to spell out "milk" in Cat, in case he still hadn't understood what they required of him.

De Glube was naturally curious. Indeed, had his manners not been so impeccable, he would have been regarded as nosy. He doubted there were whales in the area, but it could still be either someone's uncle or a werewolf.

He had observed uncles galore over the course of his life and hoped now to find something more exciting than a mother's brother.

If that was all it turned out to be, he would be disappointed.

Though an uncle with an empty jug might also possess a second jug. One still filled to the brim with beer, which he would be willing to share with a tired, thirsty traveller.

Or his original idea turned out to be correct, and it was indeed a werewolf rather than an uncle.

Well…

What a sight that would be, to see a werewolf playing a tune by blowing air over the top of an empty beer jug!

"Shall we look?" he asked his new friends.

They were young kittens, and the look they gave him made up his mind. No doubt they had never seen a werewolf *or* an uncle playing a beer jug.

It was not in him to deny them the chance of observing such a spectacle.

The whistle wafted over the fields, and the drumming rumbled like ghostly hoof beats. They would have to be ghostly hoof beats, for a real horse would have made more of a squelching noise. The ground around Nodding Dean was low-lying and remained muddy despite the fine weather.

De Glube glanced at his fine red shoes. It seemed unlikely they would survive the trip, but the cause was a noble one for which they sacrificed themselves.

Nor did the cats seem pleased.

"I have pockets," he said. He gestured towards them and a tortoiseshell kitten stood up, propping herself against his leg to examine whether the pocket was of sufficient quality for her to sit in. De Glube gave her a moment, then scooped her up to deposit her safely into his outside jacket pocket. She made herself comfortable, leaning against his side with her head sticking out so as not to miss anything. That broke the ice, and they all hopped aboard.

He invited a grey kitten to make herself comfortable in his other outside jacket pocket. The smallest, black except for yellow eyes and white eyebrows fit exactly into his inside breast pocket. The fourth, a long orange tabby with a pink nose, did not require a pocket at all. She jumped onto his shoulder then lay down, draped around the back of his neck with her tail swishing around his left ear, her whiskers tickling his right one.

Thus dressed for the occasion, de Glube made his way over the field towards the sound of the whistling, pounding mystery.

Chapter 22

Doomed, Doomed!

MRS PENGLE HAD been reading her Bible the previous night, and come to the inevitable conclusion that they were all doomed. But as one of Mr Kelby's cows was calving, she gathered her Right Handers to put Hawkinge-By-Hythe to the ultimate test. A newly born calf could not yet have been contaminated by the town's sin. It would be their final hope, for had God not spared Zoar from destruction because a single righteous man, Lot, lived there?

Things didn't look good on the farm, however, so as Mrs Pengle spied the vet, Dr Cholmmaybotham, approaching where they were gathered in the shed with the newborn calf, she felt a thrill of purest *schadenfreude*.

The dire news would serve the vet right, for Mrs Pengle doubted the woman was righteous. Who could be righteous who earned their bread in a profession requiring them to stare at animal bottoms? Mrs Pengle looked forward to apprising the vet that it was her fault they were doomed to perdition.

The Kelbys, father and son, had been unable to dislodge the Right Handers. Now they spotted the vet at the same time and attempted to prevent her from being drawn into the madness which had descended on their farm.

"I'll tell her," whispered Andrew Kelby, the son.

"Let her come!" commanded Mrs Pengle.

"A full house, eh?" said Dr Cholmmaybotham to the Kelbys, eyeing the Right Handers with irritation.

"There's nothing you can do," said Mrs Pengle.

"It's over? Well, I'll take a look at the animal while I'm here, anyway."

"It's over, alright." Mrs Pengle barked a laugh. "Sin's wages shall be paid with fire."

"Really?" said Dr Cholmmaybotham. "Talk about money burning a hole in your pocket, eh?" Indignant silence greeted her irreverence, so she knelt to examine the new calf on straw still wet from birth, its mother getting her breath back.

"Well, they both seem fine," she said eventually. "And only one head."

Hawkinge-By-Hythe set great store by omens, and Curly had been a big one, despite the Alumières" insistence he was more along the lines of a scientific marvel. Practically a supercalf, in fact, of which Nietzsche would have approved.

But not everyone in town had yet read *Thus Spoke Zarathustra*, so this was Dr Cholmmaybotham's contribution.[46]

"Fine?" Mrs Pengle turned to her group of white-smocked Right Handers. "Didn't I say there would be nothing to do?"

---

[46] Attempts to get the book for the town library had met resistance from the Reverend Gresstart, who didn't like talk about the death of God. Also, from Mrs Boff, who was having difficulty spelling ~~Neitshz~~, ~~Nietezs~~, ~~Nietchs~~, the author's name.

"You did," they confirmed. "God save us all!"

"I don't need to do anything. He just wants time to find his legs." She looked at Kelby, who nodded agreement, his lips twisted with annoyance. The reverend would be sorry the next time he came looking for funds to patch his roof.

"Can't your *science* do anything, Missus?" asked Mrs Pengle, unable to keep the gloating tone from her voice.

Dr Cholmmaybotham was a veterinarian, rather than a psychologist, but it requires only basic observational skills to understand that when a nut hangs around with other nuts, they all get nuttier.

"There's nothing to do," she replied. "I'm off to bed, and I think you should all go, too. Give the new mum some time with her child."

"The Lord is angry, Missus," said Mrs Pengle.

"It's 'Dr'," said Dr Cholmmaybotham. "And the Lord is also merciful, according to *my* sources." "Well, call Him concerned then." Mrs Pengle raised her voice. "These animals are all doomed!" "Doomed!" echoed the Right Handers. In their white tunics, they looked like the chorus of a Greek tragedy set in a flour mill. "Doomed!"

"They're an abomination, upsetting the good Lord in all his mercy!"

"Doomed, oh merciful Lord!"

Mrs Pengle saw Dr Cholmmaybotham double-check the cow and its calf, totting up the number of heads again, in case she had missed one the first time.

"Not that, Missus—"

"Doctor!"

"—Doctor. We have been testing them all day!

"All day!" moaned the chorus.

"And these animals are upsetting the Lord and making him worry."

"Oh Lord, don't worry!"

Dr Cholmmaybotham looked to the Kelbys for explanation.

"Sorry," mouthed Andrew.

"As it was, so it is, and so ever shall it be," proclaimed Mrs Pengle, milking the situation for all it was worth. Meanwhile Dr Cholmmaybotham checked her equipment was stowed in her bag, so Mrs Pengle got to the point. "As in Nineveh, so is it now in Hawkinge-By-Hythe."

"Just keep an eye out for signs of mastitis or infection, and let me know if you need me. You have my telephone number." Dr Cholmmaybotham spoke to Kelby, raising her voice to be heard.

"And as it were, so, er, should ever it be. Oh, er… you're leaving?" asked Mrs Pengle. "Doctor?"

"Oh doctor! Oh, doctor!" chorused the background singers.

"Well, what is supposed to be *wrong* then?"

"Jonah 4:11!" Mrs Pengle declaimed the mighty Biblical numbers with her arms raised to the sky.

"Right," said Dr Cholmmaybotham. She turned again to Kelby. "Well, you have my telephone number, and also Jonah's. As long as you call one of us if—"

"'And should I not have concern for the great city of Nineveh, in which there are more than a hundred and twenty thousand people who cannot tell their right hand from their left—and also many animals? sayeth the Lord,'" Mrs Pengle quoted. She eyed Dr Cholmmaybotham with disfavour, now that her conviction the vet was faithless had been confirmed.

"Sayeth, Lord, Sayeth!" Behind Mrs Pengle, the Right Handers swayed together to the rhythm of righteousness.

The animals ignored the situation. Even the newly born calf already knew better than to get involved.

"I'm afraid I don't have the foggiest idea what the problem is," said the vet.

"They've been here all day, telling the animals to go right or left," said Kelby.

"Telling the…? Ah! Now I see what's happened. That's a relief!" Dr Cholmmaybotham was so delighted to have worked out the problem that she even smiled at Mrs Pengle. "I'm in bed and dreaming this, aren't I? So, if someone would pinch me, please, I can wake up and go back to sleep again…"

"And they can't do it!" said Mrs Pengle. "Not a single animal on this farm knows the difference between right and left, just like the sinners of Nineveh!"

The cow briefly stopped licking her new calf to give Dr Cholmmaybotham a commiserating look.

"Hang on!" said Dr Cholmmaybotham.

"God has judged us and found us wanting."

"Wanting, oh Lord. Wanting!"

"We are all sinners and must repent!"

"Repent! Repent!"

"In our sin, we are ignorant of the Lord. Knowing not left from right we are as ignorant as these animals!"

The cow gave Mrs Pengle an annoyed look. As her calf now stood on shaky legs, they staggered off together for some peace and quiet.

"We must beg for forgiveness before we are struck down. Are you a sinner?" Mrs Pengle grabbed Dr Cholmmaybotham's sleeve. "Repent with me now!"

"No. I'm going to bed. Or get out of bed, then go back to bed if I'm dreaming this." But the Right Handers surrounded her and the Kelbys, pushing them to their knees in the shed. "Get off me!" demanded Dr Cholmmaybotham.

"We are saved," said Mrs Pengle. "For we have been praying for the blooded lamb's forgiveness all day!"

"All bloody day!" echoed her chorus.

"Now you must beg, too."

"I certainly won't!"

"Then—"

"Good evening, Dr Cholmmaybotham, Mr Kelby, Andrew. Mrs Pengle," came the voice of Gertrude Alumière from the door of the shed.

She seemed to be leading a posse of Wait Watchers, though if anyone—for example Victoria—were to ask, she would have insisted that she only tagged along with the group of concerned citizens who kindly allowed her to take part in their nightly patrols.

Yes, it had been her idea to see what the light on up at Kelby's place meant, in case anyone needed assistance, but that was just a coincidence.

And yes, she stood at the front of the group, and opened the discussion with the Right Handers, but she had asked and no one else wanted to do the honours. They had delegated the task to her.

So really, she was the least important member of the group, and only doing the thankless tasks no one else wanted.

A fine example of the last being first, in fact.

What else did it mean to work with people, and not boss them around? Everyone did their bit for the group.

No one said anything else for a moment. For their part, the Wait Watchers thought this looked a bit more like it.

The Right Handers thought the opposite.

Just as they were getting into the swing of things, this had to happen.

Yes, they had God on their side, but He wasn't there.

Gertrude Alumière was.

"Jonah 4:11!" said Mrs Pengle, though her voice wobbled a bit. "Nineveh, where a hundred and twenty thousand people cannot tell their right hand from their left? And also many animals?" Somehow, her argument now sounded more like an apology.

"Everybody out!" said Kelby, getting to his feet.

"The animals know not—" insisted Mrs Pengle.

"Animals…" said Gertrude, after glancing behind her to see if anyone else fancied explaining things. Which they didn't, happy to continue delegating to her. "… Don't *have* hands!"

That settled it.

The Right Handers skulked shamefacedly away, through the gap in the door left by the Wait Watchers. There didn't seem to be any way to argue with Gertrude.

Say what you like about the Alumières—and they would certainly burn in hell for being, cough, *witches*, cough, cough—but they knew how to explain things properly.

A couple of the Right Handers found themselves wondering why Mrs Pengle hadn't noticed that.

Meanwhile, the Wait Watchers' eyes had lit up as they received their first taste of action since the werewolf. They stood straighter and practically strained at the leash for more, despite it being in the middle of the night. Mr Hammond puffed out his chest, then puffed it out even more when he saw Gertrude looking at him. Mrs Lenky licked her lips and eyed up the Right Handers, as if to choose which one she fancied her chances against.

Gertrude smiled.

What nonsense Victoria talked. Working with people was *fun!*

Chapter 23

What Might Have Been

WHILE GERTRUDE WAS discovering her talent for working with people, de Glube trudged across the fields seeking the source of the eerie whistling, thumping noise in the middle of the night, miles from anywhere.

Were he still in Luxembourg, he would have assumed someone must be playing kettle music, but the English didn't go in for that, as far as he knew.

And even in Luxembourg, except for a handful of enthusiasts, the art of playing kettles has been lost. This is because, although they are not more awkward to transport than drums, it is much more expensive for a kettle player to obtain health insurance. Kettles can only be played when piping hot.

Back when de Glube had been a young man, however, kettle players still criss-crossed Luxembourg, each playing their own unique medley. Kettle playing is exactly what it sounds like. Any kettle player worthy of the name will have at least six kettles, though Master Players may have a dozen or more, depending on their proficiency. The kettles are of different sizes, each filled with water and hung over its own small fire. As they boil, the player races between them, adjusting the openings of the spout whistles to make them sing.

De Glube soon forgot all about a potential werewolf as he became entranced by the sound, which took him back to his happy childhood running across the field of Luxembourg.[47]

Back in the present, he pushed his way through the thick hedges which separated England's fields, moving carefully to avoid discomfort to his passengers. Then he crossed another field. And another, each time the bass of the sound increased, until his hair vibrated. His cats shrank into his pockets, except for the one around his neck, which dug its claws deep in his neck to warn him not to try any funny business.

And yet, all it turned out to be, when he pushed his way through a final hedge, was a wishing well. De Glube tutted at himself for his superstition. A *well*.

It occupied a small, triangular field, surrounded by more thick hedges. A high dry-stone wall ran around the mouth of the well, which was about five feet in diameter.

Which reminded him of Mrs Sniffacre. Five feet were how many feet he and Mrs Sniffacre together possessed.[48]

A disc of weathered wood, to stop people from falling in, topped it. The whistling and drumming came from the interaction of the wind passing over a circle of wood cut from this lid's centre. Except… de Glube licked his finger and held it up in the air. There wasn't much wind.

An interesting little phenomenon. De Glube regarded it as a curiosity rather than as something of genuine

---

[47] Yes, "field". It is, as previously mentioned, a small country.

[48] Once, when he had stumbled while walking with her, Mrs Sniffacre had told him he had "two left feet". He also possessed a right foot, and Mrs Sniffacre had one of each. That made five.

interest. His baby cats didn't seem to like it though, so he decided to call it a night.

He might take Jennet to see it.

He reconsidered and decided not to.

It wouldn't be right to have a strange well whistling at a respectable widowed woman.

The kitten acting as a scarf grumbled as his shoulders slumped.

The thought of Jennet, and what might have been, woke his heartache from its uneasy sleep in his breast. He sighed and made his long way home.

Chapter 24

He Who Hath Not Trimmed

"AND HOW ARE you getting on, Professor?" asked Colette Alumière coming up behind de Glube where he had briefly paused on Westarfitt Lane the next day on the way back to Nodding Dean. De Glube hadn't expected to meet anyone at 5:00 in the morning. Even the sun had not yet wiped the sleep from its eyes.

He jumped at her voice therefore, startling the kittens in his pockets and causing them to squeak. Sunk deep in thought about the changes to the Enochian Calls required to fulfil his goal, he hadn't heard her approaching. And the Enochian Calls were the one thing he mustn't let the Alumières know about.

"It whistles," he said referring to the previous night's well. It was the first other topic of conversation that occurred to him. He dished it out now to prevent Colette from reading his mind.

Not that she could, *really*. He knew that. As a sophisticated man he didn't believe all the witch nonsense about the Alumières. But they had a knack of guessing what you were thinking that would be fatal for his plans.

Of course, of the three Alumières, Colette would be the one most likely to see the lighter side of reanimating the dead, should he wish to confide his plans. But he daren't risk it.

"Does it, indeed?" Colette asked, busily dispensing tickles behind the ear to his passengers. They had followed him home and slept at the end of his bed. When he rose that morning and dressed, they hopped into the pockets of his new suit, eager for the next adventure. Otherwise he would have already reached Nodding Dean. They wouldn't leave his pockets, even for breakfast, so he had fed them with finely chopped liver delivered straight to where they sat in his pockets and on his neck.

De Glube was fussy about his clothes. And the cats were messy eaters, necessitating some intense work with a damp cloth.

Which, naturally, turned into a game of catch the cloth.

De Glube had enjoyed it immensely, though he pretended not to, as he needed to be firm for the kittens' own good.

If he spoiled them too much, they wouldn't be able to fend for themselves when they returned to wherever they lived. He needed them to understand they should regard their home in his haberdashery as temporary accommodation, not a permanent solution.

He would leave for Luxembourg soon, and they would need to stay here.

"The well whistles, I mean," he clarified for Colette. "And it smells."

"Smells, eh?" asked Colette. The orange tabby purred under her fingers, draped across de Glube's shoulders like a cruelty-free fur stole. De Glube waved his fingers in the air over the heads of the two grey cats in his outside pockets to keep them happy. The fourth cat, the black one, still slept in his suit's breast pocket.

"I assure you!" said de Glube to Colette. Despite his efforts not to think about them, the glyphs of the Enochian language wandered through his mind. Twisting into new shapes, as if they, too, didn't want him thinking about them. He cleared his throat. "Yes," he said to convince himself. "I wanted to tell you all about it. It's right up your avenue."

"You found a smelly well and thought of me?" asked Colette, looking away from the orange tabby to give him an appraising stare.

De Glube blinked. "An unusual phenomenon."

"That sounds more like it," said Colette. The kittens purred agreement. "What are we waiting for?"

It would mean passing the Church of Nodding Dean, and de Glube hoped Colette wouldn't wish to stop and have a look around at it.

Could he be sure he had covered up the traces of his activities?

But he had found the kittens near there, too, so perhaps he could finally bring them back home. Despite the animal rains, the penny had not yet dropped for him. He assumed that on the previous night they, like him, must have lost their way in the dark. Once they saw the place in daylight, they would remember where they lived, and he would get his pockets back.

"This way," said de Glube, gesturing with a hand.

Three kittens watched his fingers in case they suddenly turned into mice and needed to be pounced upon.

"Is it perhaps some new fitness fad?" asked Colette. "Or do you just like how they go with that suit?"

"The little kitties? No, they simply started following me on one of my walks. They don't *live* in my pockets!" He laughed. That would have been ridiculous.

They turned up Bark Road, just as a group of Right Handers arrived in their white tunics. They were having more success getting people to confess in the morning, when they tackled them early, before the morning cuppa. And they had their grapes ready for de Glube, as the good book commands. Seeing him not only accompanied by one of the Alumières, but liberally coated in cats, they hesitated.

They knew, as any student of the Bible did, that cats' eyes bulge from fatness (Psalm 73:7), but weren't sure whether this was a good or bad thing. The Reverend would have to advise. On the whole, probably bad.

Cats and a witch had to be bad, didn't it?

They kept these thoughts to themselves therefore, because although de Glube's pockets were obviously filled with cats, no one knew what Colette might have in hers.

Mrs Delbing, who had worked her way from Town Gossip to Town Bigot, was the last person to mention the word "witch" out loud in the presence of the Alumières. She had spent the next three months scratching herself, when, somehow, some of Colette's itching powder blew out of her pocket in such a way that it landed down the back of her neck. It remained lodged there despite baths, exfoliation, and sheep dips.[49]

---

[49] Which had been good news for everyone else. A keen adherent of folk remedies, Mrs Delbing was usually covered in so many pastes, poultices, and unguents that even Mrs Sniffacre's noisome goat found her hard on the nostrils. The recipes were passed down to her from her grandmother, who—interesting story—

As they passed now, Colette merely nodded politely to the group, who, despite themselves, nodded back. They wondered where things had gone so wrong.

Back in the good old days, witches were proper witches: frail old women, easily intimidated in the name of being a good person.

Now, they strolled about with their polite manners, air of untouchable confidence, and thick-soled, steel-capped boots that made your shins wince just to look at them.

It took all the fun out of it.

"I don't like them," said de Glube, once they were well past the group, and the danger of grapes lay behind him.

"No. They're not particularly likeable. But as long as they are not *doing* anything…"

"They smashed Spottleton's window," said de Glube. "I'm sure of it."

"You saw them?"

"I saw them grinning afterwards."

"Hmmm."

"They said the Bible forbade cutting hair, of all the ridiculous things," said de Glube.

"It does," said Colette, who had decided to give the book a go. "Leviticus, 19:27. Mind you, it doesn't specifically say 'thou shalt not cut hair', but it is dead set against trimming the corners. Beards, too. Most scholars agree you can wear it as short as you like in the back, as long as you don't touch the sides. Whether it needs to be long in front is open to interpretation. The problem, of course, is that people have round heads, so who can say for certain where the corners *are?* When I picture the

had been the reason for the 1842 Poultice Reform Bill, mentioned by the Constable.

Biblical ideal, I see fringe to the chin, and beard the rest of the way down."

"Ridiculous!" said de Glube. Back in Luxembourg, he considered his barber a friend more than anything else. "Besides, how would people recognise each other if everyone is all hair and no face?"

"Of course, Spottleton isn't a very good barber," mused Colette. "I use now the word 'good' in the sense of 'competent', rather than 'righteous.'"

"Then don't tip the man!" said de Glube. "Don't smash his windows."

"Agreed. 'Let he who hath not trimmed, cast the first stone,'" said Colette. "Sorry," she added, in response to the look the tabby on de Glube's shoulders gave her. They strolled on. The sun was so glorious that when the black kitten woke in de Glube's pocket, it needed to bask, so Colette popped it into one of her culotte's more shallow pockets. It nipped her fingers in thanks.

"It's this way," said de Glube, pointing to the bit of hedge that would take him over the field to Nodding Dean.

He still got lost whenever he took the road, and this was the only sure way he knew of getting there.

Colette passed through the hedge, followed by de Glube. It almost came as a disappointment how unsurprised she seemed.

They reached Nodding Dean easily, and it occurred to de Glube for the first time that it was odd to have a town, and a church, and nobody living there.

"So you found it!" said Colette.

De Glube's heart thumped painfully. They were just passing the church and his guilty conscience flustered him. "I do love Nodding Dean. Most people don't even realise it's here."

"Yes. Yes," said de Glube. "Not that there's much to see. Nothing really at all, in fact. That church, for example. There's nothing there. Nothing at all." He cleared his throat.

"Did you come here with Mrs Sniffacre?"

De Glube sighed. "The woman…" He paused to gather his thoughts. "The woman who threw the stone at the barbershop. The woman *I am sure but cannot prove* threw the stone at the barbershop. She gives me grapes." It didn't answer Colette's question, but he needed to work up to that.

"The usual expression is 'she gives me the pip,'" said Colette.

"Why do they give me grapes?" The free fruit didn't upset him that much, but he needed to talk about his feelings, and indignation would help him build up enough emotional speed to do so. "Everywhere I go: Damn grapes! Is that any way to treat people?"

"Most irritating," said Colette.

"Every day: grapes. And a big smile while she does it. Here you go, professor, have a grape."

"I see." Colette scratched the black kitten's head.

"And then she goes and smashes some poor man's windows. I mean…"

"You never can tell, can you?"

"Jennet! Oh, Jennet… How could I have been so wrong? I thought her the whipped cream to my *quetscheflued*, but it was not to be! Friends! That's what we are, I suppose. Or what we would be if I could stand it. I'm leaving, Miss Alumière. I must go!"

"But what happened?" asked Colette. Like everyone, the Alumières had been sure that de Glube and Mrs Sniffacre were an item. "I always thought you two were, well, you know."

"Me too, me too! It's like with the grapes all over again," said de Glube. His face contorted with anguish, and Colette wished Victoria were present.

For as much as the Alumières resembled each other physically, their personalities were very different. If an oil change, or a recalibration of his springs were all that he needed, Colette would have dismantled, repaired, and put de Glube back together in no time at all. With more horsepower than his original maker ever intended. All this emotional stuff, however, suited Victoria better.

It was their distinct personalities which led to running an apothecary shop, as the career best suited to all of them. Colette enjoyed tinkering about with chemicals and components and making people go better. Victoria enjoyed helping them and finding out more about their lives. And Gertrude, well, Gertrude enjoyed telling people what to do, and pointing out what they had done wrong to get in such a state in the first place.

But Colette decided to do her best. If Victoria could be tough, and Gertrude could be nice, then Colette could be empathetic, or whatever one called it.

Unless de Glube cried, in which case she would remember an urgent appointment and leg it.

She need not have worried. De Glube's training stood him in good stead and he composed himself again.

"I beg your pardon," he said. "I'm such a fool!"

"Not at all," said Colette. "Here." His grey cat was doing its best to climb up his jacket. Colette lifted it up for de Glube to take and the touch of the warm animal calmed him further.

"I shouldn't drag you into it, but I love her, dammit! Only to find she doesn't love me."

"A misunderstanding, perhaps," said Colette. "This matter of the whipped cream, for example. Have you mentioned it? Perhaps she doesn't want her cream whipped?"

"It's her husband," said de Glube. "She is still in love with him."

"I don't think so," said Colette.

"Oh, it's true!" said de Glube. "Whatever I do, wherever we go, everything reminds her of him."

"What rot!" said Colette. She might not have been big into feelings, but she could read people and knew it must be some minor misunderstanding.

"I assure you!" said de Glube.

"Well, let me look into it," said Colette. "In the meantime, you hang onto those cats, in case you need them. You never know."

"Fine," said de Glube. "Thank you," he added a moment later. "This is the well."

They had reached the triangular field. They couldn't hear any whistling or thumping, but the smell was present as advertised.

A very unusual smell for a well. Sulphur with a metallic aftertaste.

Colette looked into the dark of the deep well. "Well, well, well!" she said.

As if she had spoken the password, the well started whistling and making its drumming noise again, and the smell grew stronger.

A smell that Colette knew very well.
Gunpowder.

Chapter 25

De Glube's Legs

THE REVEREND'S OUTDOOR sermons continued each day, with the addition of his own signature call to the final coda. "God expects us to keep this to ourselves."

As if to underline the urgency of the matter, the service had ended only moments before a shower of various terriers. The dogs refused to be stoic about it and made their annoyance plain with barks and strategically located piles of mess all over Bagnell's Field.

So the reverend was nervous, and when people are nervous, they do foolish things. The reverend, for example, pulled Mrs Pengle aside and asked her whether perhaps her "friends" might not keep an eye on the Alumières. He didn't know what would happen next, but if Jesus were to shortly turn up, someone should be watching out for the triplets.

Just in case.

Spottleton's barber shop no longer sported the town's only smashed windows. Nor did the Right Handers feel any compunction about accosting people to demand if they were saved, even without Mrs Pengle egging them on.

When they discussed it at Swiftwater, Victoria speculated that they believed the animal rains to be a practice run for the rapture. Gertrude preferred the simpler reason that they kept getting away with it and were now "up themselves".

Still, a rain of animals, a religious mob, and a whistling well. The situation promised a juicy mystery after all, and they were delighted to sink their teeth into it. Especially as the presence of annoying Right Handers near their shop meant business was bad. Most of their customers were waiting for things to blow over, rather than risk talking to the white-tunicked ones.

So they found plenty of time to devote to finding a solution, although they did so separately, with Victoria still annoyed that Gertrude never took her seriously. Gertrude fumed that even though she worked with the Wait Watchers—without scolding anyone—Victoria still thought she only possessed the people skills of a tough old boot. And a tough old boot which had been in use during the recent shower of upset dogs, at that.

Colette knew she should do something about de Glube. He expected her to fix his relationship woes, but it took a few days before she could bring herself to do the job.

So, while Gertrude tagged along with her Wait Watchers, Colette found herself closeted in the kitchen belonging to their founding member, Mrs Sniffacre, for a heart-to-heart talk.

"I met de Glube yesterday," said Colette. "I don't wish to pry, but he seemed upset. Which surprised me, as I thought the two of you were hitting it off rather well."

Mrs Sniffacre sighed. "I thought so, too."

And there the matter seemed to rest. Mrs Sniffacre held her cup of tea in both hands and stared into the middle distance.

"And have you since decided that he is not quite the man for you?" asked Colette.

"Oh, if ever there was a man for me," said Mrs Sniffacre, "it's Lucius de Glube!"

"I see. Well, without wishing to be indelicate, what about Mr Sniffacre? I'm sorry, I don't actually know his name."

"No, you're right, pet. Mr Sniffacre is correct. My original husband, if that's who you mean."

"That's the one," said Colette. "And his first name?"

"Well, he's dead, isn't he?"

"And yet his legend lives on, if you follow me," said Colette. She bit into a biscuit and waited.

Mrs Sniffacre blinked in surprise. "What do you mean?"

"The professor, Lou, is under the impression that you are still infatuated with the late Mr Sniffacre. Mr Sniffacre, whose friends called him…?"

"Oh, but that's silly! He's long gone. And even if he were to come back, well. That was then, and this is now."

"Well, it sounds to me like there has been a misunderstanding somewhere. Have you told de Glube about your feelings for him?"

"I've tried."

"Hm. And have you ever brought up the subject of your late husband with de Glube? Your late husband who might even have a Christian name, if it's not a sensitive subject?"

"I mentioned him a few times. As a hint. A woman likes a bit of affection, doesn't she? A little hug, or what have you. *You* know." An uncomfortable pause followed.

"Well, perhaps that's where de Glube is getting confused."

"Oh no, I don't think so," said Mrs Sniffacre. "I've been very clear."

"That's good. Clarity is paramount when one discusses one's feelings."

"Exactly. 'While the baker has a dozen, the cobbler has his cousin.'"

"Right," said Colette. "There's no arguing with that. But it occurs to me now that perhaps Lou might not have understood the hints you've been giving him." How Victoria did it, she didn't know. It was like playing with dynamite.

Not real dynamite, which blew up and was exciting. Emotional dynamite, with the risk of tears and needing to pat people on the head ever-present.

"Why would you say that?"

"Remember, he's not a native English speaker. So he might not understand all these figures of speech. The meaning isn't always obvious, you know."

"Clear as cheap soup, I'd have said."

"Nonetheless, perhaps you could tell me what sort of hints you've been giving him?" Colette asked.

"Well, I've told him, haven't I? Little hints that I'm ready to love again."

"For example?"

"Well, let me see… Just the other day, I remember I said, 'Mr Sniffacre never let his tea go cold. Always quick to the table.' You know, just to let Lou know it's all right. Ginger him up a little. Lord knows, we don't have time to be prudish at our ages."

"Right," said Colette. "Anything else?"

"I mean, I've told him a hundred times. To get him moving, you know? That time we were giving Wordsworth his drops, I said—"

"Wordsworth?"

"The goat."

"The one with the digestive difficulties?"

"That's the one. Named for the spontaneous powerful overflows when his guts are bad."

"Poor Wordsworth!"

"Oh, he's alright. It's me and de Glube that have to wear the clothes pegs on our noses. Anyway, de Glube was holding Wordsworth between his legs. I mean, he was holding him between his own legs. De Glube was. Holding Wordsworth. So I could get him with his tummy drops."

"Hold on," said Colette. "I need to picture the scene. Who was holding whom?"

"Take your time," said Mrs Sniffacre.

"De Glube was holding Wordsworth?"

"Yes."

"Between his own legs?"

"That's right."

"Why was de Glube holding Wordsworth's between Wordsworth's own legs?" said Colette, unable to resist.

"De Glube was holding Wordsworth between *de Glube's* legs. Between the knees so he couldn't run away. He doesn't like those drops."

"I'm not surprised," said Colette.

"Well, they're for his own good!"

"You amaze me!"

"Oh yes. You wouldn't believe the mess when he doesn't get them."

"Really?" said Colette. "He's never mentioned this when he's come into the shop."

"What?"

"De Glube has never mentioned digestive issues to me."

"De Glube? Lou is fine, dear!"

"Then why are you giving him tummy drops?"

"What? They're for the goat!"

"Well, that proves de Glube loves you. Think about it. I mean, if he's willing to eat goat medicine just to see you smile," said Colette.

"No, no, I give the drops to the goat!"

"*Not* de Glube?"

"No. No, no!"

"Not even while he's holding his own legs?"

"Why would I, dear?"

"Ah," said Colette. "The penny has dropped. Now I understand."

Mrs Sniffacre chuckled. "De Glube holds the goat, and I shove the drops into him."

"Right! Thank you. All has become clear."

"Anyway. I said it reminded me of what Mr Sniffacre used to do when I—"

"I see," said Colette, and she did.

"Wait," said Mrs Sniffacre. Her teacup clanked into its saucer as she set it down. "You don't think he misunderstood, do you?"

"He may have done," said Colette. "Would you say Mr Sniffacre was good at picking up hints, back in the day? For example when people enquired about his more informal Christian soubriquet?"

"*Him?* Oh, dear, no! He wouldn't have noticed a hint if you nailed a mirror to his forehead with it."

"Aha!" said Colette. "I mean, you saw how confused we became just a moment ago."

"Well I'll be…. How it never occurred to me before!"

"I think we've sorted that little mystery. Don't you?" Colette was pleased with herself. "All just a simple misunderstanding."

"I'll say," said Mrs Sniffacre. "I should have realised. Poor Lou. How could he possibly be interested in a muggins like me, I don't know. I should have realised!"

"Not at all. How could you? Men are practically another species," said Colette. "Descended from apes, you know. That's what Mr Darwin says."

"Poor Lucius, God love him," said Mrs Sniffacre. "Well, I should be whipped for a fool, and that's that!"

"It's funny you should bring that up…" said Colette, remembering de Glube's comment about cream.

Chapter 26

Smug Ninnies

REVEREND GRESSTART NOW spent most nights in the bell tower of his church. Well, "tower" of the church, seeing as it didn't have a bell. The black speck—the Message, as he thought of it—appeared briefly every single night at the same time. He considered it a sign, though its exact meaning seemed uncertain. He would never presume to understand God's mind, but he hoped God meant it as encouragement. Good work on getting the faithful into the fields, it might have meant. On the other hand, the mysterious Message made him nervous. He knew by now that the object was slowing. A warning?

Mess this up, and your roof is *really* in trouble. Gresstart tried to dismiss this unworthy thought whenever it crossed his mind, for there was another, more exciting possibility. Hadn't Jesus promised to return one day?

Was He returning even now through the night sky and heading straight for Hawkinge-By-Hythe? The reverend worked hard, and his parishioners did their best. What better place to receive the Lord than

Hawkinge-By-Hythe? In his mind's eye, the black speck that whizzed overhead must be an ark, with Jesus at the wheel. Perhaps even *the* ark. He might have borrowed Moses' to pick up some more animals from whatever planet they lived to add them to Earth's menagerie. Orthodox in many ways, Gresstart's opinions on where animals came from would have shocked his bishop. In his opinion, one only needed to look at certain animals. The pyjama-wearing zebra, the outrageously necked giraffe, the cute armoured menace of the hedgehog. They surely couldn't have come from *here*.

He would mention it to his parishioners sooner rather than later. They would need a chance to prepare themselves for the Second Coming. Especially since they had started wearing white smocks, which got dirty as soon as you looked at them. They would naturally want to look their best for the Lord. Would it be too warm for wool in heaven? The reverend shook his head at his own silliness. Naturally, the temperature would be exactly right in heaven, regardless of what one wore.

He would have told them about it already, if he could have been sure that the Alumières wouldn't somehow throw a scientific spanner in the works and ruin things. They already refused to believe in all sorts of miraculous and wonderful things. It would be just typical of their modern ways to refuse to believe in Jesus, with him standing in front of them in his holy toga.

But one thing at a time was the way to do it. For now he had got his parishioners used to praying outside "where anyone can see us". In fact they loved it. They confessed all over the place. He barely opened proceedings before they raised their hands to tell him what they had done since the previous day, like naughty schoolchildren eager for his attention.

Or detention, if even half of what they claimed to have done were true.

Somehow, the reverend doubted it. Their confessions were rather aspirational in nature. Still, it was crucial to keep not just the Alumières, but also the town constable away, a man who liked to fine first, and ask questions later.

The reverend need not have worried about people (the Alumières, the constable, those smug ninnies from the Church of Atheism) coming by and poking fun, because for a change his parishioners were good at keeping it to themselves. They were having too much of a good time out in the open air to want anyone to come along and ruin things.

They would let people know. It would be selfish to keep it to themselves. But not yet.

They'd be sure to let everyone know just before the Lord whisked them up into the sky for harp lessons. That's when they'd tell everyone they should have been nicer.

Nonetheless, the Alumières knew something was going on. Gertrude, while stalking the night streets of Hawkinge-By-Hythe as part of the Wait Watcher patrols, often spotted the reverend returning from his church at completely unsuitable hours. She even went to look around once her patrol went to bed, but found nothing, as he was very careful with his precious equipment.

Victoria took up the challenge and positioned herself at Muir Hall with a telescope of her own, with which to observe the reverend.

She could confirm that he was gazing at the stars, and the three Alumières pored over their star charts to discover what so entranced him.

Meanwhile the whistling well kept Colette busy, with its unusual scent of gunpowder. And Victoria scoured the parish records, searching for a further reference of the effort to rename the constellations.

It all seemed *very* mysterious.

Around town, Curly and Chloe were heroes, rounding up and taking care of the animals who landed suddenly and unexpectedly, with nowhere else to go. The back field at Swiftwater House was almost full.

"I don't know where we're going to put any more," said Gertrude to Chloe and Curly, as she surveyed the back field which now contained sheepdogs since the most recent rain. She smiled to show it was not a complaint.

"Yes, Miss Alumière, said Chloe." Gertrude noted that while the girl smiled back to demonstrate her willingness to accept that her conversational counterpart's intentions matched those she signalled, she had not yet been won over. This, Gertrude assumed, was due to having earlier overstressed the Chancellor Churchill *motif* while getting the hang of human offspring—children. Naturally Chloe feared he might make a sudden guest re-appearance.

"You know, it's getting late, and I really think—" Gertrude tried out her softest voice. Similar to what she used with the Wait Watchers when they finally took the hint she had been giving them. Though in a higher register, for she knew that unripe adults—children— possessed a different range of hearing and reacted to it better.

"Badgers/Badgers!" called Curly as he barrelled from the far side of the field towards them.

"Curly!" Gertrude's tender voice and sweet smile disappeared faster than a bottle of whiskey in Chancellor Churchill's study.

"No, badgers!/Really, look!" He nodded his heads to where the black-and-white striped animals were falling just a couple of fields away. "Let's go!/Animal rescue!"

"Ohhh, sweet!" said Chloe.

"But bad-tempered," said Gertrude.

"Yes, Miss Alumière, they're falling out of the sky. Of course they're bad-tempered."

"No, I mean, they might be dangerous. I don't think you should go."

"But Miss Alumière, they might be hurt!"

"Well, I don't want you getting hurt, either. Either of you."

"Chloe is great with badgers/She'll have them eating out of her hand!"

"Yes, gnawing off her fingers. Really, they are among the most unpredictable and foul-tempered of all the animals."

"I think we should save them, anyway. It's not their fault they're always grumpy!"

Gertrude scoured Chloe's face for a trace of sarcasm, but found nothing. She would have examined Curly's faces for the same, except he must have just swallowed some cud the wrong way, because he kept coughing.

"It's too dangerous. I'm sure Victoria would never allow it!"

"But Victoria isn't here, and you *could* allow it. Please, Miss… Aunt Gertrude!" A final badger fell with a distant thump. Chloe looked longingly towards the sound.

"Well…" The answer was no, of course. She, Gertrude, had decided, and that was that. That "Aunt Gertrude" tempted her, though. She had waited a long time to hear Chloe say it. Dare she undo all her progress? "If we went together, then it might be fine, I suppose," she suggested.

"What on earth are you doing outside?" cried Victoria, after arriving home now from the apothecary.

"Badgers, Aunt Victoria!"

"Badgers!/Badgers!"

"Exactly, come in this instant. It's dangerous out there!" Chloe and Curly trudged inside, followed by Gertrude, whose head spun. Somehow, Victoria had laid down the law… and got away with it.

She sighed. It was hard, dealing with people.

Chapter 27

Lambs Willy-Nilly

"PSST! Come on, Curly!"

"Wha?/Whoosit?" Curly snorted out the straw creeping up his nostrils as he opened his eyes in his dark shed that night. "Chloe?"

"Let's go!"

"But it's… what time is it?/How did you get here?"

"Never mind that," said Chloe. "We saw badgers and I'm going to save them. Are you in?"

"You bet!/Let's go!"

"Come on, I have bandages and things, and some worms in case they are hungry."

"Worms!/Ew!"

"Shhh!"

"Why? Uh-oh!/How come all the lights are off?"

"Shhh! Come on!"

As it turned out, the badgers were long gone, though Chloe insisted they would be at Muir Hall, so that's where they should go to find them.

"Hey!/Hey!" whispered Curly as they passed a stray dog. He still hoped to find an animal who would answer. So far, none had replied.

Unlike the gangs of humans wandering round Hawkinge-By-Hythe, who never seemed to shut up. Curly was not allowed to talk when others were around. He could have strolled down Main Street any day this week chanting rude limericks at the top of his voices without exciting comment, though. The Right Handers were trying to outdo each other as they thought up ever more things to confess to.

Chloe and Curly had learned a lot during the first few days, including their new favourite insult, but the novelty was gone. The red-faced sweating Right Handers became implacable, insisting that their victims *must* have something to confess to.

She and Curly waited at the corner of Cairn Way for a gang of Right Handers to pass, as Chloe did her best to cheer Curly up.

"Maybe they can talk, but are waiting to be sure no one is going to come around and tell them it's a sin," she suggested. The Right Handers started running away from where Chloe and Curly were hiding, towards a sinner in the distance.

"I don't blame them. They're such adulterers!" said Curly. The Right Handers bandied the word about a lot. Not unreasonably, he and Chloe assumed it referred to the sin of being an adult. They behaved abominably.

When the coast was clear, they continued on to Muir Hall via the woods.

"Ouch!" cried Curly. Suddenly it was raining lambs around them, and one kicked him on both heads. "Watch out!/Fragile contents!"

"Oh, Curly, you're such a baby!" This hurt more than the lamb, and Curly resolved not to complain again, unless Chloe did first. In the meantime, he wondered if perhaps they should have listened to Gertrude.

Before he could mention this random thought to Chloe, another lamb arrived, knocking his white head with the black curling forelock unconscious.

Gertrude, too, was out that night, patrolling the streets of Hawkinge-By-Hythe with the Wait Watchers, who were gaining more confidence, as the menace of the Right Handers became apparent.

She dearly hoped to explain to them the error of their ways, but her hopes were dashed again and again. Every time she spotted some Right Handers, they legged it, almost as if they were scared of her.

That evening she had been explaining to her Wait Watchers that they needed to really get to grips with the Right Handers.

After saying it a baker's dozen of times, the message started to sink in.

"What we really want to do," said Mr Hammond, "really, what we want is to get to grips with them."

The rest of the group eyed him suspiciously. On a recent occasion, while investigating reports of half-naked ladies, he had suggested the same thing.

"I find wool *very* scratchy," said Mr Cormer. "So you can have my one, if you like."

"No, I mean..." Mr Hammond trailed off.

"How clever, Mr Hammond! I was just trying to think of what we should do next when you suggested showing the Right Handers the error of their ways by accosting them physically. Wasn't that what you meant? Obviously, we wouldn't hurt them, would we?" said Gertrude.

If he had run out of gold, Chancellor Churchill could have used Gertrude's smile to fix the price of the British pound instead.

"That's it." Mr Hammond assumed it must be all the fresh air and exercise making him so clever.

Pursuant to Mr Hammond's plan, the group of Wait Watchers (of which Gertrude comprised merely the smallest, least significant part) had been sneaking up on a group of Right Handers for ages. Then Mr Cormer sneezed and ruined the surprise.

"Very scratchy," he said in answer to Gertrude's look. "I felt a wisp in my throat."

"I'm going home," muttered Gertrude, and left.

Knowing she could never sleep now, Gertrude decided to walk off her irritation instead. With a little luck, she might come across some more Right Handers.

She would never have admitted it to anyone, but she had been meaning to go to Muir Hall, to see if that's where the badgers had gone. She imagined finding a small one, and then being discovered there by Chloe as she nursed it back to health.

That would teach everyone she was indeed nice. And if people still refused to think so, frankly they could go to hell.

A series of thumps and startled "Baas" started her walking faster.

When she heard Chloe call out "Curly!" she ran.

Ahead of her, Chloe knelt beside Curly as more lambs hit the ground, their fleece sparkling from the ice caught in its wool. Gertrude's heart plummeted like an express lift. "What are you doing outside?" she shouted as she raced towards them.

"What?" said Curly. "What?" But something was wrong. His voice sounded unfamiliar. There was only one of it.

"Get out of the way!" She addressed this to a lamb which bounced to its feet on the road. It shook itself, stiff from the cold, then stood blocking the way. She pushed it aside, only to be confronted with another lamb, then another as the shower continued. The more that landed, the more inclined they all were to remain motionless, for all practical purposes singing "We Shall Not Be Moved!"

She shoved lambs willy-nilly out of the way and ran the last few metres.

"Curly, get up!" said Chloe. "Help, Aunt Gertrude!"

"My brain!" said Curly. "How come there's only one of you?" he asked when he noticed Gertrude. "Aren't there normally more?"

"You banged your head," explained Chloe.

"I did not!" Curly climbed to his feet to give his best friend a haughty look. "A lamb banged it!"

"What happened?" asked Gertrude. Curly's white head hung motionless, and the weight of it caused Curly to stagger.

"A lamb rained, and it kicked him on the head."

"No," said Curly. "It didn't. I'm fine."

"On your other head!"

"Ha, ha, ha, ha, ha, ha, ha!" said Curly. Then he slumped bow-legged to the road again. "Ouch!"

"I think the lamb might have hit both heads," said Gertrude.

"You two look strange," asked Curly. "Where are your heads? Don't tell me badgers got them? Very dangerous, badgers."

"Sorry!" whispered Chloe to Gertrude. "We shouldn't have come out." Gertrude managed to say nothing. She would give them hell in the morning, but for now, they had to get home.

"Can you walk at all, Curly?" she asked.

Curly stared around him.

"Curly!"

"Hello?"

"Can you walk, Curly?"

"Who, me? Curly's the other one. I'm…. Sorry, I thought I saw something moving, and thought it might be one of your missing heads. Unless it was mine?" He looked over where his other head hung, unconscious. "No, I have mine. But, shhhh, he's sleeping!"

"We need to get you home, Curly!" said Chloe. The lambs milled around them, waiting for someone to make a decision.

"Wait!" said Curly, as he spotted the animals. His brow furrowed in thought. "Wait! This is important." His white head was still knocked out, but his black head frowned with intense concentration. His lips moved as he thought through whichever momentous problem vexed him. "Ha! I've got it!"

"What is it, Curly?"

"*Ewe'll* never guess what happened to me," he said.

"Actually…"

"No, no. *Ewe'll* never guess…"

"Yes Curly."

"*Ewe'll* never guess what happened!" he insisted.

"No, Curly."

"I got *rammed!*" He sputtered with laughter. "Ha, ha, ha, ha, ha, ha!"

"'s going on?" His white head started to move and looked around.

"You woke him!" complained Curly's black head. "Okay, my turn for a little nap, then." His eyes lost focus and his voice started to trail off. "We can continue searching for all the, the... badges, and... headers afterwards," was the last thing it said.

Chapter 28

The Divine Mrs Pengle

NOT FOR ANOTHER week did the reverend decide the time had come to break the good news to his parishioners. After careful observation of the black speck—the Message—over the previous nights, his calculations showed it was unquestionably slowing. His flock deserved time to set their affairs in order, before they were collected by the heavenly shuttle.

He didn't tell them that, though. Not quite. He knew how excitable they remained, despite all of Mrs Pengle's efforts to keep them calm.

So after the service in Bagnell's Field, he casually mentioned he thought he might have seen an ark heading to Hawkinge-By-Hythe and left it at that.

He did *not* tell them he thought Jesus might be driving it. He would let them draw their own conclusions. After all, not a lot of other people drove arks these days.

He regretted it, of course. Like sentient cream eager for *quetscheflued*, they were soon whipping themselves into a frenzy. Confessing to everything and anything. It made it even more difficult to hold the outdoor services than when animals rained on them.

Mrs Delbing had called her mother a rude word after discovering the lid off the jar of pickled frogspawn and garlic stoat blood. It kept her safe from the licentious thought of the town's single males, but dried out it became useless for protection.[50]

Mr Babbage admitted he had told the same fib about the weight of his oranges to a male customer. Straight after having told the exact same untruth to a female customer![51]

When Mrs Pengle attempted to start confessing, Gresstart reminded her of 1 Corinthians 14:34, which forbade women from speaking in Church. But she reminded him they were in a field and continued on.

It was some solace to him when Miss Tinfeld and Miss Strump then interrupted her, almost coming to blows about Corinthians 11:4-6. Miss Tinfeld insisted it forbade the wearing of a hat, which Miss Strump was doing. Miss Strump insisted Corinthians preferred that those without hats, like Miss Tinfeld, should shave their big, ugly, jealous heads.

The reverend knew the passage well. It still gave him a headache when he tried to untangle it. Rather than advise, therefore, he said a quick, ignored prayer, and left them to it.[52]

---

[50] Editor's note: Exodus 21:17: "And he that curseth his father, or his mother, shall surely be put to death." The reader will be relieved to learn that even without the pickled frogspawn, Mrs Delbing managed—somehow—to remain untouched.

[51] Editor's note: Leviticus 20:13: "If a man also lie with mankind, as he lieth with a woman..."

[52] Editor's note: The passage reads: "Every man praying or prophesying, having his head covered, dishonoureth his head. But every woman that prayeth or prophesieth with her head uncovered dishonoureth her head: for that is even all one as if she were shaven. For if the woman be not covered, let her also be shorn: but if it be a shame for a woman to be shorn or shaven, let her be covered." Regarding the question of whether Miss Tinfeld

Things got worse when Mrs Pengle took the reverend's place in front of the old oak tree. She pointed out that although *they* were now assuredly saved, most of the rest of the town wasn't. Wouldn't it be a shame if their friends and neighbours were left behind just because they wouldn't confess their sins, however small?

Even something as minor as having yawned once while she, Mrs Pengle, told the story of how her father almost… Yes. Yes! She could see the effect her favourite story was having. Already they were eager to go forth and spread the good word. Checking to make sure the reverend wasn't lurking nearby, she unleashed them on the town.

She also reminded them that if they came across Mrs Champion or any of the Alumières, they shouldn't say a word about the impending return of You-Know-Who. She wasn't going to forgive them, and didn't want them saved.

Did the Pope not once say, "Forgiveness is Divine," and Mrs Pengle was not yet so conceited that she considered herself divine.[53]

---

or Miss Strump is correct, therefore, we must assume the answer is... er... yes?

[53] *A* pope said this, but not *the* Pope. In fact, A. Pope said it, as the line, "To err is human; to forgive, divine", was written by Alexander Pope. Pope was a very successful poet because he was not averse (no pun intended) to doing what it took to sell books. For example, realising most people only prefer poetry when the alternative is toothache, he cannily titled the above poem "An Essay on Criticism". People bought essays in droves to look intelligent, but very few bothered reading them. Having it on the bookshelf was what mattered.

Chapter 29

Consepation

WHILE GERTRUDE PATROLLED town keeping the Right Handers on their best behaviour, Victoria did her best to correlate the animal rains with any sort of meteorological data without success. Hawkinge-By-Hythe was blessed with the best weather in Great Britain. Usually, when rain fell there, it fell softly, and at night, when it wouldn't upset people's plans. Colette continued experimenting with her trebuchets, to see how far something could be thrown with them. They leased some adjoining fields to house the animals which Chloe and Curly brought home, as well as a separate one for hygienic reasons. If another solution didn't present itself soon, she could use her trebuchet to offer targeted manure spraying services to the local farmers.

"It's an ark, apparently," said Gertrude, coming home breathless one evening after a patrol. "The reverend has everyone believing Jesus is coming back to say hello."

"Well, that must be what he's watching for in the sky," said Victoria, working on her weather charts in the War Room. "But where did you get that idea from?"

This was a long story, and Gertrude decided to skip it.

The Wait Watchers didn't have much hierarchy. Mrs Sniffacre acted as leader, Mrs Champion was a combination of right-hand woman and lucky charm. Both these women had quickly spotted Gertrude's potential and offered her a role with more responsibility, but Gertrude didn't want it.

She insisted she preferred to be just the smallest cog in the machine of community service. Honestly, she wouldn't know what to say if anyone asked her to make a decision. She just wanted to make some friends.

And it was therefore as the smallest friendly cog in the machine that Gertrude suggested. Simply suggested. She wouldn't want to tell anyone what to do, but if they wanted, they could wait outside Cogwell's house, while she, Gertrude, went ahead.

She thought she might have spotted someone worth talking to, but wasn't sure, and didn't want to waste their time.

Then she had dived into the hedge in Cogwell's garden and disappeared.

"Do you hear that?" asked Mr Hammond of the remaining members of the group.

They shook their heads. "I don't hear anything," said Mr Cormer.

"Exactly," said Mr Hammond. "Er, are you alright down there, Miss 'lumière?"

In fact, Gertrude was already a street away and mere inches from a posse of Right Handers outside Mrs Champion's house. They were discussing what they would like to do to her Big Toe, and it removed any regrets Gertrude might have been harbouring about what she intended to do next.

Hawkinge-By-Hythe was rich in hedges. There was the one she had jumped into. What one might term a "consepation" of hedges running through all the intervening gardens and leading to another hedge right there for her to lurk behind the Right Handers.[54]

Carefully, carefully, she stretched her hands through the base of the hedge so they wouldn't make a noise.

"What's that?" asked Mrs Hedwin of the other Right Handers. *That*, Gertrude knew, was Mr Hammond calling "Are you alright, Miss 'Lumière? Where are you?" at an ever-increasing volume. It was why she had gone on ahead: they were not natural hunters. She poised her hands around Ben Mudge's ankles, ready to grab as soon as he moved, then she took a deep breath and yelled "HOI!"

The unexpected noise, coming from right behind them, when they knew for a fact nobody could be standing there, had the desired effect on the Right Handers. They ran, unwilling to wait around to discover whether a ghost, a banshee, a ghoul, or something worse wished to make contact with them from beyond.

That is to say, they all ran, except for Ben Mudge, because Gertrude held his ankles. He splatted onto his face.

Hearing the cry, the Wait Watchers raced around the corner. Well, all of them except Mr Hammond, who continued to wait to assist Gertrude to her feet as soon as

---

[54] Editor's note: Presumably "con" derived from the Latin *cum* meaning "with", *sepes* meaning "hedge", and the ending "ation" to make it a noun, indicating a continuous agglomeration of hedges. One might indeed term this a consepation (although it would be unwise to use the word within hearing of anyone with a simple sense of humour), but one *might* also say: "there was a whole load of hedges!" I warn you, Delaney. Pull another one of these, and I shall double my rates for the next book!

he spotted her. He remained convinced she must be behind the hedge somewhere, as he hadn't heard her move off.

"Oh no!" said Gertrude, hopping over the hedge to grab Mudge by the arm before he escaped. She held him down as her back up arrived. "This poor man has slipped and hurt himself!"

"You got him!" said Mr Cormer.

"Someone shouted and everyone else ran away. Unfortunately, this gentleman fell over. I hope his woollen tunic softened his fall."

"Oh, yes!" said Mr Cormer. He might have needed a while to warm to the idea of getting to grips with the enemy but he was now all in favour.

"If he's not too hurt, we should ask him some questions," said Gertrude. "Where he lives. If he's okay. What they are doing, and what the Reverend is up to. That sort of thing."

"Ho, ho, ho!" said Mr Cormer, rubbing his hands.

"I mean, that's what I think. What do you think?"

"That's a wonderful idea," said Mr Cormer, and the others agreed.

"Might I… perhaps call you Gertrude, do you think?" came the voice of Mr Hammond from outside Cogwell's house where he still expected her to appear.

Probably Gertrude decided against telling Victoria the story because it was so long and complicated. Instead, she opted for the simple executive summary. "Pure luck. I happened to be there, when some of Mrs Sniffacre's Wait Watchers were chatting to a lonely Right Hander. Probably lonely because his friends ran off. We… they could hardly get him to shut up!" She grinned around at her sisters as she dropped into the comfortable chair given to them by the Count of Wurmbrand-Stuppach to pull her boots off.

They set up their telescopes in the front garden after that, but saw nothing that might be construed as an ark. When animals weren't raining down, the skies were clear.

"So either he's seeing things, or he's seeing something that can only be seen from the church," said Colette. "I bags first go!"

Chapter 30

Generous Chin-Tickler

"THERE YOU ARE," said Colette that night when she spotted de Glube outside St Dunstan's Church in Hawkinge-By-Hythe. He almost looked like he was lurking there.

De Glube did not answer for a moment, distracted by the replay of his life flashing before his eyes. Once again, Colette had appeared just when he really wanted nobody to see him. Normally, he found it a pleasure to meet the Alumières.

Then again, he usually wasn't contemplating trespass and floral theft. That changed things and tempered his enthusiasm.

"I spoke to Mrs Sniffacre," she said. "What are you doing out and about at this time of night?"

"Just walking," said de Glube. "And you?" The best defence was a good offence, he realised. She couldn't prove anything.

"Oh, the same," said Colette. "The good news is it's all just been a misunderstanding."

"Oh yes?" That sounded too good to be true, and like all Luxembourgers, de Glube knew that if something seemed too good to be true, it must be Belgian.[55] His cause was hopeless, but he remained polite. Besides, when she was finished talking, she would no doubt go somewhere else, and he could be miserable in peace again.

"Yes," said Colette. "We chatted about things, and I pointed out where you've been going wrong."

"I see," said de Glube.

"I have her word that yours, and only yours, are the legs she desires to steady the goat of her love. She just expressed herself badly."

"Oh?"

"Definitely. Do you mind? Puss-puss-puss-puss-puss-puss-puss!" The tabby on his shoulders wanted its chin scratched, having recognised the voice of a talented and generous chin-tickler.

Colette did the honours.

Her mission would have to wait until de Glube moved on. She needed to get into the church without anybody seeing her. All the lights were out in the rectory, and Victoria was concealed on the grounds of Muir Hall to keep a lookout with a torch to warn of impending danger. Colette carried a satchel, a powerful telescope with a selection of lenses, and her camera. She also had her own modified version of a Barlow lens, which tripled the magnification further, and allowed her to attach the camera to the telescope,

---

[55] Editor's note: The expression celebrates the 1839 Treaty of London. The Treaty codified Europe's recognition of both Belgium and Luxembourg as independent countries. The twist is that it only recognised Luxembourg's independence on the condition of Luxembourg giving up two-thirds of its territory. Which it should give to Belgium. Luxembourgers have been suspicious ever since.

All she needed was ten minutes of complete solitude to nip up to the bell tower and determine what the reverend thought he saw.

The Alumières were not witches, as anyone in Hawkinge-By-Hythe would have been happy to tell you if one of the three sisters were around. But no one could deny they had plenty of useful tricks up their sleeves to help them get what they wanted.

For instance, without resorting to any potions, spells or cackling, Colette got rid of de Glube when he appeared to be immovable, as if waiting for *her* to leave.

She did this by tending to his kittens with a smile on her face and an expression of such complete blankness in her eyes it became clear that, although her body might still be present, her mind wouldn't be returning any time soon.

De Glube coughed.

Colette continued to dreamily scratch cat chins, teasing out satisfied purrs.

De Glube cleared his throat.

"Puss-puss-puss-puss-puss-puss!"

"Well, good night," said de Glube, and moved off.

Colette hoped he would make it home safely. The Right Handers were still about, and no doubt they would try to either force grapes into him, or cajole a confession out of him. But she didn't have time to worry about that now. Covered in kittens, he should be safe. The faithful were not yet so far gone that they would hold a grudge against a respectable gentleman walking around dressed in baby cats.

She vaulted the small fence around the churchyard and wound her way through the statues and headstones towards the church. Perhaps it was just her mission, but she noticed for the first time that the angel guarding over the grave of the Reverend Hennessy also looked towards the sky. Not in itself unusual. Angels were often portrayed with their glances upraised, like schoolchildren in winter hoping to see the first flakes of snow. Colette made a mental note of it just the same. She knew from Victoria that Hennessy had made an unusually small impression on the parish's records, which may or may not mean something.

Colette hurried towards the church, which, if anyone were to ask, the reverend must have left unlocked. Did it seem likely that she would have broken in? Lock picking? Good Lord, did people really do that sort of thing?

Then she was loping up the stairs that led to the second story. From there, a quick ladder led her through a spacious hole in the floor to the belfry.

She didn't need to worry about the reverend suddenly turning up. Gertrude had encouraged Mr Kelby to call around for a late-night chat to discuss Mrs Pengle's behaviour again with reference to the City of Nineveh.

She turned to where Victoria watched and raised her hand once to confirm they could see each other, and everything was okay. Victoria's torch flashed twice in response, so Colette knew she could continue. Colette did not have the luxury of lighting a candle or using a torch, but her bag was carefully packed. She picked out what she needed by touch and moved to the aperture through which Gresstart examined the sky for his "ark."

Peace enveloped the bell tower. She set up her telescope on its mobile tripod, then connected her camera to the eyepiece. Now, by looking through the camera's viewfinder, she could use the telescope and take a picture of anything she saw. A couple of bats fluttered around, and in one lower corner an orange glow of torchlight meant Wait Watchers patrolled the town.

Colette found what she was looking for almost immediately.

A speck, too distant and moving too fast to tell, but conspicuously spherical to her eyes, which were trained to notice things. Much too regular for it to be a natural phenomenon. She took several quick photos before it disappeared again. Even in that brief instant, she doubted it could be an ark, but then she always imagined arks as being sort of boat-shaped. As a natural consequence of them needing to move through water. That wouldn't apply to an ark designed for space, of course. Space was famously empty of water.

Then, she risked adding a flash attachment to her camera, after removing it from the telescope. She took several quick photos of the bell tower. One never knew where one would find a clue unless one looked for it.

Victoria's torch flashed three times in concern and Colette quickly raised her hand again to confirm things remained under control. She let her eyes adjust to the dark again and left. If her camera flashes had created a commotion among the local nocturnal wildlife, the way she packed her bag, slid down the ladder and strolled outside again without a single sound, won approving murmurs from them.

That, felt a nearby owl, was the way to do it.

Chapter 31

Cats Or The Power Of Life And Death

BACK AT HIS own cottage, de Glube continued hatching his own secret plans in the small front room with the fireplace that didn't work. He had come to Hawkinge-By-Hythe on a bit of a busman's holiday, while visiting his old friend, the Reverend Aubrey Gresstart.

Once there, he realised what the Alumières had already known. Hawkinge-By-Hythe was a *very* interesting place. Barely a day after he arrived a plague of rats descended on the town. And the witch, of course.

A real one, not an Alumière.

And then he discovered that people were misreading the Enochian Calls, the language of the angels. He translated them properly, causing some embarrassing side-effects to prowl around town and knock on people's doors.

Yet, he himself hadn't even believed in the language of the angels which John Dee jotted down after waking one morning to find that the angels were talking to him (or rather, his sidekicks). Which he, by a great stroke of luck, understood more or less perfectly straight off the bat.

Unlike the Alumières, de Glube preferred to avoid the arcane. His only purpose in looking into the matter in the first place, had been to write a paper rubbishing Dee's claims because one of his colleagues at the University in Fontissen liked the man. Writing a disparaging report about a figure held in high esteem by one's colleagues is the academic equivalent of sticking out one's tongue and saying "nyah, nyah, nyah-nyah, nyah!" Normally a peaceful chap, de Glube had been spurred to action after this colleague made rude remarks about the swag on de Glube's best formal gown during an excellent dinner. True, the port had flowed freely, but de Glube had sworn revenge.

Yet it turned out Dee's claims were true. Now, having interpreted all the Enochian Calls—including the forbidden one—de Glube wandered around town with the power of life and death in his pockets.[56]

He would have been content to wander there forever, but there seemed little point anymore. Despite Colette Alumière's reassurances, he knew Mrs Sniffacre wanted nothing more than to be his friend. Pshaw! Well, they could be pen-friends when he returned to Fontissen.

He had been nominated for an award, which included a stipend for his university department, and he wanted to return and make sure they received it. Despite them all having laughed at the dinner gown joke, he liked his colleagues.

---

[56] Normally he walked around with the power of life and death in his pockets. Back when he carried his notebook with the Enochian translations. Now, he walked around with his pockets full of kittens. Giving him the power to make a room full of people go "awww!" or endanger dog walkers, should their charges get a sniff of his cargo.

He had already bought his ticket, leaving him but a short time to finish things up in Hawkinge-By-Hythe. He knew the Enochian Calls and where Mr Sniffacre was buried (one advantage of epigraphy was that no one could *ever* get away from you).

It hurt even just thinking about leaving Mrs Sniffacre. But a man in his position had no option other than to return to her the man she loved.

He worked on the precise sequence of calls, then looked up from his kitchen table when the light came on in Jennet's kitchen beyond the fence that separated their gardens. He sighed. Gone were the days when he looked forward to seeing it, believing she loved him, and they would sit out their insomnia together.

He resumed work.

Chapter 32

Pea Break

THE NEXT MORNING, de Glube could not stay away from Jennet any longer.

After retiring to bed, Colette's words circled around and around his brain. Woken by the hopeful yellow sun, he decided to see if perhaps by some miracle Jennet really did love him.

Because once Mr Sniffacre returned, there would be no going back.

It took him a long time to dress that morning. He wanted to look good to impress Jennet, and boost his confidence.

He had been a bachelor all his life. Less by choice, more a combination of being kept busy by epigraphy, and being too shy for his own good when it came to the ladies. As a spotty teenager he used to confront his mirror with a single anguished question. *What*, he would demand, *do I have to offer a woman? Other than spots?*

Even as a boy, he had been kind, intelligent, and a good listener. But these things cannot be viewed in a mirror. Now, older and wiser, he had gained a modicum of confidence. After Jennet failed to recoil from him on that first occasion, despite seeing him in a repellently drab outfit of blue and purple trousers, with a red waistcoat, and a blooming nasturtium in his buttonhole, he became so confident that he could have eaten a horse!

Since that auspicious occasion, however, Mr Sniffacre had been thrown in his face so often that his confidence died, and de Glube reverted to the spotty teenager of yesteryear. Why should anyone, this teenager wanted to know, especially such a wonderful woman as Jennet Sniffacre, care a fig—or even a grape—for him?

Then the voice of reason chimed in, boosted by Colette's assurances. Why shouldn't a widow mention her deceased husband? No doubt she meant nothing by it. All she said was "like my husband." Well, he would do his best! He loved everything else about her. No doubt, if he put his mind to it, he could even learn to grow fond of her husband, if that would make her happy.

He shouldn't read more into it.

It was human to discuss the past. No doubt even Goldilocks, while trying out the bear's porridge and chairs, made the *faux pas* of comparing them to other porridges and chairs from her chequered past. He must learn to be less sensitive to the mention of Mr Sniffacre if he were to win the heart of the woman of his dreams.

Finally, he stood ready, in a simple suit of red, white, and blue stripes (she would recognise the significance), with a yellow shirt, discreet salmon-coloured tie and straw boater. He intended to visit Jennet alone, but his cats insisted on coming with him.

Only as far as the door of her cottage, however. Once it became clear that Wordsworth, the goat, was having a bad tummy day, three of the four cats insisted he drop them back home before he approached any closer.

After performing this errand of mercy, he returned to Mrs Sniffacre's door armed with only the grey cat for support.

*　*　*

"Well, isn't this wonderful!" said Mrs Sniffacre after opening the door to find him on her doorstep.

De Glube smiled and seemed to grow before her eyes.

"Almost like you read my mind! Like my husband..." She trailed off. "Come in!"

De Glube shrank a little and entered. "Can I help you with Wordsworth?"

"Let's have a cup of tea first," suggested Mrs Sniffacre. Just a moment before, he had seemed full of beans, but now his voice sounded hollow, like a member of the jazz generation going through a particularly gritty patch of ennui. A cup of tea would sort him out before they tackled the goat. And it would give her a chance to pull herself together. Bearing what Colette told her in mind that he was finding it difficult to understand her, Jennet once again dared to hope this wonderful man did love her. That the last weeks were nothing more than a terrible and painful misunderstanding. But she had been alone for a long time and fallen into the habit of talking the way she did. She would need to be extra careful, so as not to scare him off again.

They went together like, like... well, like his suit and shirt. The colours were unconventional and bold, not for the faint of heart. But if one liked that sort of thing, then the pairing couldn't be better.

No doubt there were people who thought that he and she were too different to suit each other, but, oh, they were wrong! She might have been a simple countrywoman who couldn't hear "epigraphy", without thinking of bacon and wiggly tails, and he might have been from Luxembourg, but neither of them could help that. What mattered was that when they were together, the sun shone brighter, the birds sang sweeter, and life itself seemed to pick them up and hug them to its soft bosom for joy.

But she would need to watch her words around him for a while. Until he got the hang of how she spoke.

She had almost done it again at the front door just now. She stopped herself just in time, from saying, "Almost like you could read my mind. Like my husband used to say: 'If you've got two peas in a pod, you've not got a lot of chat!'" The idea being, that both peas understood what the other was thinking, because they were so alike. But as with the "letting your tea go cold" business, de Glube wouldn't understand such a funny colloquialism. She must make allowances for the fact that English wasn't his first language.

Luckily, he hadn't noticed. She must remember that he was a foreigner and not aware of all the finer points of English language. She needed to rein in her quaint sayings. The Lord only knew what he must have made of her attempts to make him keen by dangling her dead husband in front of him.

"I'm wondering if it might be the fish," said Jennet when they were sitting at the table, shielding themselves with their dainty china cups of steaming tea. "The goat, I mean. He's worse than ever."

"Meow!" The grey cat poked its head out of his pocket at the mention of fish.

"Oh! I don't have any now, puss!" said Mrs Sniffacre. "Here." She poured milk from the jug into her saucer and set it on the floor. De Glube said nothing. If she didn't have Colette Alumière's word that he loved her, she'd have been confused all over again.

He'd dolled himself up, given her a big smile. Now he just moped.

Finally, he cleared his throat and spoke. "You mentioned your, ah," de Glube swallowed, "your husband at the door."

"Ex-husband," she corrected him.

"Ex-husband," amended de Glube.

"Yes," said Mrs Sniffacre. "It doesn't matter. I only wanted to say..." She licked her lips nervously. The cat looked up from its saucer of milk. Oh, why had she said anything? It had seemed to her a minor miracle the way de Glube arrived, just as she wondered what she could do about Wordsworth on her own. He hated the drops. Without help, she would have to either ambush him or chase him around the garden until he grew tired.

And chasing Wordsworth meant being downwind the whole time.

Then de Glube had rung the doorbell, as if he aware that she needed him. She must choose her words. Speak carefully so there would be no misunderstanding. She couldn't afford to beat around the bush... there! That was the kind of expression that would get her in trouble. And the pea-pod-no-chat bit went right out the window! If she used that one, he might think she wanted him to shut up while she had a pea or something!

She needed him to understand that she loved him as much as she used to love her husband. That, in fact, if he *became* her husband... well. That would float her boat right up to the top.

No!

No boats! Plain speaking was the order of the day.

"Just the way you turned up right when I needed you," she said.

"Oh?" said de Glube.

"And it made me think of my ex-husband." Jennet gulped.

"Oh."

"He used to say..." Peas swam around Jennet's head, preventing her from coming up with an easily understood alternative formulation. She gave up. "Look, if we're going to do it, then let's just do it."

"Right," said de Glube. "The goat?"

"Yes!"

"Oh! Then once we have assisted Wordsworth, perhaps we might take a walk together?" suggested de Glube.

"I'd love to!" said Mrs Sniffacre. She loved fresh air. Especially after dealing with Wordsworth.

"Splendid!" said de Glube. He whipped his jacket off and rolled up his sleeves. "Then I shall look forward to the excursion, but first: let's do it!"

Mrs Sniffacre realised he had just handed her the perfect line to allow her to help clarify another matter.

"Of course, sometimes when my husband said 'let's do it', he *didn't* mean the goat," she said.

"I see."

De Glube did not ask for clarification, so Mrs Sniffacre assumed he finally understood her hints that they should make the most of what time remained to them.

Although the conversation dried up, that was only to be expected as they tackled the goat. De Glube held Wordsworth steady while she administered the bolus with his tablets in it. Then he left.

Jennet assumed he went to freshen up and waited for two hours for him to reappear, before her heart broke all over again.

Chapter 33

Gone Gertrude

OTHER THAN FEELING sheepish, Curly had suffered no serious injuries. Once they were sure he did not suffer from concussion, he would be back on his feet.

"Unless, you keep eating these eclairs. Then Chloe will have to roll you down the streets!" said Gertrude standing over him where he lay in his stall. Paying off her sense of guilt with pastry tubes filled with cream and covered in chocolate.

"Need to keep my strength up/My whole life flashed before my eyes!"

"Well, one more, then." Gertrude knew Curly was taking advantage. But it had somehow been her fault, after all. It would have been nice to call him a malingerer and order him up off his bed of straw, but that's what the old Gertrude would have done.

She was *nice*, now.

Somehow, she didn't enjoy it as much as she thought she would. Because Curly wasn't the only one whose behaviour needed correcting. That Mr Hammond at the Wait Watchers…. He infuriated her, though he did nothing other than be nice. She didn't like it. Are you sure you can manage, let me do that for you, and do be careful. As if he thought she were feeble.

He was lucky she was nice, or she'd have punched him by now! "What are you doing, Gertrude?" Victoria came into the shed to check on the patient. "Why are you still in bed, Curly?"

"Just finishing breakfast!/Five more minutes?" said Curly, already getting to his feet, but making as much of a production out of it as possible.

"Don't hurt yourself!" said Gertrude.

"Ooh!/Ow!"

"I'm not surprised you can't get up with all the rubbish you've been stuffing yourself with!"

"Victoria!" said Gertrude.

"Victoria!/Victoria!"

"It's very naughty of you to take advantage of poor Gertrude like this, Curly!"

"Me?/Sorry!" Curly continued to gasp with exertion until he found Chloe waiting for him outside in the sun.

"Aw, the poor widdle calfy-walfy! Do you have a booboo, poor baby?" she mocked.

"Oi!/I'm injured!"

"Oh. Then you won't want to check out the sheep."

"What sheep?/I'm starting to feel better, actually." He burped a creamy burp.

"Last night's sheep. There's a group of them that hang around together at the back. I thought if any of them can talk, it's probably those. But if you're *hurt?*"

"Let's go!/We'll ask them about Chancellor Churchill!"

"Ha ha! Shhh!"

The sound of footsteps and hoofbeats faded away into the distance.

"Chancellor Churchill?" asked Victoria. "What's wrong with you, Gertrude?"

"I'm just working *with* people." Gertrude sniffed.

"You're giving nice a bad name, is what you're doing," said Victoria and stormed out of the shed, feeling dreadful. Since her fight with Gertrude she was being as tough as possible to prove the point, and the tougher she became, the less she liked herself. There might be something to be said for being tough and having people obey your every command, but it didn't suit her. It even got in the way of her research. She liked to observe people, to understand them better, but how could she observe humanity when every time she went close, it edged away nervously. No doubt Mrs Pengle kept spreading the word of her having "gone Gertrude" at the Records Office, and they were all nervous in case it happened again.

She didn't feel bad about being tough with Gertrude, however. It was Gertrude's fault Curly had been hurt. That was the thing about being nice. You didn't have to be nice to everyone. Let Gertrude find that out the hard way.

In the meantime, Victoria put up with people giving her worried glances whenever she turned up. Hopefully thick-headed Gertrude would learn her lesson soon, and everyone could go back to normal.

Chapter 34

A Hell Of A Bell

"WHAT I LIKED best about these photos?" said Victoria later on that day, during a quiet spell at the apothecary while they examined Colette's photos from the previous night. "Was the photo of the bell."

"There was no bell," said Gertrude, trying not to snap.

"No, but there should have been."

Business stayed quiet. The Right Handers remained on the street, though no longer directly opposite the apothecary, where Gertrude could stare at them. Close enough to dissuade most of their customers, however. The photos were spread out on the shop's counter and the three Alumières pored over them.

Someone came in, letting in calls of "Confess!" with them.

"Good morning, ladies," said Alderman Fawsick.

"Morning Alderman," said Gertrude sweetly, causing him to blink sharply. "What can we get you?"

"Oh, I'm fine, I just thought I'd enquire whether you had any ideas about, er…" He came from the Town Hall, where the council members were giving him that look again. The one that suggested they thought he should do something. Which he would, once someone told him what it was. Someone other than the Constable who was putting together a list of crimes of which the animals might be charged if the alderman let him.

"A couple," said Victoria. She had returned to the town's archive to make certain of her facts. In 1753, Hawkinge-By-Hythe had celebrated—bragged might have been a more suitable word—about the installation of its church bell. The newspaper made it clear that at two and a half tonnes, it was a hell of a bell, of a size guaranteed to give other bells an inferiority complex.

Victoria had copied out the article, though there was little information in it. Mostly just Mayor Catchpleen, the Reverend Hennessy, and Lord Collopy Muir banging on about the size of their bell.

"Catchpleen!" said Fawsick, spotting the name. He pretended to despise the man, but really he was jealous. Rumours persisted Catchpleen had been a pirate before turning up one day and insisting they vote for him to be mayor. Which everyone did! He used to keep a pistol on his desk, and a stable of horses, which, according to rumour, no one else could ride. And he fired members of his council if they as much as looked at him sideways. And on one occasion, he had closed the town for two weeks to sleep off an epic drunk. It was just after some men came to town with a cart. Friends of his, said Catchpleen and started buying rounds of drinks for everyone. It was irresponsible of him, but mayors were only human, too, felt Fawsick.

"You won't find the bell," continued Fawsick, indicating the article they were reading. "No one knows what he did with it. Probably melted it down to pay his gambling debts." He sighed. "Dreadful man," he added wistfully, and stalked off between the glass cases to take his mind off the matter.

The Alumières switched their attention again to Colette's photos. There were several of the black speck in the sky from which little might be deduced. A photo of the trapdoor into the bell tower revealed, judging by the disturbance of the dust, that the reverend used his elbows to help him climb up.

"That's what you think happened to the bell, is it?" Gertrude asked Fawsick, still using her friendly voice, which worked so well while dealing with her... Mrs Sniffacre's Wait Watchers.

"Or he may have given it to Hennessy or Muir. Thick as thieves, the three of them." The final photo on the counter showed the yoke where the enormous bell should have been hanging.

It seemed unlikely that even the legendary Catchpleen could simply have nipped in and stolen the thing, though. At two and a half tonnes, it wouldn't have fit through the trapdoor, even if someone had been strong enough to steal it. The tower roof would need to be dismantled, then rebuilt again afterwards. Not something that could be done in a hurry, or, one would think, without attracting a lot of notice, yet Victoria had found no mention of it anywhere.

A mystery, therefore.

Another one to add to their list.

What with the fauna-based precipitation, and the onset of religious fervour, things were getting interesting.

Of course, the biggest mystery remained the question of why the pasty-faced righteous of Hawkinge-By-Hythe thought that white would be a good colour for them to adopt.

"Lord Muir!" said Colette. "That gives me an idea. I need to go look at something."

"So I suppose that means that I'm left looking after Curly and Chloe?" said Gertrude. She did her best to sound annoyed.

"I'd be happy to stay and help," said Victoria.

"No, no, it's fine! You need to get to the archives before they close."

"I'd love to see how they're getting on, too," said Colette. "Poor Curly! If you need to go somewhere, then I can—"

"It's fine!" snapped Gertrude. "Both of you get off. I can't stand around here chatting all day."

"I'll be going too if you don't need me any more?" said Fawsick.

"We'll let you know if we discover anything." Victoria walked him out.

Gertrude lost no time shutting up the shop. It was time for her rematch with Chloe and Curly, and this time she would win.

Chloe was already in the back field with Curly when she arrived home at Swiftwater. "Now then," said Gertrude, bringing out the tray to the terrace. "I have milk, eclairs, and thick custard with apple mousse for you, Chloe."

Curly galloped towards Gertrude as soon as the tray came into view, with Chloe on his back. They weaved through the tanks of fish, the cats, and dogs, and the sheep all making themselves comfortable in their new home. Possibly there were also voles, but nobody saw them.

"Thank you, Aunt Gertrude." Chloe smiled, in case Gertrude still intended to shout at her for breaking Curly out after curfew.

"Oof!/Whew!" said Curly, sniffing the treats.

"Something wrong?" asked Gertrude.

"The air is rather…/Did I step in something?" asked Curly, showing Chloe his hooves.

Chloe shook her head.

"Oh, it's just poo," said Gertrude. "What?"

Chloe giggled.

"Nothing funny about it. Everybody poos. Even animals."

"*Especially* animals," said Curly. "I… I don't think I can eat these eclairs."

"What?" Chloe and Gertrude looked at him wondering if perhaps the recent accident had damaged him.

"The smell is rather strong, Aunt Gertrude," said Chloe. "We saved a *lot* of animals."

"What about if we moved our picnic to the War Room?"

"And close the window!/Yayy!"

"I want to sit next to the mummy's head!" said Chloe, running into the house, followed closely by Curly.

Children? thought Gertrude. *A piece of cake!* She looked around at all the animals, and all the little messes they had made. Nothing wrong with poo. It was perfectly natural.

Inspiration struck her. Mr Hammond thought she needed help, did he? Well, he could help to cart off all this stuff!

Chapter 35

Shower Of Shetland

EVEN AS A boy, while his friends tried to decide whether they wanted to grow up to be farmers, police officers, or train drivers, Old Smith already knew that when he grew up, he wanted to be retired. With admirable single-minded devotion, he dedicated himself to making this dream come true. He progressed from sucking on lollipops to sucking at brown bottles of ale almost with no time elapsing between the two. He passed through puberty as soon as the biology teacher explained what that was.

While still in school, he worked as a paperboy, a scrap metal collector, and a milkman. He married, got divorced and married again without his parents noticing and grounding him.

All this enabled him to claim at his graduation at the grand old age of sixteen that he had done enough. He would devote the meagre time that remained to him on Earth to contemplation, walking his dog, and complaining about how lazy young people were.

On the morning the Alumières discovered the church bell was missing, Old Smith fulfilled the second of these promises, walking Russell, his dog through town. Russell was getting more exercise than usual, for Old Smith liked a bit of fish for supper, and you couldn't beat the super low price of free. He tutted as he and Russell passed the ruins of what used to be the town's best pub, the Damme Billett.

It was all the fault of Lorry Tassel, showing moving pictures upstairs in the "do" room over the pub, until things escalated as they usually did.

The landlord wanted to rebuild it exactly the same, but progress was slow.

The Groat and Ball did its best to soothe the town's thirsty drinkers, but Old Smith did not like the Groat and Ball. He had tried it out, but unwillingly. He felt too old to get used to new things, finding a new stool to sit on, and all that palaver.

As much as the sight of his ruined pub pained him, he stared at it a little longer for, out of the corner of his eye he noticed Mrs Delbing and her young son approaching him from the other side of the street.

"Easy, Russell," he said. Russell grew agitated when he noticed Mrs Delbing because, thanks to the home-made "remedies" she used to ward off sickness, evil spirits, and foreigners, she always smelled interesting.[57]

---

[57] The author must reluctantly confirm that although, like the Alumières, he does not believe in witchcraft or any of that nonsense, the remedy against foreigners seemed to work. Other than de Glube (who was a tourist, rather than a proper foreigner), and the Alumières (who might have been foreigners, but also somehow kind of didn't count because they were probably also witches, and so you couldn't do anything about them), Hawkinge-By-Hythe remained free of any. Mrs Delbing often had coughs, red eyes, and a runny nose, but she insisted that her remedies against colds worked, and these were merely allergic reactions to her anti-flu medication, which included plenty of onion, ginger, and a healthy dash of sulphur.

Her son, Delbing Junior, was an attractive little chap who made good money advertising items in the local newspaper.

Russell liked the boy, and Old Smith didn't want to stand in the way of their friendship, so he continued walking so Russell could greet them when they met.

Russell wouldn't move. Instead, the dog looked into the sky and whined. Old Smith followed his gaze, hoping for fish.

Something much bigger than a fish sped straight for the Delbings.

"Run!" shouted Old Smith.

"What?" asked Mrs Delbing, for she had twists of boiled newspaper in her ears to keep out headaches.

"Run!" He doubted they would make it, anyway. He couldn't look. His gaze travelled upwards to the mass of legs heading towards mother and son. Russell whined.

When Delbing Junior heard Russell, he pulled free of his mother and ran to pet the dog.

A second later, where he had just been standing, the latest animal rain poured down.

It didn't take long. A reddish Shetland pony with a thick corn-coloured mane landed on the spot Delbing Junior had just left. It neighed, coughed, then raced down the street.

Old Smith left Russell to look after the boy and lumbered towards Mrs Delbing. "Are you all right?" he asked. He didn't think the pony had hit her, but one could always hope.

"Oo-*ooh!*" said Mrs Delbing, struck by an idea. "Fine, fine!" she continued, in response to how everyone fussed at her. All this time, and she had never known! As soon as she reached home, she would add "pony repellent" to the list of things her onion-sulphur concoction was good for.

Yes, she might smell like an unmarried house painter's lunch box. But that was a price to pay to avoid influenza and ponies!

Chapter 36

Permed Valkyrie

DE GLUBE FELT guilty on his way back out to Nodding Dean to dig up the rest of his catapult. His original intention had only been to dig enough to confirm what he thought it was. He should stop, but archaeology turned out to be irresistibly more-ish.

Meanwhile, Colette started excavating the whistling well. As an Alumière, she had the advantage of not needing to worry about being caught. When people think you are a witch, they let you get on with things, to avoid being turned into a frog. First off, she removed the lid covering the well's hole, then set up the camera with a flash. Carefully, lest any powder fell in, preparing to take the photo which would confirm her suspicions.

The well didn't seem to mind having her mucking about in its mouth. It whistled to keep her company while she worked. She took some measurements of the outer and inner circumference of the stone wall comprising the well's head and used a plumb line to measure its depth.

Afterwards, she examined the field. There had to be another piece of the puzzle in the field.

She headed home once she found it.

"So this is where you've been going," said a voice behind him.

"*Hell giel!*" said de Glube.[58]

A certain irritation was natural. This was the third time Colette had snuck up behind him, and he had bitten his tongue. Then a terrible suspicion grasped him with its icy hand around his neck, and he gulped with difficulty.

For it was not Colette behind him, but Gertrude, combing the local countryside for a Shetland pony at Chloe's request.

"What you must understand," said de Glube. "Is that I didn't intend to desecrate any graves!" Gertrude turned to leave.

"If you only knew how often I've heard that excuse. Come along!" She had climbed in behind him under the lattice of branches and down the small ladder into the hole he stood in, all without him having heard a thing.

What with the lantern, the confined space and the galloping of his heart, de Glube found it warm and wanted fresh air. He followed her out without further complaint. At least she didn't have any grapes. It was the only bright side to the matter he could think of.

"Hello!" said Chloe Dunsloe, waiting on the road with Curly. "You haven't seen a pony, have you?"

De Glube did the honourable thing and looked about him. "No," he said. He would have patted his pockets, too, but he knew they only contained kittens.

---

[58] Editor's note: This translates literally as "bright yellow". Although it doesn't sound rude in English, it is considered strong stuff in Luxembourg, ever since Philip the Handsome banned yellow for "making me look 'girly'".

"The professor has found a trebuchet!" said Gertrude.

Chloe gave him a polite smile, Curly two disdainful ones. "The pony might have run into the church." Gertrude did not need to say any more. Her two companions shot off without a further word.

"Tell me about this trebuchet," she said, settling herself on a nearby headstone.

"Well, I would guess it's easily fifty years old, and it's been hidden, rather than lost. You can tell because the 'headstone' turned out to be concrete pressed into the bucket to disguise it. I haven't really examined it, but I'm confused about its purpose, as there seem to be traces of animal waste in the bucket."

"Animal waste?" asked Gertrude. "Do you mean poo? If so, then please say so."

"I do," said de Glube. "I mean poo." He said it, but reluctantly. He was not particularly religious, but the vestiges of a religious upbringing—his mother a fervent Calvinist, and his father a Seventh Day Hopper—made him shy about referring to what his parents both insisted was the main flaw in God's design for humanity.

Furthermore, Gertrude said it with a relish, which did not seem proper.

"Would you be able to hazard a guess as to what sort of poo you found?" asked Gertrude. As her commanding eye dared him to say no, he hazarded a guess.

"I would say a goat," said de Glube. He did not pick at random. His family used to own a goat, and he found its stool sample to be uniquely shaped and coloured.[59] Furthermore, the size of the catapult's bucket meant that a goat would just about fit on there.

____

[59] Although not as unique as Wordsworth's samples tended to be...

Pure conjecture, but Gertrude was experienced at evaluating conjecture. "And do you have any idea what somebody might have used a catapult capable of firing a goat for?" she asked.

De Glube knew when to admit defeat. "No," he admitted frankly. Then he remembered something. "But Aubrey told me everyone hereabouts is very keen on winning the choir competition. Perhaps the catapult and its load were part of these machinations against each other?"

"Colette has a catapult," said Chloe, after finding nothing of interest in the church.

"Mmm/Mmm."

"No sign of the pony in there?" asked Gertrude.

"No."

"Oh, dear! Well, at least it means it's not injured. Come on!" Gertrude gathered them up and away they went. To de Glube's surprise, however, rather than returning to town, she led them all to the field he previously had brought Colette to.

They heard the well whistling when they were still a couple of hundred metres away. It sounded eerie, and the vibrations shook his skin until it came out in goosebumps.

"This wall is built at an angle," Colette said to Gertrude when they all arrived. Gertrude and de Glube walked around until they spotted it. It wasn't much, but Gertrude looked to where it must be pointing.

"Did *Aubrey* tell you anything else interesting recently?" she asked de Glube.

"Not much," said de Glube. They hadn't spoken since the reverend told him about his concerns regarding the church roof.

Gertrude had asked, because she found it significant that the well pointed directly at the church in Hawkinge-By-Hythe, several miles away. She looked for confirmation at Colette. Colette nodded. A straight line drawn from the well to the church at Hawkinge-By-Hythe would also perfectly describe the arc described by the black speck in the photographs.

As they made their way home, they stopped again to look at de Glube's catapult—and double check for ponies. "Mine's about the same size," Colette informed him. "But the power on this one is astonishing. Absolutely astonishing. What I couldn't do with one of these…."

After that, they all privately followed their own thoughts until they reached the outskirts of town, when they heard people shouting. They walked faster.

"Take Chloe and Curly to Swiftwater," said Gertrude to de Glube. "Then go check on Mrs Sniffacre." De Glube hurried off with the two youngsters.

The people of Hawkinge-By-Hythe were a spirited bunch, always willing to take a bruise or two for what they believed in. And they believed in a *lot* of things.

No longer content to accost pedestrians on the street, the Right Handers had organised into groups. They knocked on people's doors and demanded of anyone who answered whether they were saved. It seemed a rhetorical question, however, for they would assure the responding householder they were not. The only way to be saved was to confess all sins *right now.*

The method proved effective. Most people were doing something when they were at home. Whether they were cooking tea, changing a nappy, or reading the football scores, they were in a hurry to get back to it. If the only way to get rid of people at your front door is to confirm that you have been eating the weekend's leftovers,[60] then most people will confirm it in order to end the inopportune interview.

Even if you were keeping out of trouble and eating a brand-new cheese sandwich, it's still more interesting to talk about yourself than listen to somebody else.

With everyone agreeing to every suggestion they made, Reverend Gresstart's Right Handers were soon aghast at the depth of depravity they found within their hometown.

It's hard not to believe you live in a modern Sodom and Gomorrah when practically every person you meet admits to coveting their neighbour's ass.[61] It was this kind of excess that persuaded Noah to nip into his garden shed to draw up plans for a big boat.

The Wait Watchers had watched the Right Handers from a distance, keeping an eye on things and growing nervous. With Mrs Sniffacre depressed and Mrs Champion resting her Big Toe, Gertrude had moved into the power vacuum. Without her to guide them, they weren't sure what to do. Not that Gertrude would have told them to do, if they were to ask. She would have just made a suggestion.

The Wait Watchers even overlooked the smashing of Mr Carde's window. It had only been a little one. But when Mr Hammond overheard one of the Right Handers mention witches in the same breath as Gertrude

---

[60] Editor's note: "And if it be eaten at all on the third day, it is abominable; it shall not be accepted." Leviticus 19:7.

[61] In case American readers are confused, it is not what you think. In England, the word "ass" refers to a type of donkey, considered by the British to be the pinnacle of animal beauty.

Alumière, he sprang into action like a berserker with brand new batteries.

By the time the Alumières reached town, the brawl covered the entirety of Main Street. So intent were the participants, that they didn't even notice that a particularly heavy shower of cats and dogs pelted them from above. Gertrude, Colette, and de Glube watched the fight.

"Just the perfect weather for a riot, isn't it?" said Colette.

The scene below them was reminiscent of an Hieronymus Bosch painting, with dozens of tiny figures clutching at one another, reinforcing their arguments with brute force.

Mrs Warner sat on Mr Hammond's back, hitting him over the head with her Bible.

Mr Cormer was punching Mr Evans in the stomach.

Mrs Efney poked Mr Carde on the breastbone and shouted about hellfire.

Mrs Jumpage was restraining Mrs Tinfeld from attacking Mr Oaten with her handbag, (an item large enough to hide a member of Parliament in).

Mr Dale twisted Mr Nooney's ear painfully, while Mr Ball used two fingers lodged firmly in Mr Dale's nostrils, to attempt to wind his nose off his face.

The Constable rested against the wall near the post office and bided his time. He wouldn't start making arrests until everyone got a fair go. Mrs Pengle stood beside him, looking pleased.

The Alumières prided themselves on always being prepared. They weren't expecting to find Hawkinge-By-Hythe locked in a kind of battle royale fight to the death. They had only been gone for a couple of hours.

Nonetheless, they were ready. Keen cyclists, and wearing multi-pocketed culottes, they lost no time in grabbing hold of their preferred peacemakers and wading into the fray.

Gertrude drew her reinforced steel bicycle pump from a thigh-pocket in a manner which reminded those who saw it of King Arthur unsheathing Excalibur.

Regarded as the nice one, Victoria showed how she earned this epithet. Her method was simple. She would tap someone in the back, then say "Excuse me!" in a chirpy, friendly voice, to get their attention. When they turned around to see what she wanted, she pinched their collarbone in a Touch of Death, sending them into a pleasant sleep.

With her two sisters engaged in effective melee fighting, Colette provided ranged support. A connoisseur of itching powder, her mix of rose, velvet bean, and cat hair was now perfect, and she looked forward to testing her improvements to its means of delivery.

She had seen a blow pipe she liked the look of while visiting Sarawak, and withdrew from her pocket a slim metal tube. Narrow at one end, wide at the other. The major innovation lay in the tissue-fine paper carrying the itching powder. This would carry its load to the target, before bursting and delivering a fine cloud of non-lethal agony.

You can't fight—not even with God on your side—if you urgently need to scratch the back of your neck and all the way down to the top of your belt. She picked off seventeen targets before the reverend showed up. He stopped with his back to her. One little puff from Colette and he would have been wriggling all night. She refrained from doing so, however. It looked like he, too, wanted to calm people's inflamed passions. She didn't lower her blowpipe, but she didn't use it either.

"What are you thinking?" he demanded. He moved through the crowds of fighters, his hands raised, using his best pulpit voice to get people's attention. "Stop this! Stop this now!"

"That's enough!" shouted Mrs Pengle.

People stopped. Some looked towards the reverend, some looked towards Mrs Pengle. Reluctantly, they each released their opponent's necks, and gave each other sheepish looks instead of another punch.

"This is madness! Do you not understand what you are doing?" He cut an impressive figure, like a respectably dandyish scarecrow ready for a funeral, with his black hair flapping around his ears. It would be hard to hit the back of his neck, thought Colette. But his arms were raised, and a pellet on the back of the hand would certainly trickle down his sleeve. "Good people of Hawkinge-By-Hythe. You must desist. *This* is why the Lord is coming!" cried Gresstart.

A few people craned their necks to check the road behind the reverend.

"I have seen him!" continued the reverend.

"You haven't," muttered Gertrude. If the Lord did come to Hawkinge-By-Hythe, he would certainly stop at the Alumière Apothecary first. Victoria continued to watch the crowd. Those members of it dressed in normal clothes looked abashed. Those wearing white tunics looked confused and sought out Mrs Pengle for guidance.

"I have seen his vehicle: the ark! He flies over us every night, looking for a sign that we are fit to receive him!" said the reverend.

"Or looking for a spot to park," mumbled Mr Softly, giving the constable a dirty look. He had been caught numerous times parking his cart without a licence and believed in holding grudges.

"Hush!" hissed Mrs Pengle.

"You said the reverend would be pleased," said Mr Nooney.

"Hush!" said Mrs Pengle again. Mr Nooney and Mr Ball gave each other meaningful looks. This wasn't the first time she had got things wrong.

"We are fit!" cried out Mrs Goyle to the reverend. "We are pure and white."

"It's not your clothes that matter, but the purity of your hearts," said Gresstart, but it was too late. Hawkinge-By-Hythe enjoyed its second riot of the day as those without tunics did their best to remove them from those with them. Those who had them did their best to keep them.

While it might be the purity of their hearts that mattered in the end, the tunics would help them nab a spot on the celestial ark. Once on board, they would have an opportunity to charm the Lord before he noticed their souls weren't quite match fit.

Sick of moping around at home, Mrs Sniffacre now rounded the corner into the street at the head of a dozen more Wait Watchers. They wielded mighty notebooks and pencils, with which they would take down the names of anyone caught creating a fuss.

When the rioters saw the notebooks, they calmed down immediately. Nobody wanted the constable calling around asking awkward questions with Jesus due any minute.

Mrs Sniffacre made for an impressive sight. A permed Valkyrie. Luckily de Glube had gone the other way around and missed her, for he would have otherwise fallen in love with her all over again.

Chapter 37

Sins Committed To Paper

"WELL, THIS IS everything I've found." Victoria had compiled every reference to the craze of attempting to rename star constellations. She'd even included those in the newspapers stuffed up the chimney.

Covering the walls of the Alumières' War Room at Swiftwater and draped over the tables were numerous charts. Where space allowed, they were set up in pairs. On the left, the constellation and the name by which most people would recognise it. On the right, the alternative suggestion funded by Lord Muir's campaign, though increasingly a passion project of Mayor Catchpleen.

For example, the constellation otherwise known as Orion, named after the mighty hunter of Greek myth, hung next to a rather more amateurish effort detailing Lord Collopy Muir's rebranding of the constellation as The Bells.

According to this document, one viewed the bells from below. "Orion's Belt" became the yoke from which the bells hung. One bell was formed by the stars Betelgeuse, Bellatrix, Alnitak, and Mintaka (which more traditionally represented Orion's upper body). The second bell comprised Alnitak, Mintaka, Saiph, and Rigel (Orion's lower half).

And where the rest of the world saw Orion's Sword (the Orionis stars, including astronomer favourites Theta, Iota and 42, plus the Orion Nebula), Lord Muir saw the bell's clapper.

This suggestion was an outlier, however, as most of the suggestions tended towards the animals of England, with some Scottish and Welsh ones thrown in.

For, according to the visionary astronomers of Hawkinge-By-Hythe's past, the constellation that the rest of the world knew as Cassiopeia, should thereafter be known as the Kent Goat.[62]

There was the constellation of the Tench, the Shetland Pony, the Red Grouse, and the Scilly Rabbit.[63]

As might be expected, however, people quickly lost focus, and things became personal as people attempted to name constellations after beloved family pets. That, at least, was the Alumières' interpretation to explain constellations such as Dash, Fido, Cesar, Lady Whiskers, Snuggelums, and Uncle Rascal.

"Well, there we go," said Gertrude. "I think it's obvious what's been happening here."

"Catapults and rains of animals? Yes, it's all too obvious." said Colette.

"It's an interesting approach," said Victoria. "Is it possible to build a catapult—or trebuchet—strong enough to fire something into space?"

---

[62] Despite the praise the people of Kent heap upon their goat (the majesty of its bearing, the sweetness of its nature, the keenness of its mind), many biologists insist it looks like any old regular goat to them. Experts, eh?

[63] Editor's note: Not a typo. One of the earliest recorded mentions of rabbits in England is on the Isles of Scilly off the Cornish coast in 1176. Yes, it's pronounced "silly".

"Difficult," said Colette. "But if someone knew the right people at the Astronomy Society and had money to spare… One could fire animals into the air so anyone looking through a telescope at the right moment would see them, then ram the change in the constellations' names through."

"Catchpleen!" Gertrude did her best to sound shocked, but it didn't work. She had a soft spot for people who got things done.

"So why are the poor animals only coming down now?" asked Victoria.

"Well, they'd have to be fired pretty high to be visible between a telescope and the constellation Catchpleen wanted to rename."

"Ouch!" said Victoria.

"Yes," said Colette. "But the Earth is spinning all the time, and gravity is weaker the further away you get."

"They've been falling all this time?" asked Victoria.

"Probably," said Colette. "Shot fast enough to get them close to the edge of the Earth's atmosphere, and then forgotten. They've been falling ever since they launched, but because gravity is so weak up there, they haven't been falling down. Just going around and around."

"Until?" asked Gertrude. The animals all seemed fine to *her*.

"Well, it's a matter of balancing speed and gravity. Get it right and you could, in theory, have something spinning around the earth forever. High enough up, the impetus of the launch would keep it going forward without enough gravity to pull it down. Put another way, the thing would keep falling, but would keep falling *forward*. At the right height, there would only be just enough gravity to prevent it from floating off into space, not pull it back down to Earth."

"So Catchpleen messed up the calculations?"

"If his intention had been to keep the animals up there, then yes."

"And now gravity has remembered they're there, and wants them back? Er, the poor little things," said Gertrude.

"Exactly," said Colette, looking puzzled.

"It is a lot of effort to go through for such a small reward," said Victoria.

"I wonder how he did it."

"Haven't you just explained that?" asked Gertrude.

"Yes," said Colette. "But the mechanism on de Glube's trebuchet. That's way ahead of what anyone should be able to do."

"Is it powerful enough to explain the elephant, or whale, or whatever Gresstart thinks is an ark?"

"No," said Colette. "And how did the animals survive being shot into the air, floating around for years and years? We're missing something."

"Maybe someone stuffed them full of eclairs to keep them going," said Victoria.

Gertrude sniffed.

"Maybe," said Colette. "I have another idea, though. I'll be right back."

"It's dark," said Victoria.

"Which means I must be heading off to see if Mrs Sniffacre needs me to make tea for her Wait Watchers, or anything. I do enjoy working with people!" said Gertrude.

"Meaning I'll stay here and read to see if I can come up with anything else, shall I?" She loved reading but tried to sound annoyed for the sake of it.

Reverend Gresstart would have preferred not to reschedule church services for the middle of the night. But it was necessary to prove to the unbelievers that it really was Jesus, which disappointed him. He would have preferred to shake Jesus by the hand when he arrived. And tell him that his flock was one that had not seen, and yet had believed (John 20:29)

For another thing, he enjoyed sleeping. He liked to get his eight hours, and if he could get nine, he liked that even better.

And for a third thing, it caused friction with Mrs Gresstart. The reverend was always in great demand, and nights were the only time she could count on having him to herself. She let him know in no uncertain terms that she did not approve of even this little time being encroached upon. They might all be going to heaven, but Gresstart would find it decidedly chilly up there with the mood Tabitha was in. And being out after their usual bedtime seemed to have the worst effect on the group that hung around with Mrs Pengle.

It encouraged them in the most terrible way.

"Where's the ark?" demanded Mrs Pengle, once they were all assembled, yawning in Bagnell's Field. The reverend had hoped it would show itself, but clearly the time had not yet come. He told them that, after which they ignored him. Instead, they raised their faces to the night and confessed all kinds of crazy things at the tops of their voices so any passing high-flying messiahs could hear them.

Having worn out all the usual sins, they were getting more and more inventive. Mrs Pullbore confessed to reading the newspaper before she brought it to her husband in the morning. On hearing this, her husband confessed to getting up an hour early, going out first, reading the newspaper, then leaving it in front of the door so she would bring it to him. And so on. The reverend could barely make himself heard above the noise. They seemed to be trying to get the Lord's attention, and the reverend decided they would be more successful if they sounded penitent, rather than proud of their "sins."

Only Mrs Pengle kept silent, but he didn't like the look on her face.

Mrs Sniffacre and Gertrude, who were watching discreetly from the sidelines, didn't like any of it. But they had their notepads and pencils and committed all the sins to paper, in case it might be of use to the constable.

Chapter 38

Ecuadorean Orange Eagle

ONE PERSON NOT taking part in the midnight masses was Prof de Glube, hurrying towards Lorry Tassel's cottage that night as a prerequisite to his secret project.

"This is the eagle, is it?" said de Glube as Lorry displayed the cage.

"This is she," said Lorry. "Won't you come in? We're just about to have dinner."

"We? Oh, excuse me, I don't wish to intrude if your young lady is here."

"No, I meant myself and the eagle. She informs me she wishes to partake of a cracker."

"I see," said de Glube, entering the cottage. "She is rather more brightly coloured than I was expecting."

"Ecuadorean Orange Eagle," said Lorry, refraining from noting it seemed a case of the pot calling the kettle black for de Glube to complain about colourful plumage. De Glube wore a yellow suit and hat, with brown shoes and a bronze waistcoat. Lorry himself also followed the trends of fashion, but he tended towards the subtle. A part-time private detective, he found simple greys and navies more suitable.

"And this eagle wants a cracker, does she?"

"So she tells me. I have no reason to believe she lies. Sit, please!" The two men, Hawkinge-By-Hythe's best dressed bachelors, sat at the kitchen table in Lorry's cottage to better examine the eagle. The eagle, which bore a close resemblance to a parrot in a certain light (for example, in the light of Lorry's kitchen), bobbed her head to examine them both right back.

"I didn't know eagles talked."

"Nor I," said Lorry. "One of the most intelligent eagles he's ever seen, according to my birdman." "Boah! Shut your face!" screamed the bird.

"But unable to take compliments."

"Crackers! Crackers!"

"I might just put a towel over the cage for a second, if you've seen enough?"

"I have," said de Glube.

"So. Here, have a sip of this." Lorry poured de Glube a shot of whisky. "And let's talk terms. I'll be sorry to see her go, but a deal is a deal. No doubt you are keen to take possession of this very clever, and colourful eagle?"

"Yes. Unless you have another, more typically eagle-like one?"

"Most humorous! No, when I saw Polly, I knew she was perfect for you."

"Polly?"

"That's right."

"Polly?"

"And a very pretty Polly she is, too. That's the main reason I'm so keen to get rid of her. I'm finally making progress with Ruth after a mix up—"

"Another mix up?" De Glube knew how that felt.

"—another mix up, and I can't conjecture what the effect of Polly will be when Ruth sees her. She may be jealous. She may be all for it. All I know is that I didn't have an eagle the last time we spoke. I don't want to take the risk that the sudden bird might cause her to fly off the handle. So if you would…"

"Polly the eagle?"

"It sounds odd, doesn't it? But I'll tell you what. The first time I met this bird, I remember thinking this bird doesn't look like a Polly. You know how it is. You meet a 'Constance' or a 'Eustace' and the name either clicks, or it doesn't. Yes, you think, that's what a Constance looks like. Or, no, that chap is never a Eustace. A Eugene at a stretch, and more like a Wilmot than anything I've seen all year, but never a Eustace. Now, though, I can't imagine calling her anything else."

"But Polly," said de Glube. As often happened when Lorry talked to people, de Glube's resolve melted into a sense that perhaps things might somehow be alright, after all. "It's an unusual name for an eagle."

"Oh, I don't know," said Lorry. "My contact tells me he knows all sorts of birds called Polly."

Once he returned home, de Glube retired to his bathroom, attempting to teach the fish in his bathtub to swim. A difficult undertaking, because the fish was dead.[64]

[64] Difficult, but not impossible. It had been done before, according to the apocryphal Acts of Peter. This text details a competition between Saint Peter and Simon Magus to prove who had the most powerful magic. Simon expected to win, as he had a very good levitation trick, but Peter outsmarted him. Spotting a herring hanging upside down in a window (where it was being used as a form of primitive curtain), he brought it back to life. Although the trick was not spectacular, Peter could maintain the illusion for several hours. Long enough for Simon to fall out of the sky, upon which Peter was declared the champion.

It was the fish he had saved during the original shower, but the poor thing did not survive long. Although, looked at another way, it survived longer than the other fish, now residing within the stomachs of his four kittens. Soft tapping at the door of the closed bathroom told de Glube that they were with him in spirit. Also they were prepared to dispose of his remaining fish whenever he had tired of it.

But de Glube needed this fish. He believed he knew the correct sequence of Enochian Calls in order to bring it back to life. Dee had been clever, and provided a mistranslation of the Enochian Calls, knowing full well that humanity could not resist being able to take them for a test drive. Even the accompanying warning that the angel Nalvage had given Dee that the last Call was dangerous and should be ignored would have made no difference.

It would be like telling a child not to set off a firework because it would make a very loud bang.

Instead, Dee had robbed the Calls of their potency by swapping out the syllables. The *meaning* remained the same. But they weren't supposed to be said in simple English.

Take the eleventh call, which de Glube paraphrased as follows, for example. "A Mighty Seat groans. Five thunders go East and the eagle speaks with its voice. Come away and be the House of Death. Yet on the 31st, come away from the House of Death. I am the servant of God, and the worshipper of the Highest." It was like poetry, one needed to know where to put the emphasis

It quickly became his signature trick. So much so, that when the time came to be martyred, he insisted the authorities crucify him upside down in honour of the original Peter's Herring.

when reading it. And then translate it back into the *real* Enochian, in order to make it work.

Well, de Glube had worked it out. Most of it. He wasn't sure about the Mighty Seat (Alderman Fawsick?), but the rest seemed simple. There would be a storm on the last day of the month (the thirty-first). Which is when he would use the eagle, to make Mr Sniffacre come away from the House of the Dead.

As for the last line, about proving his faith was true? Well, he couldn't have put it better himself. Mrs Sniffacre was *his* Highest, and he worshipped her!

Nothing would stand in his way.

This was the time.

And this, so to speak, must be the plaice.[65]

Under Polly's eye, de Glube summoned up all his resolve and spoke the incantation.

Nothing happened.

Unwillingly, he danced. He examined the illustrations in his notebook one last time. They came from an old forbidden book and detailed the *other* way Morris Men dance.

Most modern Morris Men are in it for the bells and hankies, but in its early days, there used to be another side to it. A darker side, and this is what de Glube wished to emulate.

There were no bells, for these dancers did not wish to be heard when they were about their work. There were no white hankies to wave, for they did not wish to be seen while dancing their devilish steps.

---

[65] Editor's note: Checking Chapter 13, I find it must, in fact, have been either a pike or a bream. But this is typical of Delaney. He'll go on about Irish-French economists and consepations, but won't check the nonsense he jotted down barely an hour ago. And if you're reading this footnote, then I'm right in supposing he skimps on the proofreading, too!

Instead, there were only the bunches of fresh graveyard flowers—tulips—and the movement tending ever widdershins until the dance terminated.

De Glube picked up his flowers and started to move. He shook the flowers in his left hand, he shook the flowers in his right hand, and closed his eyes to concentrate on the incantation.

He wasn't a natural dancer, but it wasn't a natural dance. As he moved in sinister circles with wilting tulips plucked from a grave, he felt, well, not like a Morris Man exactly. But a little bit Morrissey, all the same.

"*Wayeth balgam Elach, r Elach fullmes! R Elach dsushk, mes teg a par! Thoren lyck a vell, tsallith ga granbar!*"

"Crackers!" commented the eagle. Nothing else happened.

A plaintive meow from the door did its best to convince him that he was wasting his time.

"Unless," said de Glube. "I were to 'carry the one', so to speak…"

"Shut your face!" said Polly from her cage in the sink.

Another meow from the door.

"Well, it's worth a try. *Elach balgam wayeth, Elach r fullmes! R Elach par, mes teg a dsushk! Thoren lyck a granbar, tsallith ga vell!*"

A mini-thunderclap accompanied the final word, and the parrot seemed to flash. "Crackers!" it swore, but when de Glube checked, the bird was fine. His incantation had merely caused a single tail feather to self-immolate, unleashing an unpleasant smell like burning hair.

He couldn't swear to it, but de Glube thought he the fish might have moved, too. Barely a twitch, but something. A ripple rolled across the surface of the water in the bathtub. Then it came again as the fish jerked its tail and shot across the bathtub to hide under de Glube's sponge.

He threw in some flakes of fish food and watched the fish for a moment to make sure it seemed okay. After the first startled quiver of life, the fish now seemed quite relaxed. It bounced around the tub, letting the water eddies carry it, but this seemed normal to de Glube. Fish are not noted for their curiosity. So when it didn't spontaneously combust, or give a sign of discomfort, de Glube decided his experiment could be considered a success. He edged out through the bathroom door carefully carrying the "eagle", and provided it with plenty of food to distract it from the singed feather in its tail.

So the fish would not grow lonely in his bath tub, he left it in the company of his sponge. An original *Sienipummi* from Finland. It had always been a good friend to *him*, and he hoped the fish would appreciate it. He would have kept the fish company himself, but needed to continue excavating his catapult. When he reached Nodding Dean, however, he discovered someone had beaten him to it. It was gone.

Chapter 39

Weapons Of War

DE GLUBE'S CATAPULT currently sat behind Swiftwater House, where the Alumières had put it. Like the fish in de Glube's bathtub, it was in good company.

The author can think of no better example to demonstrate how enterprising the Alumières were than to show the reader the half a dozen catapults Colette found, brought home and set up before de Glube even got his first one out of the ground. Furthermore, she had located a further half-dozen, too flimsy to bother moving.

The catapults (or trebuchets) had been hidden around the countryside in various fields after the failure of Lord Collopy Muir's attempt to rename the star constellations. Originally determined to name more constellations than de Lacaille, the urge to immortalise his own pet had overtaken him, as it had everyone else. When he clashed with Catchpleen as both wished to rename the same constellation, the scheme was doomed.

Never a man to do things by halves, Catchpleen invited everyone to a party, got them drunk and stole their catapults. No doubt he only closed the town for a fortnight to buy enough time to bury them all.

Presumably those "friends" of his who turned up with the big cart one day had helped move everything.

Impetuous, he would not have cared that the catapults, all marvels of engineering, and based on his own designs, were among the most powerful things around, capable of shooting their loads to a distance of almost fifty miles to the outer edge of the mesosphere where they floated *almost* free of gravity. If Catchpleen's beloved Catchmouse, a Chartreux with whisky-coloured eyes, could not be immortalised in the stars, then no other animal should be, either.

"I have them set up in chronological order," said Colette as the three Alumières inspected the line of catapults. "As you can see, the first ones aren't as powerful. Capable of reaching the upper limits of the atmosphere thanks to this interesting little device like a dynamo on the axle. It's ingenious, for every half-turn the beam makes, the device spins several times, increasing the force of the throw. I'm looking forward to taking it apart. Anyway. Powerful enough, but only for small loads. And the sling's bucket, that's this spoon-shaped bit, looks clean. But if we add some of this liquid and sniff... ah! Fish!"

The other two Alumières sniffed and concurred.

"We have several more with fish," said Colette.

"Shall we skip them?" asked Victoria.

"Let's," said Gertrude.

"Well, then. Here's the next biggest model. We note the larger area for the payload, and larger counterweight, again with this dynamo device. Thanks to the use of harder woods for the beam however, larger loads can be sent into the atmosphere. This one is—"

"From the size, and the scratches, I would say cats?" asked Victoria.

Colette picked out a hair. "Cats, with a dog or two mixed in."

"This dynamo gadget looks like it goes *through* the axle," said Gertrude, peering at it.

"Exactly. It would have to, but how they managed to do it is beyond me. It's locked in an endless coil. The technology still doesn't exist to do that sort of thing.

"Almost as if they had some kind of help," suggested Victoria.

"Exactly." Colette did not need to say only Carfax could be behind it.

"I recognise this one. It's de Glube's. Goat, he thought," said Gertrude.

"Yes," said Colette. "But we can sniff to make sure." She waved the bottle which would reactivate the scent.

"No, thank you," said Victoria. "So which of these launched whatever Gresstart thinks is the ark?" "None of them."

"That doesn't help us much," grumbled Gertrude.

"Oh, but it does. It's the same basic progression as found for weapons of war. So, like warlords around the world, Catchpleen—or Carfax—gave up on trebuchets and moved onto the next thing."

"Well, what's the next thing?" asked Victoria.

"Projectile weapons," said Gertrude.

"The whistling well?"

"Exactly," said Colette. "It's a cannon!"

Chapter 40

What Did You Call Them?

WHATEVER THE REVEREND saw in the night sky, it could not have been an animal. From its size it must have come from a cannon, and you couldn't shoot living things from a cannon.[66] Not without creating more mess than it was worth, anyway. Filling a cannon with fish, cats, dogs, voles, badgers, and a Shetland pony might have been a cheap way for a psychopath to quickly paint the walls of his house red, but didn't suit their current requirements.

So the Alumières bicycled out late to the whistling well together that evening with their telescopes, some sandwiches, and flasks of tea to find out what the reverend thought he was looking at.

"By the way," said Colette, once they were sitting comfortably on blankets. "De Glube and Sniffacre were having a spot of bother, but I sorted it out. "

"You?" Gertrude didn't mean to sound surprised, but she knew her sister's distaste for that sort of thing.

"Me. It turns out her attempts to spur de Glube on achieved the opposite when she kept talking about the late, great Mr Sniffacre."

[66] Except for Luxembourg's famous human cannonball, Captain Pol Scholl-Kroll, naturally.

"So that explains why he's been looking so sad," said Victoria.

"But I told them to snap into it."

"It looks like he'll be around for some time then," said Victoria. "Good."

"We might need to make sure we keep a bit of a closer eye on him. In case he starts anything else." Gertrude sniffed.

She might be nice, but she'd hate for anyone to think she was *soppy*.

"It should be along any second now," said Colette, standing and lining her eye up to the viewfinder of her camera, connected to her telescope. "Here we go!"

The other two applied eyes to their respective telescopes and watched. The speck, almost a blob at this stage, whizzed overhead.

It flew over the cannon, towards Hawkinge-By-Hythe and out of sight. It whooshed as gravity slowly caught up with it to pull it cautiously out of the atmosphere, like someone with a cold extracting a hard lump from a blocked nostril.

"That's not an ark," said Gertrude.

"It's a bell," said Victoria, remembering the photo in the newspaper.

"It's the bell from Hawkinge-By-Hythe's bell tower," said Colette.

"Of course," said Gertrude. "To rename the constellation."

"And as they didn't get it quite right, it's been circling the earth ever since, its orbit slowly deteriorating."

"Due to come down right about... Here!" Victoria tapped a spot on the map in front of her.

It was a good job that the Reverend Gresstart could not be present at this juncture. He would have been disappointed to find out the Lord was not returning in an ark, as he told everyone. He would have been even more upset by the fact the bell wished to crash-land on the ill-fated roof of its old home: the roof of the church in Hawkinge-By-Hythe.

Mrs Pengle stared when she saw the Alumières, all three of them, walking up the path to the rectory the next day.

Victoria took the lead and walked past Mrs Pengle. "Good morning!" said Victoria.

"Morning," said Mr Nooney and Mr Ball involuntarily.

"Don't!" hissed Mrs Pengle.

"Morning!" said Gertrude, as she walked past.

"Good morning!" said Mr Nooney and Mr Ball, straightening up and smoothing out their smocks.

"Stop it!" said Mrs Pengle.

"Morning!" said Colette. "When the rest get here, just let them know we've already gone in. Don't let anyone else in, though, will you?"

"No, Miss," said Mr Nooney.

"Miss," said Mr Ball.

"The rest...?" asked Mrs Pengle.

They rang the doorbell and entered as soon as Gresstart's maid, Dilly, opened up. The three Right Handers then spent a very uncomfortable morning outside, wondering if any more Alumières would turn up. They were pretty sure Colette had been joking, but couldn't be certain.

"What is the..." started Aubrey, when Dilly led them into the parlour, where he had been reading the Bible in one chair, with Tabitha reading a crime novel in the other. "That is to say, to what do I owe the, er…?"

"Oh!" Tabitha blushed bright pink with pleasure. She seldom received visitors, and she liked the Alumières. And she had just finished a mystery novel about twins. It had been terribly exciting, and triplets must be fifty percent more exciting even than twins.

Besides, the Alumières always seemed to be in the thick of things and having fun, which Tabitha Gresstart would like to do. As long as it was respectable fun, of course. Fun compatible with being a reverend's wife.

"Do sit down!" She bustled around until they were all sitting at the table.

"It's rather serious, I'm afraid," said Victoria.

"Of course," said the reverend. He only talked about serious matters. The ice having been broken at de Glube's house a few weeks ago, the meeting was not as awkward as it otherwise might have been.

"Sit down, Aubrey!" said Tabitha, and Aubrey did so. He only realised he was standing when she mentioned it.

"What can I do for you?" he asked after Tabitha dispatched Dilly to the kitchen to prepare tea. Tabitha Gresstart thrilled once again with excitement. Tea with witches!

"It's more a matter of what we might do for you," said Victoria.

"Oh yes?"

"We heard you mentioning that the Lord is returning," said Victoria.

"Oh yes?" said Gresstart, puffing himself up.

"Yes," said Victoria. "We're not convinced, to be honest."

The reverend laughed. "Well, that is a surprise! Did it occur to you that perhaps he's not returning for everyone?"

"Yes," said Victoria.

"Aubrey!" Tabitha looked shocked.

"It's fine," said Victoria. "We're not here to argue about it. But we would like to show you some photographs, if you don't mind. It'll be easier to explain once you've seen them. Have some tea first, though."

Photos! Tabitha Gresstart barely managed to sit still. This was turning out to be the most exciting day of her life since their honeymoon in the Cotswolds!

Colette laid out a half-dozen photos. She had only brought the ones from the field near the whistling well, so as not to alienate him. He might not like knowing they'd been up his belfry after hours.

"What is this?" he asked, examining the pictures.

"Well, this is a bell," said Victoria.

"And those are clouds," added Colette helpfully, tapping the photos. "In the sky."

"Where on Earth did you get these?"

"And this is the top of the Town Hall, and this is a bit of your church spire through the trees," said Gertrude, pointing towards the bottom of the photo.

"I don't understand," said Aubrey Gresstart. And for a change, he didn't sound stuffy, or pompous. He sounded like he didn't understand, so Victoria explained.

"Colette took these photos with a telescope and a camera."

That immediately caught the reverend's interest. "What sort of telescope?"

"Never mind that," said Victoria. "We're interested in the bell."

"It might not be a bell," said the reverend. "It's rather dark." He scratched at the photo, as if to scrape away the shadows to get a better view of the object.

"And if you look at the photos in chronological order, you can see the bell is travelling this way."

"Towards me," said the reverend. He saw the tiniest glint of light from the church belfry, which he imagined must be the moonlight reflecting off his own telescope. "Oh my word, it's going to hit the ark!"

"This *is* the ark," said Victoria. "Look again at the way it is travelling. This is what you've been seeing in the sky." She handed him one of the close-up photos taken with Colette's magnifying lens attachment.

"But…" The reverend stared at it. "That's my bell!"

"Your bell?"

"Well, the church bell. I've been looking for it everywhere."

"How did you lose it?" asked Colette.

"I never saw it. They promised me a bell, but I never got one."

"And the bishop didn't help at all, did he?" said Tabitha.

"He did not! Well, that's a weight off my mind, at any rate."

"Yes…" said Victoria. "Would you like to look at these photos again? I don't think you've absorbed their full significance."

"Oh!" Tabitha had been examining the photos while the others were speaking. She rose now to stand behind her husband, holding his shoulders to comfort him. She herself would be happy to meet the Lord when she passed and reached heaven, but she understood her husband saw things differently. There wasn't anyone for him to talk shop with in Hawkinge-By-Hythe.

"My bell…" said the reverend.

"You see, it won't hit the ark, because there is no ark," continued Victoria. "But we think it will hit…"

Colette laid out a map of the area, then placed a sheet of onion paper on top. On the onion paper she drew the bell's trajectory and marked its landing place: the roof of St Dunstan's Church.

"My roof!"

"And that," said Gertrude. "Is where we come in."

"But first," said Victoria. "It might be an idea to let Mrs Pengle and her Reverend's Right Handers know."

"I beg your pardon?" said the reverend.

"Don't be like that. They are making quite the nuisance of themselves. All the broken glass is playing havoc with the soles of people's shoes."

"Looking after soles is supposed to be your job," chimed in Colette.

"No, I mean, what did you call them?"

"The Reverend's Right Handers."

"I see," said the reverend. He raised himself to his full height and inflated his lungs. "Mrs Pengle!"

Chapter 41

Her Luck Limped Out

THE ALUMIÈRES LEFT after excusing themselves from the interview between Mrs Pengle and the Reverend.

"I trusted you, Mrs Pengle," said the reverend, while alone with her in the parlour. "Yet now I have been given to understand that—"

"'Trust the Lord with all thine heart; lean not unto thine own understanding'," said Mrs Pengle. "Proverbs 3:5."

"'Let every man be swift to hear, slow to speak'," thundered the reverend at this insolence. "James 1:19!"

"'… and, slow to wrath'," said Mrs Pengle. "That's how that one ends." She was starting to get the hang of the Bible.

The reverend sighed, regarding Mrs Pengle the way Dr Victor Frankenstein must have regarded his monster when it demanded a bride.

"You've been very busy, haven't you?" he asked.

"A lot of sinners need saving before the Lord comes back. 'And whatsoever ye do, do it heartily,' Colossians 3:23."

"Yes, yes," said the reverend. "I wanted to talk to you about that."

"You're annoyed, aren't you?" said Mrs Pengle. "I wanted to tell you."

"About the *Reverend's* Right Handers?"

"They do it all for you. We want to be pure."

"For when the Lord comes?"

"For when the Lord comes, blessed be the hips of His Mother who bore Him!"

"Quite. I imagine your… what shall I call them, your adherents, will be disappointed if he doesn't show up?"

"They're *your* adherents. I have been merely as your cosy, keeping the teapot of their faith warm for you, Reverend."

"Thank you, but there shall be no tea."

"What's that, your reverendness?"

"There shall be no tea. The whole thing seems to have been a bit of a mix-up. Still, at least we were able to get some practice for when the time comes."

"You're not saying…"

"I am," said the reverend. "The Rapture has been postponed indefinitely."

"But why?" Mrs Pengle turned white.

"Hard to say, but all the Deceit flourishing under My very Nose couldn't have Helped!" The reverend tended to capital letters when excited.

"It was in a good cause."

"Well, Thank You Very Much For Lying To Me In A Good Cause. No Wonder We Have All Been Banished From Eden."

"I thought we were all going to heaven," said Mrs Pengle.

"Well, We Aren't Now!" The reverend calmed himself. Anger would not help him, and was unlikely to make God look more kindly on Hawkinge-By-Hythe. A bit of expiation of sins, on the other hand, might. "So, I Shall Leave It To You To Explain That To Everyone."

"But…!"

"Dismissed!" said the reverend. The maid ushered Mrs Pengle out. Dilly hated it when the reverend capitalised things. It made her think of those advertisements for cheap hair tonic in the back of the newspapers.

Mrs Pengle scurried home instead. Nooney and Ball followed her, no doubt wondering what was up after all the shouting at the rectory. She couldn't bear to lose her position as their leader. By the time she reached home, she understood what had happened.

The Reverend Had Been Tempted.[67]

No sooner did the three-headed snake of the Alumières visit him, when suddenly the charabanc to heaven was cancelled.

The time had come for her to assume her Whites.

She left her right-hand men outside to don her uniform with modesty (wishing the Bible passage mentioned the lion lying down with the cotton boll, rather than the lamb. Or that the Lord might have booked his return date for late autumn. The tunics were *hot!*)

The Lord helped those who helped themselves. Mrs Pengle clung to that. *She* hadn't done anything wrong, it was the reverend who had lost his faith.

But sin remained sin. It would have to go.

The Alumières were behind it, of course. That's how witches worked. But even in her Righteous Whites, she didn't quite think she would be able to tackle them.

---

[67] Capital letters are contagious.

What other enemies did the Lord have in Hawkinge-By-Hythe? She put the kettle on and went to talk to her followers, waiting—grumbling loudly—in her front garden. She needed to give them something to do, but nothing occurred to her.

As she stood in the doorway, desperately trying to think of some scapegoat to save her bacon, she spotted Mrs Champion walking down the road. Her with the Big Toe, who was getting all the attention. While the Alumières might be responsible for damning the whole town to hell, Mrs Champion represented Mrs Pengle's own nemesis.

Mrs Pengle grinned, then did her best to twist the evil leer into a beatific smile. "Get her!" Mr Nooney and Mr Ball looked at each other, then at Mrs Pengle. They shivered at the expression on her face, then ran to catch Mrs Champion.

She heard them coming and limped away as fast as possible, but she didn't stand a chance. Her luck had finally run out.

Chapter 42

Shoot!

AFTER VISITING THE reverend, the Alumières made their way to their apothecary shop rather than returning home, sure that something would happen soon. The sight of Mrs Champion lolloping past their window at a high rate of speed proved them right. Victoria sighed. Gertrude pressed her lips together in grim satisfaction. Colette did some stretching.

When, seconds later, Mr Nooney and Mr Ball flashed past, they were ready and saddled up.

Victoria headed off to let the reverend know his Right Handers were once again causing trouble. It so annoyed her to see Mrs Champion being harried, that she would find no difficulty telling him what she thought of him. She had done her best to be nice and break the bad news about the bell gently to him. As if to prove Gertrude's point that no one took nice people seriously, he had ignored her. Well...

Gertrude sped towards Mrs Sniffacre's home which doubled as the Wait Watchers' headquarters, to let them know they were needed. She also intended to ask—nicely—if anyone would mind if she came along with them. She looked forward to seeing Victoria's face when she turned up, not bossing anybody about.

Colette headed straight to Bagnell's Field to monitor matters. She knew she could get everyone to see the funny side of things until her sisters turned up.

By the time she arrived Mrs Champion was already tied to the Hanging Oak.

This caused considerable consternation among the rest of her Right Handers until Mrs Pengle explained Mrs Champion was the reason they would have to wait a while longer for Judgement Day. She gave everyone time to let that sink in.

It was terrible news. They had confessed to some pretty awful things, believing they wouldn't have to face their neighbours for too much longer afterwards.

When they thought about all the asses they had claimed to covet…

It suited Colette that her sisters weren't around. Victoria would have wanted to save Mrs Champion immediately. Gertrude would have wanted to show everyone the error of their ways. Colette wanted to see how things played out.

"Repent, Mrs Champion! Repent!" cried Mrs Pengle.

"Please repent," said Mr Nooney and Mr Ball. After grabbing Mrs Champion, they expected Mrs Pengle to simply exhort her to confess. They found the bondage a bit much. "We'll let you go as soon as you do!"

Mrs Champion, however, remained calm. She hadn't enjoyed being chased. Being tied to a tree was only marginally better. But she believed in her luck and expected some good to come of it.

"Perhaps we should let her go?" said Mr Nooney.

"She is the one who has stopped the Lord from coming!" said Mrs Pengle. "With her false idol! With her Lucky Toe, she has scared away the Lord!"

"What's this now?" asked the assembled Right Handers.

"The Reverend has spake unto me," said Mrs Pengle. She fancied she was getting pretty good at the old biblical phrasing. "And whereof he hath spake, spake I now even unto you!"

"Spake! Spake!" said Mr Nooney and Mr Ball, once more getting into the flow of things. It looked like Mrs Pengle knew what she was up to after all.

"With her Biggeth Toe, hath Mrs Champion revolted against the Lord! She hath chosen the way of the idolator. Let him that hath understanding count the size of the Toe, for it is the Biggeth Toe, and none in Hawkinge-By-Hythe hath a Bigger Toe than she!"

"Except for Big Tony," said Mr Hampton.

That stopped the crowd. Big Tony's toes were very big.

"Fine," said Mrs Pengle. "Except for Big Tony." She paused, in response to Mr Nooney's meaningful glance. "And, possibly, Tim Thumbs," she allowed.

The crowd murmured again. Tim Thumbs had very big thumbs. It seemed likely he might also have big toes, though, nobody knew for certain.

"But neithereth of them, doth swanketh about the placeth, ashoving of their toes in our faceth!" said Mrs Pengle.

This was true. Both were shy men who would never dream of swanking in public.

"I never swanked in my life!" said Mrs Champion.

"You dideth, too! All the time!"

"Never! People asked to see my toe, and I showed them. *You* wanted to see my Big Toe!"

"She admittedeth ith…it!" said Mrs Pengle. "Idolator!"

"Rubbish! It was either that or listen to you ramble on again about your father and how he failed to invent putting condiments on taters. The number of times I've stifled a yawn!" The mention of a yawn stopped Mrs Pengle. Could she have finally found the one?

"Ooh!" It stopped the crowd in its tracks, too, but for a different reason. They still believed in Mrs Champion's lucky toe. It only now occurred to them, that the toe had been lucky for them too. It had been ages since Mrs Pengle told that story about her father. Still, they did want to go for a ride on the ark to see if heaven was as good as everyone said. If Mrs Champion was responsible for the trip being called off, well…

"How *dareth* you!" said Mrs Pengle.

"On and on, and on, and on," continued Mrs Champion. "Everybody in town knows the story. Everyone is *sick* of the story. Won't you finally put a sock in it?"

"It wath… it was *you*," said Mrs Pengle. "Wicked woman!"

"Silly moo cow," replied Mrs Champion equably. Any time now, her Big Toe would kick in and get her out of this mess.

Mrs Pengle expected to hear her followers refuting the suggestion they had been bored. Their silence told her things weren't going according to plan.

"What Is The Meaning Of This?" boomed the reverend's voice as he appeared in the field with Victoria. She had coached him the entire way here, and been as nasty as Gertrude about it, so he wouldn't dare mess up again.

"I was just telling Mrs Pengle we're sick of hearing that story about the potato and the bad wine," called Mrs Champion from the tree.

"Mrs Champion!" The reverend's eyes bulged Byronically.

"Yes, Reverend?"

"What are you doing tied to a tree?"

"She's telling Mrs Pengle you're all sick of hearing that story about the potato and the bad wine," said Colette, materialising behind him to join Victoria.

To his credit, the reverend barely jumped when she spoke. "Untie her at once!" he demanded.

Mr Nooney looked at Mr Ball.

Mr Ball looked at Mr Nooney.

They both looked at Mrs Pengle, pale with rage. They glanced away.

"Mrs Pengle. Untie That Woman At Once!"

"Is it true, Reverend?"

"Is what true?"

"You find my poor Da's story boring?"

"The story is fine," said the reverend, falling out of capital letters to sound soothing.

"Yes, it's more the way you tell it," said Mrs Champion. "Again, and again, and again…"

"I…" Mrs Pengle did not know what to say.

Luckily, a rain of exceptionally woolly sheep coming in softly to land at that moment spared her from needing to say anything. The Right Handers scattered, and the field filled with "Amens", "Ars", and "Baas" as the two groups—both clad in wool—attempted to scatter. The

Right Handers wanted to be elsewhere before the reverend shouted at them. The sheep followed, assuming they knew where they were going. Mr Nooney grabbed Mr Ball's hand, and they fled together. Then Mr Nooney came back with the sheep he had been escorting. A few tense moments later Mr Ball turned up with *his* sheep. The men grabbed hands, checking this time that another sheep wasn't coming between them, and ran.

Mrs Pengle stood motionless as her world fell apart around her.

The arrival of Chloe and Curly did nothing to rouse her. Not even when Chloe told Curly to turn right to catch a stray sheep and he did so.

She barely noticed when the reverend started giving out, listing all the ways she had let him down.

That's when Gertrude turned up with her group of Wait Watchers to find everyone else already on their way home to dig out their old mint sauce recipes.

Even Colette and Victoria were gone, chaperoning Curly and Chloe to Swiftwater.

That's when the local newspaper reporter decided to make his move. "Excuse me," he said, heading towards Mrs Champion.

"Yes?" said Mrs Champion.

"Would you like to get your name in the paper?"

"Oh Lord!" said Mrs Champion, who thought that sounded lovely. Ideally, she would need her own dedicated weekly column, but they could start with an interview.

"I just have a couple of questions."

"About what, young man?"

"Well, what do you think about being tied to a tree and accused of idolatry?" Amazing, thought Mrs Champion.

Her Big Toe never let her down. And without Mrs Pengle, this would never have happened.

Mrs Pengle eyes had tracked the reporter's progress with hungry eyes and now she howled.

"First, however, let me ask you a question," said Mrs Champion to the reporter.

"Shoot!" said the reporter, who read American crime thrillers.

"Can you untie me, please?"

"I can," said the reporter. "But how would you like to get your *photograph* into the paper, too?"

Chapter 43

Bags Of Guts

AT SWIFTWATER, COLETTE and Victoria put the sheep in the field, and Chloe to bed in the extra cot in Curly's shed, before relaxing in the War Room with a good night cuppa to ponder what they had so far discovered.

"I don't know what you said to the reverend, Victoria, but he was furious when he turned up!" Colette poured herself and her sister another masala chai.

"I imagine it's been a long time since anyone talked to him like that," said Victoria. She closed her eyes. Being strict wore her out. "I wish I could get my hands on Catchpleen. I'd do the same to him!"

"Take the scenic route, did you?" Colette asked as Gertrude finally showed up. "Have some chai. The cheese fingers are almost ready, too."

Gertrude dropped into her seat. She pulled her boots off and threw them into the corner of the room. If she had simply *told* the Wait Watchers what she wanted, she wouldn't have missed the fun. But no, she thought she could do it "being nice", and had missed everything. If only Victoria would admit her mistake, they could go back to normal. All this smiling played merry hell with her cheek muscles. She sipped some chai and closed her eyes.

"Here we are, ladies!" Colette returned with the cheese fingers and chutney dip. Gertrude and Victoria shook themselves awake for the piping hot brain food. "I'll just come out and ask, will I? Are we going to save the reverend's roof?"

"We did say we would," said Victoria.

Gertrude shrugged.

"Just checking. What do we suggest? Now, we know the bell was shot into the sky with the cannon in the field near Nodding Dean, correct?"

"Why?" asked Gertrude.

"We'll get to that, but time is of the essence. The bad news is that shooting a bell which weighs two and a half tonnes, with a circumference of sixty-one inches and travelling seventeen thousand miles an hour is the simple part. Getting it down again—safely—is where things get interesting."

Victoria and Gertrude thought about it for a while. "Some kind of net, to act as a brake?" tried Gertrude.

Colette meanwhile was in her element. "I'm thinking—and I'm happy to bow to your suggestions— but my idea would be to shoot it out of the sky."

"Shoot it?"

"It's the simplest solution. And it would teach it a lesson so it doesn't do it again."

"Have the thing explode in the sky above the town?" Even Gertrude considered this a mite rough.

"Not necessarily," said Colette. "We know the path it takes on its orbit, so we shoot it enough to knock it off course. Have it land in a field or something."

"Well, let's do that," said Victoria.

"The problem is: what do we use to shoot it down?"

"Hmmm!" Everyone chewed on cheesy fingers as they thought it through. To shoot a bell out of the sky itself would not be tricky. One loaded up one's machine with something hard enough and heavy enough to make a lasting impact on said bell. The problem arose when one considered that as something became more suitable for shooting an enormous bell out of the sky, it became less suitable for use over a populated area. Succeeding in knocking the bell out of the sky, they would then need to worry about where their ammunition landed. Or whether it caused the bell to shatter, raining down devastation.

"Soft," said Victoria. "Something soft."

Gertrude sniffed.

Colette nodded. If they used something soft, then the bell would remain intact, and the soft thing, whatever it might be, wouldn't be dangerous either.

Of course, if they opted for soft ammunition they would need a lot of it.

So. Something soft, and in plentiful, immediate supply. According to their calculations, the bell would last only another rotation, two at most, before it fell out of the sky onto the town.

"This might not be a popular suggestion, but hear me out," said Gertrude.

"No," said Victoria. All three of them were thinking of the animals which had fallen from the sky over the past several weeks. They were undeniably soft and in plentiful supply. "Absolutely not."

"I agree," said Colette.

"Oh, so do I," said Gertrude. "Just wanted to make sure we know our options. And we have to do something with them."

"The smell?" asked Colette.

"The smell," confirmed Gertrude.

"Chloe and Curly are finding homes for them," said Victoria.

"Perfect," said Gertrude. "Forget I said anything."

"I hope they find homes before we drown. Really," protested Colette, "I knew animals went, but these do nothing but!"

"Mr Hammond will get rid of it for us," said Gertrude. "What?" she added, in response to the looks her sisters were giving her.

"I'll tell you what, though," said Colette, staring into space. "Let's hang onto it a little longer. Chloe told me a story that I think might be relevant."

The next morning Colette took her sisters to the whistling drumming well, which they now knew was a cannon. De Glube's explanation of the sound had been incorrect. Neither uncles, nor werewolves, nor empty beer jugs were behind the unearthly sound. It was the wind howling over the open mouth of the well. Simple Helmholtz resonance.

The well, or cannon, was tilted slightly. When the wind passed over the opening, some passed over it and some became trapped inside. The ripples caused by the two separated streams of air colliding against each other as they flowed. They made the sound. Not by themselves, however. The volumes of air passing over the mouth of the cannon were too low to create a perceptible sound.

But as Colette explained, there was an underground chamber and a passageway to tend and fire the cannon. And when the wind blew from the west, then quite a large amount of air pushed through the passageway and up the bore of the cannon, which caused the noise. Similar to what caused a kettle's whistle as water boiled: more air attempted to leave the vessel through the spout than there was room for. The energetic jostling created vibrations, which created the noise.

"An underground chamber?" asked Victoria as they approached it.

"This way," said Colette. A trapdoor hidden at the edge of the triangular field led down. A wooden ladder took them into a long underground cave where air whistled and thrummed around them. Crates lined the walls, and Colette plucked two oil lamps off the closest crates and lit them. "Follow me!"

"It's in perfect working order," said Colette, as they reached a larger cave dug out around the bottom of the cannon.

"Isn't she a beauty?" said Colette. From here, the cannon's slight inclination to the south towards Hawkinge-By-Hythe was more obvious.

More crates, as well as tools and bits of machinery lined the walls.

"Enormous!" asked Victoria. "One could blow Hawkinge-By-Hythe off the face of the Earth with this. Why do you say 'she', though?"

"Because she's beautiful," said Colette.

"Men can be beautiful,"

"Really?" Colette stopped and thought. "'The beautiful Mr Hammond?' Yes, I see what you mean."

"And this is how they shot the bell into the sky?" asked Gertrude loudly.

"Yes. Crucially, this is how we shoot it down again."

"How?" Gertrude looked around. "And what's in the boxes?"

"Something called goldbeater skin," said Colette. "It's like thin, rubbery silk."

"I found the receipt for goldbeaters's skin. I wondered where it went," said Victoria.

"Also, several tanks of hydrogen."

"Hydrogen? At the base of a cannon? With these lit torches?" Gertrude looked aghast.

"I know," said Colette. "Isn't it exciting?"

"Of course!" said Victoria. "So that's how Catchpleen did it!"

"Did what?"

"Well, we were wondering how the animals survived so long up there. This explains it. He'll have bagged the animals in goldbeater skin, then filled the skins with hydrogen. To help them float. It's less dense than even helium, which people use now to fill those party balloons. So, they'd be up in the air long enough for his astronomer crony to spot them. They use goldbeater skin to contain the helium in airships, you know. It's incredibly impermeable. That the hydrogen would freeze the animals is just a side-effect."

"But the crony will only have seen bags of guts if Catchpleen packed the animals in it," said Gertrude.

"Not at all, it's impermeable, but also quite transparent. Look." Colette opened a crate for Victoria to pull out a sheet. They could see her hand through it. Then she pulled at it. For all it looked so delicate, the material withstood the pressure. "*That's* how the animals are still alive. They've basically been frozen alive until they started to fall again, at which point the atmosphere warmed them up and brought them back to life."

"A lot of effort for such a minor cause," said Gertrude.

"But he was almost certainly working at Carfax's behest. Catchpleen won't even have realised the real reason for doing what he did."

"Well, what's Carfax's motivation, then?" asked Gertrude, looking grim.

"We'll find out, I'm sure," said Victoria. They stood in silence for a moment at the thought of what the return of Carfax might mean.

"To cheer up, let's all go visit Alderman Fawsick. I'll tell you the story Chloe told me, and explain my brilliant plan!" said Colette.

Chapter 44

Pigeon Vendetta

TO START THINGS off in the mayor's office at Town Hall, Colette told them all Chloe's story. It seemed her brothers celebrated Guy Fawkes Day after their own fashion. The whole thing started as part of a vendetta against a family of stubborn pigeons which illegally occupied a particular tree to which they had no right. A series of experiments were undertaken, and the boys discovered that fireworks, mixed with a generous helping of cow manure, could achieve what nothing else did. The manure did little for the bang, but the full flavoured brown cloud of exploded manure which followed acted as a superlative bird deterrent. Enjoying how the stuff evaporated, they kept making their pungent signature fireworks, long after they had rescued the tree.

"I see," said the alderman, looking worried from the official side of his enormous desk. He always looked worried when people tried to explain things to him.

"They don't do it anymore, of course," said Victoria to prevent the Dunsloe boys getting in trouble.

"Good," said the alderman, looking even more worried. No one ever explained things to him when it was good news.

"We've rescued a lot of animals recently," said Gertrude.

"Thank you," said the alderman. "Much appreciated." Did they want medals? He wasn't allowed to give out more medals without running it past the council first.

"And they keep pooing," said Colette.

Alderman Fawsick choked at the word and spluttered into a glass of water. He sometimes forgot how *modern* the Alumières could be.

"It's a good thing," Colette continued. "We're going to save the town with it."

"Crops?" asked the alderman faintly.

"Bells," said Colette, and explained everything. The time had come to put him out of his misery.

All the poo around the back of Swiftwater, and wherever else they had been housed, made for the perfect *matériel* to shoot the bell out of the sky without physically endangering anyone. They would need a lot, and they would have to stuff the enormous cannon with it. Really stuff it down to compress it. Then make the calculations.

Light the fuse, and launch it as the bell flew past.

Thereby coating it with sufficient stuff to increase its matter enough for gravity to drag it out of the sky in a controlled landing before it crashed into town. Anyone who has ever done it knows that things don't fly as well when covered in thick sticky poo from a wide variety of animals.

"It's equivalent to radically altering the density of the earth's atmosphere localised around the bell," said Colette. "But we don't have time to do that. So hopefully this quick and dirty version will work just as well."

"You said 'hopefully'," said the alderman. "Why did you say 'hopefully'?"

"A figure of speech," said Colette. "What could possibly go wrong?"

"Wait." The alderman was not yet ready to face facts. "Why are you telling me about this interesting, hypothetical experiment?"

"It's not hypothetical," said Gertrude. "We intend to shoot as much poo as possible over Hawkinge-By-Hythe tomorrow night, and we need your help."

"My help? You don't mean…"

"My dear Alderman, *someone* will need to break the news to people. Stop shaking your head!"

Fawsick groaned. "I won't do it. What would I even say?"

"'The night is dankest before the dawn?' And Mrs Sniffacre has some incredible clothes peg tips she'd be happy to share with you," said Colette.

Sensing he wasn't yet completely on board, Gertrude stayed with him to talk him round, while Colette and Victoria returned to Swiftwater to work on the calculations.

They first separated to visit the Dunsloe and Kelby farms with offers to buy any spare manure they might have lying around.

While the alderman felt that things had reached a new low, the need to convene an emergency meeting to warn people meant the constable got to drive around town. He loved beeping the horn of the alderman's Wolseley, proving there was a silver lining to every cloud, regardless of how brown it might initially appear.

By the time everyone arrived for the meeting, Fawsick knew his lines. With Gertrude's help, he had prepared a long speech.

To a connoisseur's eye, it might have struck the "you can't blame me" note a little too heavily and often, but he thought it pretty good, under the circumstances.

But two-thirds of the way through it, he decided all the polish in the world wouldn't help improve the complexion of the remaining part. So he skipped it. "Which brings me to the other reason I invited you here today," he said instead. "I have decided we will have fireworks tomorrow night."

"What's the occasion?" asked someone.

Fawsick silently cursed them. "It's… a surprise," he said.

"Ooh, lovely," said Mrs Goyle. "I love the smell of smoke!"

"Yes," said the alderman, neglecting to mention the smoke might smell riper than they were accustomed to. "So stay indoors. These are special fireworks, and very dangerous."

"Dangerous?" The crowd murmured.

"No! Sorry. I meant they sound better than they look. That's it. Dangerously ugly fireworks, with a beautiful bang. Awful looking things. They'll give you nightmares. Sound like angel farts, though. Stay indoors!"

Gertrude started the standing ovation that followed, though the alderman was unable to enjoy it. No sooner had he stepped off the podium than the constable asked about permits until the alderman got a headache.

Gertrude removed the constable from proceedings by claiming to have seen someone hanging around the Wolseley, then enquired if she could do anything else to help.

"Anything *else?*" asked the alderman.

Realising he couldn't be pushed much further, she left to make her own way home.

Gertrude easily spotted Mrs Pengle on the roof of St Dunstan's with Mr Nooney and Mr Ball. Unwilling to accept that the Lord had given up on them, they were refusing to come down, despite the reverend's frantic pleas.

After much negotiation they were allowed to stay, on the condition they removed their shoes, to avoid damaging the roof more than necessary. There was no talking to some people, Gertrude realised.

Besides, if Colette's plan worked, they wouldn't be in any danger. They just wouldn't smell very nice for a while…

Chapter 45

Bosworth Was Better

"BETTER SAFE THAN sorry," said Colette, as she and Victoria carried another few bags of gunpowder down the stepladder to the underground base of the ridiculously over-sized cannon. She started to whistle.

If she were honest with herself, Victoria had to admit she also looked forward to it. This kind of opportunity—exploding several metric tonnes of manure—usually only came around once, maybe twice, in a lifetime.

Still, they would need to work feverishly to get things prepared. They started shovelling.

Chloe had enlisted her father to deliver the stuff as fast as possible to the field and forbade him from asking questions. Not that he would have done, anyway. From his perspective, the Alumières were stuffing poo down a well. Fine. He knew, as everyone did, that sometimes witches poisoned wells, but the Alumières were definitely not witches, so why would he have questions?

He and his men shovelled their cargo into a steaming pile at the edge of the field, waved back to whichever of the Alumières was currently on duty—having swapped their hats for gas masks, they were difficult to tell apart—and hurried off to get more. It took all sorts to make a world.

The cannon itself had already been prepared, with plenty of train lubricant coating the cannon's bore. All the stuff needed to go in, and they couldn't have any of it sticking. "Better out than in," said Colette, mixing in a fifth dose of sticky synthetic hydrocarbons with a dash of whale fat because she still had rather a lot and needed to use it up.

The rest was easy enough, though exhausting. They needed to pack the cannon with the stuff as tightly as possible. 12.431 metric tonnes were needed for the bell, and the cannon could barely hold that much. So, the stuff needed to be *compressed* to an unbelievable extent. Once they had filled the cannon (using up everything from the grounds of Swiftwater and Dunsloe's farm) Colette added a thermochemical solution to separate the mixture into its component parts. Stirring it then allowed the densest materials to sink to the bottom, and the lightest to rise to the top to be skimmed off. Then they packed it some more. What they needed for their plan to succeed was basically a constipated cannon, so they kept packing, mindful of Dunsloe's warning that Kelby had little left on his farm either. Eventually the groaning of the cannon told them it couldn't take any more.

With that done, they were free to concentrate on the trebuchets, for the cannon alone would not suffice. Victoria and Gertrude would take command of two trebuchets plus a Wait Watcher of their choosing, stationed further back to set up the bell.

Colette could predict her own missile's behaviour, but her estimates of the bell's were limited. She knew its path and forward momentum, but could not account for other variables. Such as spin. Even the tiniest miscalculation might turn the bell's spin into a wobble. And a wobble into a disaster if the bell's trajectory deviated from its expected course too much.

Which is where Victoria and Gertrude came in. Using the four most powerful trebuchets, they would each fire two pony-sized poo pellets in quick succession. The first two pellets would strike the bell from either side squarely in the middle (of its lateral axis) with enough force to negate any existing spin. The second pellets would strike on the same axis, Victoria's would hit it higher up and Gertrude's lower down. The concurrent blows would give it a new, stronger, and pre-determined spin. Its flight path would be more stable for Colette's missile, while removing the uncertainty of this variable.

Having set up the cannon and the trebuchets, they assisted Chloe and Curly evacuating the animals from Swiftwater. Just in case. Gertrude spoke to Mr Sporkmann who housed them on the grounds of Muir Hall, well out of the way of danger.

Then it became a matter of waiting.

A hush fell over the town as night fell. Almost everyone was at home, though nobody slept. What would be the point? Although they still weren't clear why they weren't allowed to see the fireworks, they looked forward to hearing them.

And the alderman had promised everyone that they would all be getting a free bucket, mop and rubber gloves as part of the secretive celebrations.

"You're sure Jesus is coming?" asked Mr Nooney on the roof of St Dunstan's Church. "Sorry for swearing."

Mrs Pengle sighed. "Just saying His name isn't swearing!"

"But He is coming?"

"Of course! And we three will have pride of place in His ark. Right up beside the driver."

"Cor!" said Mr Ball.

Nothing happened for a while. "These righteous woollen smocks came in handy after all, didn't they?" said Mrs Pengle.

It was chilly on the roof. The idea had been to pray until the Lord rescued them, but they'd already said all the prayers they knew and begged for forgiveness several times. It seemed pointless to keep doing so. The Lord wasn't deaf. He'd have heard them the first time and they didn't need to bang on about it. If He wanted to save everyone, He would. If He didn't, He wouldn't.

To take their minds off the thought that perhaps He wouldn't, Mrs Pengle's remaining Right Handers switched from prayer to small talk.

"Warm," agreed Mr Nooney, trying to find a more comfortable position on the roof.

There wasn't really any more to say, so Mr Ball, a man of few words, didn't say it.

"It'll be like camouflage!" said Mr Nooney after the lull in the conversation.

"What's that?"

"The smocks. Up in heaven, we'll be surrounded by clouds everywhere, so it'll be like camouflage when we're wearing our uniforms."

"Heaven isn't clouds," said Mrs Pengle.

"Of course it is!" The night grew even quieter around them to see how Mrs Pengle would deal with this doubter.

"Heaven," explained Mrs Pengle. "Will be more like Church except a lot bigger, with that lovely incense smell and—"

"Hate that smell," mumbled Mr Ball.

"—and everyone will be there, including my father, and all our loved ones, and it will be perfect."

"*All* our loved ones?" said Mr Nooney.

"All of them who are saved," said Mrs Pengle.

"Even Jennifer Bosworth?"

As the Devil did tempt Jesus in the wilderness, so now did Mr Nooney tempt Mrs Pengle on the roof.

"Who?"

"Jennifer Bosworth. She… Well, she… I mean…"

"Ah!" said Mrs Pengle. "I understand. And you want to know if you will see her again. Yes, if she was a good girl, then you will see her again in heaven."

"Right. Good to know." How good did one have to be? That was the question on Mr Nooney's mind.

The trio returned to their thoughts, though not for long. "Your wife will go spare," said Mr Ball to his friend.

Mrs Pengle did not hear him, lost in her own dreams of heaven. "And my Da will be there."

"Really?" This was the only thing capable of rousing Mr Nooney from his depression. If Alfred Pengle was good enough for heaven, then the standard must be a lot lower than he had assumed.

The same thought also struck Mr Ball. "Ho, ho, ho!" he said, pointing at Mr Nooney. "*Denise* Bosworth!" He bit his woolly sleeve in mirth, imagining the scene when they arrived in heaven and Nooney tried explaining things to his wife.

Jennifer Bosworth might be good, but her sister Denise was better.

Mrs Pengle ignored them. "And he'll tell us how he almost invented putting vinegar on chips." Her voice trailed off, and she didn't notice her followers getting up. "It was like this..." she started.

Mr Nooney and Mr Ball left her to it and climbed down from the roof.

"Heaven!" said Mr Ball.

"Exactly." Mr Nooney pulled off his white smock. "Tell you what, let's get a drink."

"Where?" said Mr Ball.

"I can find some bottles at home." They linked arms and headed off down the road.

"Not...?"

"Yes," said Mr Nooney. "Porter!"

Chapter 46

Terrible Pressure

"THIS IS NICE," said Tabitha Gresstart.

"Yes," said the reverend. And he meant it. They were in the sitting room with the lamps on, and the room smelled of apple. Tabitha had sliced one up and arranged the segments around a little bowl of sugar on a large plate. One dipped the apple bits into the sugar to bring out the sweetness and add some crunch. Only force of habit made him wish he could be in the belfry looking up at the stars.

While his wife read a book about criminals, he tried to concentrate on parish paperwork, but it was hard, knowing that the stars were all alone without him. And that bell! What if the Alumières let it crash down? His poor roof!

With Mrs Pengle on it. It's an ill-wind that blows nobody any good, he thought and once more attempted to focus on more prosaic matters.

"We could go to bed, Aubrey," said Tabitha.

"We'll only be woken in a couple of hours."

"Yes… if we were asleep…"

"Tabitha!" The reverend looked indignant. "You know what I think about reading in bed!" Still, she might have hit on something. He wasn't able to concentrate on his work anyway, and who knew? Just because he was a priest, didn't mean he would automatically get into heaven. And the stars wouldn't care what he did. As for the Lord. Well, He would turn up when He wanted to. It would be a shame to waste the precious time He had given them.

And Tabitha was still the most attractive woman he knew. Though they hadn't yet managed to have children, miracles did happen. If one helped God to make them happen. He cleared his throat, and she looked at him, over the cover of *Strangler in a Golden Cage*.

His roof could look after itself for one night. "Time for bed, Tabitha," he said, though it came out like a hopeful question.

The doorbell rang as he stood.

His heart pounded. Had Jesus turned up after all?

He should have known better than to trust the Alumières!

But after he had smoothed down his suit and slicked back his hair with sweaty palms, it turned out to be only Mrs Champion wanting a word with Tabitha.

He swallowed down the uncharitable things he would have liked to say at this unexpected visit and took himself off to the church to check bats weren't gnawing holes in his roof.

When the reverend felt disappointed, he liked to really wallow in it.

Alderman Fawsick was so tense that night in bed one might have thought *his* roof was in danger. But while the reverend feared that something *might* happen to his roof, the alderman knew for a fact that the following day would bring his greatest challenge to date.

To prepare for it, he had tucked himself into bed with one of his housekeeper's steak and kidney pies for moral support.

Tomorrow, if things went well... He swallowed a forkful of pie and allowed himself a bitter laugh. If things went well, he would be alderman of a town covered top-to-toe in poo, and would need to supply answers to people. And could he rely on his council members to back him up?

He could not!

Fawsick knew what kind of behaviour he expected from his council members. He expected them to back him up, to nod and applaud when he said something important, and avoid asking questions in public that were better answered in private. If at all.

He also knew that his council took a diametrically opposed view of their duties. They saw it as their duty to hang back and use him as a shield to deflect attention from themselves. The only time they spoke in public was to ask him infernally troublesome questions! When he didn't have his notes to help him find the answer.

And the only time they applauded was when he blew out the candles on his birthday cake. Which was, admittedly, nice of them.

At that moment, the alderman could have been forgiven for thinking that his only friend in all the world was Mrs Wells' steak and kidney pie. And he could not even rely on that friendship for long. Almost half the pie had disappeared already. But Mrs Wells knew a good pie provided strength, and as the alderman ate, it strengthened him.

What would Mayor Catchpleen have done? He'd have told the council to go boil their heads. And if they complained, he'd have boiled their heads for them. The pie's magic conjured up an image of Fawsick standing behind his desk at Town Hall, telling Mr Oaten to boil his head. Telling Mrs Jumpage to boil her head. Mr and Mrs Cornigan. All of them, individually and then collectively, should go boil their heads, and not stop boiling them until he, Alderman Fawsick, informed them that all the rannygazoo was boiled out of them!

He wouldn't tell the reverend to boil his head, of course.

But all the rest of them. He ate another forkful of pie and his imagination gracefully provided him with a riding crop to slap against his thigh as he spoke to make his meaning clear. "You don't like poo all over the place? Then go boil your heads!" That's what Catchpleen would have said, no doubt about it.

Fawsick sighed. He would never do it. On the morrow, he'd be peppered with questions and would find himself sputtering answers that he hoped would fit the bill.

And that was if things went well!

If they didn't…

He ate another forkful of pie. The future might look hazy—to put it nicely—but tonight he had steak and kidney pie.

***

De Glube felt nervous in the dark of his kitchen.

He detected no sign of an impending storm, yet he needed those five thunders to make his plan work. He would have to pray they were coming.

After all, the only bit of his plan beyond his control seemed to be the thunder. The Enochian Call insisted he must have five peals of earth-shattering thunder, if he wanted to wake the dead.

He gazed through his kitchen window. Perhaps it was his imagination, but even though the kitchen light was off, signalling Mrs Sniffacre lay in bed, he believed he could feel her presence anyway, reaching towards him through her kitchen window.

All that could be seen, however, was Wordsworth, glaring back in at him.

Through the glass, he heard the first rumble of the poor goat's digestion.

De Glube sipped at his tea, long since cold, and remained where he was. He lacked the energy to move. Could barely stand to lift his eyes from the window, but his pile of luggage would not be ignored.

He had a lot of luggage. There were his clothes, of course. His notebooks. His etchings and engravings. The flowers and the little tie pin given him by Mrs Sniffacre. A handkerchief she once lent him, which retained the scent of her perfume.

The patch of wallpaper he would take with him, because it contained some notes about Saint Hermagoras that might interest the Bollandist Society. He had scribbled them down in a fit of inspiration. They were too valuable to leave, and his handwriting was too awful for him to decipher in his current mood.

He intended to take everything of value with him, leaving behind only his sponge and his heart.

As soon as he heard the "thunder" he would make his way to the train station on Mr Hyssop's cart. He would take the slow milk train to Folkestone, and from there make his way to Luxembourg and home.

On the table in front of him all he needed lay in readiness. Graveyard tulips, consecrated earth, updated notes on the Morris dance, and an eagle too worried about its remaining tail feathers to say much.

"Farewell, Jennet," de Glube said to her dark, empty window. As if in reply, Wordsworth's guts gave a tremendous rumble. Then, under the terrible pressure of the wind contained within, his Mighty Seat groaned.

Chapter 47

Since Forever

"NICE NIGHT," CALLED Mr Hammond from where he waited with an axe to cut the rope on his trebuchet. He and Gertrude were in a field a couple of miles further away from Hawkinge-By-Hythe than Colette's cannon. Victoria and her helper were two fields away to their right.

"Fine," said Gertrude with her own axe. She needed to sever her rope first, before Mr Hammond sprang into action, and wished to concentrate, worrying that they might have missed something. She hated this bit: waiting to see if things would work out. Because it was Colette's plan, she didn't even have the satisfaction of knowing if something went wrong, it would be her own fault. It might not sound like much consolation, but she liked being in charge. It was easier than expecting other people to know what they were doing, even if those other people were her sisters.

She *knew* Colette would have accounted for everything possible, but as she stood in the dark, an axe in her hand, and Mr Hammond watching the skies for the bell, she didn't *feel* it. Being forced to rely on Mr Hammond made her stomach churn. She consoled herself with the fact she didn't really need him. She had been keeping the time in her head since leaving Colette earlier that evening. If only Mr Hammond wouldn't keep *talking!*

She prided herself on how well she had worked with the Wait Watchers. Something about Mr Hammond made her uncomfortable, however. He seemed to like her, and she couldn't explain why. It wasn't the sort of mystery she liked, either. It was too odd. She and Victoria had called around to Mrs Sniffacre's house to request the assistance of two patrol members. Victoria selected Mr Grunnion to help her out, and before Gertrude had the chance to say anything, Mr Hammond had jumped up and *volunteered* so fast that he almost choked to death on his biscuit! It was her own fault, really. That's what she got for being so good at being nice.

"I was worried the other night," said Mr Hammond, exactly 138 and a half seconds after his last comment, according to the clock in Gertrude's head.

"Why, what's wrong with you?" said Gertrude. "If it's indigestion, I'm not surprised, considering how you deal with biscuits. It's not a sign of weakness to masticate your food before swallowing it."

...Fifty-four, fifty-five, fifty-six seconds passed.

"About *you*," said Mr Hammond.

"Me?" The surprise almost caused her to lose count.

"You slipped over that hedge so fast, I thought you'd hurt yourself." Gertrude was once more silent, this time as she attempted to work out what he meant. The suggestion that she, Gertrude, might have hurt herself sounded like an unnatural one. So much so, that if some Right Handers were to pass at that moment, she would have insisted they stop to hear Mr Hammond's confession for having made it.

"Oh," she said. A possible explanation dawned on her, and she didn't like it one bit.

His volunteering to spend time with her.

His concern for her well-being.

The way he looked at her with his eyes out on stalks, like a snail speeding towards a ripe patch of strawberries.

The countdown in her head rescued her. She just had time to say, "Any sign of the bell?" to distract him.

"I see it!" he shouted, as they bell made its circuit, noticeably lower than before.

Gertrude swung her axe. It bit the trebuchet's rope. The trebuchet rumbled, the beam spinning. The packed manure whistled as it shot after the bell.

"Now!" she called, and Mr Hammond swung his own axe. He didn't normally go in for physical exercise, but with Gertrude watching him, he swung like a circus strongman doing the Harlem Shag.

Gertrude held her breath. Mr Hammond puffed.

Would their missile hit the bell? Had Victoria and Mr Grunnion done their bit? Could Colette really have thought of everything that might go wrong?

BB-b-OOO-oo-NN-GG-ggg….!

The unmistakable double warble of a revolving bell being simultaneously rung from both sides at once!

Then, a moment later:

BB-BB-oo-OO-oo-nn-NN-gg-GGG….!

The equally unmistakable sound of a bell which is *not* revolving being hit twice in such a way as to spin it just the way they wanted it!

"We did it!" said Gertrude, smiling at Mr Hammond.

If anyone asked, he would have sworn he heard a third bell ringing, but it was only his delighted heart.

From the underground control centre at the base of the cannon, Colette heard the four strikes of the bell and waited for Chloe and Curly to provide visual confirmation that the target was now overhead.

Hopefully, it really was a bell, rather than a bell-shaped ark. It would get them off on the wrong foot if the reverend had been right after all....

"Now!" confirmed Chloe. Colette touched the spill to the hole in the cannon's breech.

She raced for the ladder as the fuse fizzed. A moment's silence, then the cannon blasted with a rumbling bang.

Colette ran to the top of the stairs and put her arms around Chloe and Curly.

She knew she had thought of everything. She must have. In her mind's eye, she saw her missile speeding towards its target.

What if an owl got in the way?

Anything could yet go wrong, and they only had this one chance...

A split second after she was sure something had gone wrong, she heard it:

A sticky wet DDDDDTTTHHHOOOOONNNGG! as the cannon's soggy bullet struck the bell, ending its decade's long journey.

Chloe and Curly hollered with excitement when they heard the sound, and Colette grinned in relief. The reverberations of the blow continued for some time, allowing her to track the bell's progress.

As liquid poo coated the bell, it started to wobble and slow down, no longer heading for town, but to an empty field nearby.

It crashed down with a terrifying noise, both hollow and damp at the same time.

Hawkinge-By-Hythe was saved.

Colette also grinned because she was looking forward to the next bit.

The bell's rapid spin meant that while enough poo coated it to drag it out of the night sky, most of it was sent spiralling off into the night sky.

Any second now, it would start pouring down.

Victoria, Gertrude, Mr Grunnion and a red-faced Mr Hammond turned up before the smelly rain started, and they all settled companionably around the observation post with the large tarpaulin roof set up near the steps to the cannon and waited for the air to clear.

It would be some time before the brown rain finished fertilising the surrounding countryside for miles around.

"What's that?" asked Chloe, breaking the silence. "Ugh!" She pointed to a spidery "X" twinkling at them through the brown mist that obscured their view of the night sky. An unusual looking "X". Thin and wavering, glowing purplish red, like a mouth with four lips.

Two grinning with evil delight, two turned down in infernal rage.

"Oh!" said Victoria and looked at her sisters.

"It looks like someone cut a hole in the sky," said Chloe. "And the scar became infected."

"That," said Gertrude. "Is bad news."

"Is it Carfax?" asked Chloe, who paid attention.

"Yes," said Colette, after a moment. There was no point lying to the child. If Carfax turned up, *everyone* would know about it.

The "X" faded.

"He's getting brazen," said Gertrude.

"De Glube's notebook?" asked Colette.

"The Enochian Calls," confirmed Victoria. It seemed the only explanation for Carfax's interest in Hawkinge-By-Hythe. He must know by now de Glube had deciphered the Enochian Calls. Naturally, he would want that power for himself.

And it explained the whole thing. Carfax saw time differently. He might have set the whole thing up, Catchpleen and the rain of animals, the bell, de Glube's arrival in town, long before the Alumières came to Hawkinge-By-Hythe.

Carfax could have been planning to have de Glube discover the Enochian Calls since *forever*.

And he would have known that with the terrible pungent rain falling, de Glube would be powerless and unprotected at home, ripe for the plucking.

It looked like they would have to head out into the unpleasant weather, after all.

"Mr Grunnion?" called Victoria. "Would you look after Chloe and Curly until it clears up enough to take them home?"

Curly looked at the butcher and exchanged nervous glances with himself before backing behind Chloe.

"I'll do it," said Mr Hammond, looking at Gertrude.

"Thank you," said Victoria.

"Are there biscuits here, Chloe?" asked Gertrude, who couldn't take any more.

"If Curly didn't eat them all!"

"Moo-ee?/Moo-ee?!"

"Well, don't give Mr Hammond any. He can't be trusted with them," said Gertrude. *There*, she thought, *that'll let him know where he stands with his shiny red face.*

It did indeed. Mr Hammond heard her words and almost swooned. *She cares!* he thought.

"Of course," said Chloe. Mr Grunnion was staring at Curly and rubbing his chin. She gave him the dirty look she usually reserved for people who suggested she might even look pretty, if she wore a dress for a change.

"Right. Let's find de Glube!" said Colette.

They ran for their bicycles.

In the graveyard at St Dunstan's Church, there was movement where no movement should have been. Despite the unpleasantness of the weather, the earth stirred over a grave. A tired figure raised himself to his feet and shambled into town.

Chapter 48

A Miracle

"I CAN'T BELIEVE Carfax thinks he can taunt us! Why weren't either of you paying more attention?" said Gertrude, as they sped towards town on their bikes. She didn't need to worry about anyone hearing them fight, for everyone stayed safe indoors out of the terrible rain.

"Shut up!" said Victoria. "Sorry, but really! It's as much your fault as anyone else's."

"My fault?"

"If you'd been managing the Wait Watchers properly, instead of... of..."

"Flirting?" suggested Colette helpfully.

"Flirting with Mr Hammond, then you might have noticed what was going on. When I suggested being nicer, I didn't expect you to go that far!"

"Well, you've certainly taken *my* suggestion to stick up for yourself more to heart!"

"You've both done very well," said Colette, "but I don't think you're enjoying it very much."

"I hate being rude," said Victoria.

"I can't stand being a pushover!" said Gertrude.

"Pushover?"

"Rude?"

They cycled on for a while in silence.

"I don't mean to be rude," said Gertrude. "I just like plain speaking."

"And I'm not a 'pushover'," said Victoria. "I just like helping people to help themselves."

"If they were able to help themselves, we wouldn't be here," said Gertrude.

"So once we teach them how to help themselves, we can move on. 'Give a man a fish, and you feed him for a day. Teach a man to fish, and you feed him for a lifetime.'"

"Well, it sounds like you both learned a valuable lesson," said Colette, then grinned as her sisters stared daggers at her back. "By the way, Victoria also worked out why Catchpleen switched from animals to bells, and then buried the catapults. While you were, um, *busy*, Gertrude."

"The Reverend Hennessy petitioned Lord Muir to stop the whole renaming enterprise before Catchpleen could immortalise his cat. So Catchpleen confiscated all the catapults and buried them."

"Hmph," said Gertrude. "Makes me glad we're dealing with Fawsick rather than Catchpleen." "Fawsick would be just as bad if Carfax were leading him."

"And the creatures already shot into the air?"

"They were simpler times. People hung around for a while, waiting for them to land. When they didn't, they assumed God must have taken them and forgot about it."

"And the bell?"

"Well, guess who built the cannon?"

"Catchpleen?"

"Correct. And if you thought the trebuchets were good, you should see the mechanics of the cannon!"

"After it's had a wash, perhaps."

"Good idea. But there were notebooks for its construction in one crate. It's clearly Carfax's doing, though Catchpleen thought he was getting revenge on Hennessy and Muir. He wanted to blast Muir Hall with the reverend's bell to teach them not to spite his cat in future."

"They don't make 'em like that anymore," said Victoria.

"No," said Gertrude.

"As to who Catchpleen really was…," said Victoria.

"Not a local, I'm guessing?" said Colette.

"No. Just appeared one day with a lot of money and even more confidence."

"And set this whole thing in motion. A trap for de Glube when he finally turned up?"

"It's possible," said Gertrude. "Carfax…" She didn't need to finish the thought. They had unfinished business with Carfax, but weren't looking forward to resuming it. They pedalled faster to de Glube's cottage, hoping they weren't too late.

Mrs Pengle only noticed she sat alone on the church roof when the stuff started coming down.

"It's a sign!" she called and looked around, but there was no one there to heed her. When she heard the ringing of the bell, she assumed it must be the opening of the gates of heaven. She raised her head to heaven and started to pray.

Then the rain hit her. A lot thicker than usual.

She got up, carefully, and took a step towards the ladder she, Mr Nooney, and Mr Ball used to get onto the roof.

The stuff poured down around her, thick and slippery. It made walking difficult.

She took another step.

And slipped.

Shot down the slanted roof.

She would have plunged to her death in the graveyard if she hadn't had the great good luck to plunge through a hole in the roof created just seconds before by a particularly crusty shard of brown rain.

Her life flashed before her eyes, mercifully distracting her from the hard stone floor of the church rising quickly to meet her.

"Boah!" said a lightly smoked parrot as it flew past.

Mrs Champion sat in the rectory's parlour, talking to Tabitha Gresstart.

Tabitha Gresstart, thought Mrs Champion, was the kind of woman they needed at OWCHH events, and it would do her good to get out of the house. Mrs Champion had only gone in for a brief chat about the OWCHH, as she didn't want to miss listening to the fireworks, but had found it impossible to get away, as they chatted for simply hours.

On one thing, however, Tabitha would not be moved. She would not take part in any meetings without first running it past her husband. She didn't think he would regard a monthly tea and scone event as a cult, but couldn't be sure. He sometimes had silly ideas.

"You can wait here," she said to Mrs Champion, who had risen to her feet and looked like accompanying her to the church. Mrs Champion still limped and Mrs Gresstart didn't want to put her to extra bother.

"I need the exercise," said Mrs Champion, and they puffed their way together into the night.

Tabitha was glad of the company as they passed through the graveyard.

"Tabitha!" Having finished his sermon for the following week, the reverend had been pottering around the church before closing up for the night, when he spotted her. Normally this time would have found him at his telescope, but he had gone off it since it let him down so badly. "And Mrs Champion?"

"It's about the OWCHH, Aubrey," said Tabitha.

He examined Mrs Champion's walk. "Perhaps a doctor would be of more use," he suggested.

"We'd love Tabitha to come to our meetings. The Official Women's Club of Hawkinge-By-Hythe. OWCHH."

"Oh." he seemed put out, then rallied. "Of course." As if to applaud his decision, the heavens rang with four celestial gongs.

Then one more. The reverend bit his lip. Everyone looked up and waited.

When nothing happened for a full ten seconds, they breathed again.

The reverend grudgingly admitted that it seemed the Alumières had done as promised. The bell would not destroy his roof. He mastered himself and remembered his two visitors.

"Give you a hand, Reverend?" asked Mrs Champion, limping over.

"Thank you," said the reverend. He had been sorting out his sheets and tarps—of which he owned dozens— with a view to getting rid of some older ones before the builders returned.

Which might not be for a long time now, he decided, and almost smiled.

Then the roof cracked. Dust rained down on him, followed by Mrs Pengle.

The smell hit him almost as hard as Mrs Pengle did.

Luckily, his arms were still full of tarpaulin sheets, which absorbed most of the blow, though he found himself sitting on the ground with Mrs Pengle in his arms.

"Reverend!" she cried out.

"What?" The reverend couldn't understand what had happened. He only understood that Mrs Pengle was somehow suddenly back again. "What?"

"You saved me!"

"Yes," he said. He did his best to save all his flock. It registered that she had *fallen* on him.

"Oh, Reverend, I'm so sorry!"

"Never mind." He tried not to snap, but he wasn't happy. First Mrs Champion, then Mrs Pengle. How many other people were going to drop in on him before he could get to bed? He looked around to see if the door to the church was open. She had hit him hard. She must have fallen off the roof, but how had she then landed *inside?*

He found it hard to think. His back ached from holding Mrs Pengle, and he found it hard to breathe because his lungs didn't like the air and were refusing to take it in.

"It's a miracle," said Mrs Pengle.

"Well, I just came out to, er. If Mrs Champion hadn't called around, I wouldn't be here."

Mrs Pengle's wondering gaze took in Mrs Champion. This time without animosity.

"I'm glad you're alright..." said the Reverend dazedly, wondering if she had any plans to get off him at some point. The smell seemed to be getting stronger, and it was the sort of smell that did not belong in a house of worship. Also, his ears insisted they could hear something going splat, splat, splat all around him.

He noticed Tabitha and Mrs Champion were still looking up. He decided to do the same.

"My roof!" he groaned.

Chapter 49

Tenerife

IT IS DIFFICULT to describe what Hawkinge-By-Hythe looked like as Colette, Victoria, and Gertrude arrived at de Glube's cottage on their speeding bicycles.

The author would therefore like to start things off by drawing the reader's attention to a common, often unremarked, contradiction.

On the one hand, we are told things were always better in the past. They were the "good old days". The men were real men, the women were more womanly. Egg yolks were a brighter and tastier orange, delivered by happier hens. There was always something good on the radio.

And, of course, the air was miles better. Fresher. With more ozone. More volume. More *taste*.

Yet, when we examine the past, we sometimes feel it must have been drab. A glance through the photo collection of one's grandparents confirms it. People wore simple colours. Such as brown. They ate brown bread with traditional soup flavours such as oxtail. Which was brown.

On Friday nights they would let their hair down and treat themselves to a drink. The preferred drink was ale. Brown ale. And so on.

So the past was better *and* browner. Is there a way to reconcile these two statements? In fact, there is. All one needs to do is take a look at Hawkinge-By-Hythe at this moment.

By now the poo had stopped falling, and the streets, roofs, gardens (and hedges) were brown. Everything was a beautiful uniform brown, just the way people used to like it.

And the air? Why, it was packed with as much taste as anyone could want. Just a single breath, if that, was about all anybody could take.

Not that the Alumières paused to enjoy it. De Glube's cottage lay in darkness, and time was of the essence. They gave him a moment to respond to their knocking, but Colette already had her hairpin at the door's lock.

Inside, other than a missing patch of wallpaper, there was no sign that Luxembourg's pre-eminent epigrapher had ever been there.

"He must be with Sniffacre," said Colette.

"He's gone," said Victoria, noticing the ripped wallpaper.

"Didn't you say you fixed things between them?" demanded Gertrude.

"I did," said Colette. "He must be with her, I fixed it!"

"I hope so. Because that wallpaper makes it look to me like he's gone."

"Carfax got him!" said Gertrude with relish.

"...*or* he's with Mrs Sniffacre," said Colette.

"It's possible." Gertrude didn't wish anything bad to have happened to de Glube. But it would have made things more exciting. They ran, more grateful than ever for the non-slip soles of their boots.

Mrs Sniffacre had waited up for several hours. The fireworks didn't interest her. She hoped to glimpse de Glube. If only she could think of something to say, she would have gone to see him at his cottage. And yet the whole time she sat in her kitchen, she imagined he might be sitting in his kitchen looking back out at her.

Until, at some point, she didn't. He was gone, if he had ever been there at all.

She retired to bed. When at one point she heard noises downstairs she didn't even bother to shout, "Who's there?"

Eventually she rose again. Her hot water bottle had turned into a cold water bottle, and she needed more tissues to blow her nose. And she could detect a smell as if something had gone wrong with the plumbing.

She didn't notice the envelope on her kitchen table until the kettle was already boiling.

Her heart sank when she saw the handwriting. Lou's unmistakable scrawl. It seemed unlikely to be good news if he was sneaking around to leave her notes in the middle of the night.

She crumpled into a chair to read it.

> *"My dearest Jennet,*
> *Though it pains me to do so, I leave Hawkinge-*
> *By-Hythe alone. More alone than I could ever*
> *have imagined, for I leave without my heart.*
> *I wish for nothing more than to stay with you,*
> *to love you and worship you forever.*
> *The Lord required seven days to create the*
> *world and everything in it. You needed but a*

moment to create an Eden for me. You transformed the cold star of my soul into a burning passionate sun, and raised me to life from the death of my solitary existence.

Please excuse my words, which I share with you only for the sake of my sanity. I make no claims on your affection nor expect you to reciprocate my feelings. I realise you love another.

Know I desire only your happiness. As you raised me to life, I return the favour, and leave you now in the capable hands of the man you desire most in the world.

Sincerely, and forever yours,

Lou"

P.S. I have made arrangements with Mr Tassel for him to provide any assistance you might require giving Wordsworth his medication in future.

Mrs Sniffacre read it again. It was gibberish.

Lou admitted, finally admitted, that he loved her.

And was leaving for that very reason.

Her blood boiled and the whistling in her ears prevented her from thinking clearly.

What did this nonsense mean?

What was wrong with him?

And then, to top it off, that senseless drivel about leaving her with the man she loved?

Who else could that be but Lou?

The kettle whistled for several more minutes before she remembered it. Her hands shook as she made tea. When her doorbell rang, she ran to it. She hoped to find de Glube on her step, so she could fling herself into his arms.

No, first she would give him a good tongue-lashing for the fright he had given her. Then she would fling herself into his arms.

"Oh." It was the Alumières outside. All three of them, with no sign of de Glube anywhere. "Come in."

"Sorry to disturb you," said Victoria.

"Is de Glube here?" asked Colette.

"Oh!" said Jennett Sniffacre, with a catch in her voice. She led them to the parlour to park them while she prepared more tea and regained her composure.

But when she opened the door to usher them in, a strange man sat in one of the two armchairs.

And not de Glube.

Mrs Sniffacre stared and realised he wasn't a strange man. "Oh?" She knew exactly who he was. She just hadn't been expecting him.

"Won't you introduce us?" asked Colette.

Mrs Sniffacre did so. "This," she told the seated man, "is Colette, Victoria, and Gertrude Alumière." She indicated the ladies beside her.

The man blinked.

"And this," Jennet indicated the pale but undeniably animate individual in the armchair, "is my dead husband, Tenerife Sniffacre."

The Alumières considered the matter and came to the same conclusion.

For a corpse, he looked well.

Well.

Well-ish.

Hawkinge-By-Hythe Wants You!

When a demon takes over the body of a two-headed calf…
it's time for the heavy-duty rubber gloves.

You get two exclusive ebooks free, plus regular updates from the author.

Find out why rubber gloves are needed to exorcise a demon from a two-headed calf, what the ghost trapped in a telephone booth wants, and how Ireland's miraculous moving statues became a nightmare.

Get *The Devil Rode Out,* and *People Skins, Volume 0: Hidden Cuts* free, EXCLUSIVELY for subscribers at

morgandelaney.info/newsletter/

Acknowledgements

Yes, another book dedicated to Nadine. Of course! If you're wondering why, then you've obviously never met her. All my love and thanks, Nadine. Always.

And thanks again to the proud German tribes of Traber-Jahn and Weidemann. It's great to have a family. It's wonderful to find one.

Speaking of which, I'd like to thank my sister, Anita, for all her help working out colour schemes for the new Alumière covers. If you bought this book because it looked so nice and enjoyed it, you should thank Anita, too. If you bought it because of the cover and hated it? Well, now you know about the 1839 Treaty of London. You could win a pub quiz knowing that. Say thank you to Anita.

This book would have been possible—but not very good—without the efforts of Julian Barr, Editor Extraordinaire. He doesn't use body doubles or stuntmen for even the most dangerous editing tricks. Thanks, Julian!

Finally, a huge thank you to everyone who offered to read an advance copy to provide feedback or reviews. Writing a book is a slow, lonely process. Finding like-minded people who want to read it makes it all worthwhile.

About the Author

Morgan Delaney is an Irish writer of dark, strange, and fantastic fiction, has appeared in Not One Of Us, ParSec Magazine, and Fraidy Cat Quarterly.

He reads peculiar bedtime stories on YouTube on his Sleepytime Supervillain Theatre channel.

You can support him—without having to deal without any of that feckin' stuff he writes—by buying the t-shirts he designs here: morgandelaney.threadless.com

If reincarnation were a thing, he would come back as a lizard.

His best friends say it is.

And he has.

Get 2 free, exclusive ebooks when you sign up to his newsletter here: morgandelaney.info/newsletter

Also by Morgan Delaney

**Light Fantasy in the Alumière Sisters'
Adventures**
The Devil Rode Out (a subscriber exclusive)
The Phoenix
The Squared Circle
The Forgotten Creatures
Whispers Behind the Mirror

**The Resurrection Men Historical Fantasy
Horror Mystery Mashups**
A Grave and Dreadful Business

**Darker and Stranger with People Skins. Dark,
Strange and Fantastic Stories**
People Skins, Volume 0: Hidden Cuts (a subscriber exclusive)
People Skins, Volume 1
People Skins, Volume 2

Pure Horror: Short, Sharp Horror Shocks
Sour Milk
Quick Deaths